# Lord Ashley's Beautiful Alibi

## Scarlett Affairs
### Book 1

# Cerise DeLand

## ARE YOU SIGNED UP FOR DRAGONBLADE'S BLOG?

You'll get the latest news and information on exclusive giveaways, exclusive excerpts, coming releases, sales, free books, cover reveals and more.

Check out our complete list of authors, too!

No spam, no junk. That's a promise!

### Sign Up Here

www.dragonbladepublishing.com

*Dearest Reader;*

*Thank you for your support of a small press. At Dragonblade Publishing, we strive to bring you the highest quality Historical Romance from some of the best authors in the business. Without your support, there is no 'us', so we sincerely hope you adore these stories and find some new favorite authors along the way.*

*Happy Reading!*

*CEO, Dragonblade Publishing*

# Additional Dragonblade books by Author Cerise Deland

**Scarlett Affairs Series**
Lord Ashley's Beautiful Alibi (Book 1)

**Matrimony! Series**
If I Loved You (Book 1)
Because of You (Book 2)
You Made Me Love You (Book 3)

**Naughty Ladies Series**
Lady, Be Wanton (Book 1)
Lady, Behave (Book 2)
Lady, No More (Book 3)
Lady, You're Mine (Book 4, Novella)

**The Lyon's Den Series**
The Lyon's Share
The Lyon's Perfect Mate

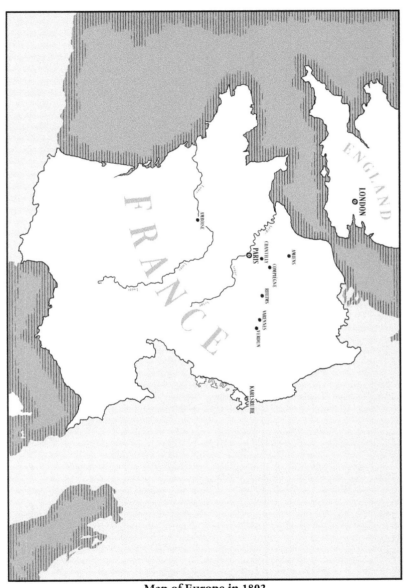

**Map of Europe in 1802**
**Designer, Xenia Sukhareva**

# Prologue

*June, 1800*
*Malmaison, the road from Rueil*
*France*

IT WAS A hell of a day for an ambush. The rain. The cracks of thunder. The sounds were enough that they'd frightened off the two feral cats who lived on the edge of this forest. Kane chuckled at how bad the weather was if those animals did not dare to come near his sack of mice.

Not a bad idea to use mice to run amok, clog the road, and surprise Bonaparte. But it was one thing to have a great idea to abduct the man and another to execute it. Better yet if the leader of the group showed up!

But Juvenot was not here, was he? He was late, the bugger. Not that Kane could impartially admonish a man who did not keep good time, but still. How could one be a proper assassin if one came late to the party?

Kane winced, lifted away his cap, and swept his long curls from his eyes. *Where are you, Juvenot?*

Kane had taken his position minutes after four this morning, hiding among the sodden underbrush and hoping his bag of mice did not all die in that double-lined sack. After he finished this bit of nasty business, he was headed straight for the Seine, the barge to Rouen, and home to Dover. He could not be caught here. Even though his French reflected his six years spent at the superb *Ecole de Bordeaux*, he never counted on too much circumstance to set him free. Especially not from the torture the French chief of police meted out to any British lurking in the shrubbery. Fouché and his lackeys had murdered his cousin Fabien Lamartine last year and had the audacity to send the sad remains to his Aunt Justine in Amboise. The woman had fainted at the sight and not recovered her wits for days.

To take Kane's mind off Fouché's bloodthirsty *gendarmes*, he pulled open his smaller sack and took out yesterday's baguette. He tried to take a bite but had to gnaw at the stale loaf. When he finished this bad bit of work this morning, first thing he'd order would be a large cup of coffee, a slab of bacon, and a fat chunk of Bûcheron cheese.

*If I live.*

He scoffed.

*I will. What else can I do but go after the next target on Scarlett Hawthorne's list? It's not like anyone else pays as well or as promptly.*

And then, as if the sun complied with this mission, the rain stopped. A rainbow instantly appeared over the tops of the trees. Aunt Justine had taught him the power of good omens. She believed in signs for every turn of events. Sunshine was one.

He, however, believed only in results.

He tried his baguette again, but stopped to save it for later. He stuffed it in the back pocket of his ragged pants, then cursed the man who was missing from this plan to block the road and kill Bonaparte.

The sound of horses on the road had Kane shrinking backward into the shadows of the dense green copse.

Horses! How many? He shut his eyes and counted hooves. Three horses. No, two riders headed for Malmaison.

Where was the carriage with Bonaparte? Had Juvenot gotten his details wrong? Was Bonaparte on a horse? Or if this *was*

Juvenot on horseback, why did the idiot come openly in the thoroughfare?

Kane stepped back further into the cover of the forest. The tree branches around him rustled and shook. Nothing like the density of a French woodland. He raised his hand and could not see it beneath the veil of green leaves and heavy vines.

This could not be Juvenot approaching. He would not come with an entourage on the road. These riders had to be some advance guard of the first consul. Bonaparte never traveled without protection. He was a smart man, this Little Corporal who was hailed as the newest savior of the French Republic.

Kane mouthed his dislike of Juvenot and the Corsican alike. But, being a good man, he gave the signature whistle of *chuck-chuck-chuck* to notify his comrade Alphonse, down the lane at the Malmaison gate, that some stranger came.

*But why didn't Pascal whistle to alert Brussard and me we have intruders?*

Pascal and two others manned the firewood piled up beneath an old oiled tarp. Whoever came along the lane had passed those three men hidden near the clearing.

Had they seen the three? The firewood? Had they realized how it was to be used?

After *the Terror*, everyone feared a pile of wood or furniture or street lamps. Barricades were the engine of any revolt. Or assassination.

If these riders had seen or suspected anything, they would gallop toward the house and guards.

He froze at the sound that met his ears. They trotted…and *laughed*! In fact, *they giggled!*

They had not seen the wood, the tarp, the men, nor perceived the intent.

He parted the leaves of the trees and squinted through the slits.

The riders came into his view. Two horses and…

*Two…women!*

*Merde.* Girls, they were! One buxom and raven-haired, with breasts that jiggled as she trotted forward. Her friend, a flame-haired witch, was a slender reed with bright white flashing teeth.

He drew back into the shadows.

They came up the road from Rueil. No villagers lived near Madame Bonaparte's beloved house this far down the road. Bonaparte's guards discouraged casual visitors or gawkers so near Malmaison. And Pascal should have taken out any strangers when first they entered the lane.

Kane was stumped. No one had passed him this morning. Certainly not these two. He would have noticed. They were too young, too carefree, and too damn beautiful not to make a man drool. Why were they out so early?

He knew. He stilled. They rode bareback. Their journey was nothing but a lark. They stayed at Malmaison and were either guests of Madame Bonaparte or that lady's servants out for a quick jaunt. They had gone out for a ride, early in the morning, escaping the house and all responsibilities. They were dressed in muddy riding boots and thin muslin shifts bunched up around their shapely thighs. No hats, no coats. No riding crops. Their derrieres were pressed to smooth leather and their chats were open to the slick...

Kane shook his head. *Business, man, not pleasure!*

Wincing, he spread apart the greenery once more and fought his urge to waylay them. But he was only one. They were two. Did they have pistols?

He froze at another thought. They had to have passed Pascal, the first man on the watch. The same man who had not whistled to the next man, Brussard, of approaching danger. And Brussard had not whistled to him either.

"I will race you, Augustine." The redhead circled her prancing horse around her friend.

"My aunt's ruby ring says you lose, *ma cherie.*" The raven-haired girl chuckled, then tossed her mane of unbound black tresses over her shoulder.

Kane wanted a handful of those windblown curls.

"Not this time!" Her friend jabbed her horse's belly with her boots and galloped off down the lane toward Malmaison.

Raven did not care. She arched an elegant black brow and serenely sat atop her mount to stare at the departing figure of her friend.

A whistle, loud and clear, rent the air.

*Damn. Who was that? No whistling now!*

Raven cocked her ear. Lifted her pert chin.

*Hell.*

She danced her horse around and scanned the woods as she bent low to her horse. *"Qu'est-ce que, Mirage?"*

Alphonse, at Malmaison's gate, gave the signal of the *chuck-chuck-chuck* of locusts.

*He warns me of what I already know.*

Raven spun toward the sound. Her dark eyes went wide. Her body stilled.

Kane was already lunging at her horse and reaching for the reins.

She yelped and snatched them from him.

But he had one arm around her waist, another attempting to cover her mouth. "No, you don't," he ground out, and hauled her off her horse.

*"Arrêt! Arrêt!"* She swung her head to and fro and evaded his hand. She clung to the reins of her horse so dearly, he had to pry her fingers off.

Once he did, and she was in his hold, the animal took off toward Malmaison.

*Shit.* A riderless horse would alert them all!

He clamped her plush little body to his and struggled to get a good grip on something other than one of her breasts. She cursed him roundly in a smattering of loud gutter French.

"Colorful." He snorted as he reached around for his baguette and aimed it at her mouth. *"Ferme la—!"*

*"Laisse-moi partir!"* She spat the bread out in bits. *"Fils de pute!"*

*Son of a...?* A girl with a dirty mouth. He huffed and jammed another piece of the old roll in her open mouth. *"Silence!"*

Her eyes blinked up at him. They were big green and gold orbs, and for a split second, he opened his mouth, dumbstruck, and then he went blind. But she wrestled him like a wounded cat, writhing and digging her heels into the soft muck of springtime soil—and he subdued her with arms she could not budge.

Still, he had to give it to her—she fought like one of Madame Josephine's well-muscled guards. All limbs, all energy, she pummeled him when she could, but he wrapped her flush to him and dragged her further off the trail. Caught by branches and leaves, she sputtered and cursed. But he had her to ground finally and managed to turn her around. Clamped in the vise of his arms, she stared up at him. Once more, for one stupid moment, he was mesmerized by the beauty before him.

That was when she lifted her knee to aim for his balls.

But he squeezed her so tightly she fought for breath, lowered her leg, and gagged. Then she surrendered to his power and went limp.

"You must stop," he told her quietly in his very good French. "Be quiet."

She choked and pushed more breadcrumbs from her mouth with her tongue. Her long black hair curled around her face and shoulders, and her green eyes popped with indignation. "Let me go." She did not beg or plead, but simply ordered him. In English.

Good English. Without any French accent.

Who was she?

"Quiet." He raised his head. He had to listen...but the woods were silent. Too silent. As before, he heard no bird calls that were not the normal early morning chittering of robins.

"Who else was with you and your friend?" It was silly to think she might tell him, but he could ask and hope for an answer.

"Only us two."

"Out—?"

*"Oui!* Before the morning toilette."

Whatever that meant, he could only wonder as he fell into the verdant green of her eyes and wondered once more who she was and why she spoke perfectly fine English but lived in the home of the new first consul.

His bevy of mice slithered around inside their sack and around her ankles.

"Ew. Eww. What…what is that?" She folded up her legs, bare and sleek, and tried to inch away. She only wound up more deeply in his embrace.

With one booted foot, he pushed part of the sack away from her. "Nothing for you. Don't worry."

A loud whistle of *chuck-chuck-chuck* hit his ears. Brussard, north on the road.

"What? What is that?" she asked, her round face strained with shock. "You… What are you doing here?" She was scrambling away from him, but he hauled her back into this embrace.

"Be quiet. Let me—"

"No!" She pounded his chest, and he clamped her to him again. "Hell." She burst into angry tears.

"Quiet!"

Another bird call came from the north. Brussard. Loud and…broken.

Meaning what? *Was he discovered?*

Whatever Brussard's message, it was now time to go!

Kane looked at his lovely captive—and something in his face told her she was both angry and afraid. He understood. But she didn't. He did not kill people. But she could not know that.

She opened her mouth to scream, and he did the only thing he could to shut her up. He kissed her.

Her lips were everything a woman's should be—warm and supple, her breath sweet with mint—and when he plunged his tongue inside, she let him. The fright drained out of her. She came into his arms like a lover should, eager and mewling. Compliant and dragging his collar closer so that she could kiss him more easily…

And bite him!

*Bitch!* He tore away and licked his lip. The taste of iron and sweat. Blood. *Of course.*

"No time to give you all the love bites you should have, *ma cherie.*" He clutched her shoulders and pushed her against a tree stump so hard, she grunted. He shot to his feet and admired the prize he'd captured, if only for a second. She was everything a man could want, and if he had hours this morning, and a big, broad bed, he would show her the good time she deserved.

Alas, another time, perhaps. His gaze fell to his farmer's sack, then he locked his eyes on hers with devilish glee. "Be sure to open that bag before you run home to *madame.*" He pushed to his feet, grabbed her hands, and caught her up against him, breasts and belly, legs and lips—and kissed her. Hard. Fast. And done.

She blinked, her green-gold eyes dazed.

He was just as stunned. But today was not what he'd planned. He bowed as elegantly as if he'd been knighted a chevalier of St. Louis. *"Adieu, mademoiselle. A bientôt!"*

# Chapter One

*April 1, 1802*
*Grosvenor Square*
*London*

"SHOW HIM IN, Friendly. I am as much prepared for the man as I will ever be."

Kane watched the old butler hobble away and grinned at the clickety-clack of the man's wooden teeth. Friendly had lost his ivories so long ago no one in the family recalled him with real teeth. But everyone knew the sound of Friendly talking to himself. For the man mumbled night and day, and no one knew exactly what his topics were. But Kane's father had speculated that Friendly did it to keep his sanity in his service to the Whittington males, who through the ages were known as brawlers, gamblers, and notorious rakehells.

Friendly had never muttered a distinguishable word in criticism of his masters. He was, among household staff, dubbed an angel because God had preserved him to celebrate the other day, his seventieth birthday. Hardy ancestry or luck, if not adherence to the Good Book, had aided the man to work here for nigh on half a century, bowing and scraping to Kane's grandfather, his father, and his two older brothers in turn.

*Now the poor fellow bows to me. May I be worthy of him...for as long as I live. Which, given my summons to Hawthorne Trading in an hour, foretells my forthcoming departure from this house, this country, and perhaps this world.*

He snorted.

*Irony.* It was how Kane had lived. And now that he had inherited, through unnatural means of accident for Reginald and pneumonia for Arthur, he was called away, and only Scarlett Hawthorne knew if his mission was to kill...or be killed.

He clicked his tongue and marched around the library once more. What in hell was he supposed to do with the solicitor, Mr. Roberts?

In Kane's twenty-eight years on this earth, he had never sat in on a discussion with any of the Whittington retainers. He was fortunate his estate manager of Ashbrook, Will Gardener, had come to London from Kent last week to notify him of his brother Arthur's demise. Otherwise, Kane would have learned of his new responsibilities from the *Times.* Kane had last seen his next eldest brother a year ago upon the occasion of the catastrophic carriage accident that had killed their father and his eldest brother, Reginald. Kane and Arthur had not talked in years. Family love had always been in short supply.

Kane paused before the huge astrological globe at his feet and gave it a dolorous, slow spin. He marveled at the large blue-black sphere behind which he had hidden to play hide-and-seek with his two brothers and sister.

The hundreds-year-old books, smelling of ink and mold and old leather, still marched along the shelves in higgledy-piggledy order. Reginald, his eldest brother, to Kane's knowledge, never took down one. Arthur read only the lurid tales. Most likely memorizing a few choice phrases and useful positions. *Whereas I hungered to read each one, stole moments with the tomes, but was hounded by the boys to abandon the nook near the fireplace and cavort with them.*

Now both of them were gone, as were their parents and their

young sister, Louise. *And I am left with what they taught me. How to fight like a bare-knuckle boxer. Drink like a bosun. Curse like a fishwife. Cheat like a knave. And swive.*

In none of that had he ever met his brothers' standards.

That was why he'd abandoned playtime in favor of employing his dubious talents in the pursuit of valuable results. For the country. For the Crown. Yet after the fiasco along the road to Malmaison, when one of his friends was brutally killed, Kane had asked Scarlett Hawthorne for less perilous duties.

"No more abductions or assassinations," he'd told his director and head of her own trading company in the city. "My skills at lying are best."

"Deception is your forte," she had argued—gutsy of her to do so, since she had just recently taken over her trading company and her job running her father's intelligence operation. She was also terribly young. Twenty-two and quite beautiful. A lady with a veiled past, who some said had once been wed and had the marriage annulled. Whatever her personal problems, she kept all her secrets to herself—and Kane ventured they numbered in the thousands.

"I care not where you send me, Scarlett, nor what you wish me to find. But leave the killing to those who have a taste for blood."

For two years, she had.

"Lord Assshley," intoned old Friendly as he stood unsteady at the threshold and fought to fit his teeth to his gums. "Mishtur Robertss, shir."

Kane welcomed the man in. Noting the sprightly little fellow had walked toward him in wet shoes that squished, he immediately offered him a chair near the fire. "Terrible spring storm out there, Roberts. Good of you to come. Brandy, perhaps?"

"Kind of you, my lord. Yes, I will, thank you."

Kane raised his gaze to Friendly, who clacked his teeth together at the same time as his heels—and off he went in search of a bottle and glasses.

Kane licked his lips. "I know this is quick notice to you to bring me the family investments and legal bits. I am grateful you agreed to this."

"I am happy to serve, sir." The little man's dark eyes went to Kane's sleeve, where the black armband signified the loss of Arthur. "My condolences on your loss, my lord."

"Thank you." Kane nodded, grateful for the solicitor's felicitations. There had been so few offered by his family to any others that Kane appreciated those who observed the niceties. He wished to observe them, too. Even though Arthur had been less than kind to him, Kane would miss him for what they *might* have been for each other. "I am at a loss, Mr. Roberts, as to what we have, what I am responsible for, and how I can help you. I was never included in any discussions of the family holdings or finances. You must guide me—and do it quickly. You see, I am called away. Urgently. I fear I have no time to learn or to decide complicated matters."

"Well, sir, there is not much you need do."

"Mr. Roberts, you need not coat this with sugar, sir. I am well prepared to hear the state of the family finances. I know my father had turned running of the estate to my oldest brother Reginald. He, unwise fellow, was less than attentive to Ashbrook, and many tenants abandoned their plots during his tenure."

"They did, sir. But your oldest brother bought four new ploughs the year he died, and he sold four of his racing horses. The ploughs enabled the tenants who remained to produce sizable crops. Even though we had a drought that year and the next, he made a profit on the sale of his wheat, sir." Roberts extracted from his bulging portfolio a sheaf of papers. "I have brought you the sales numbers, sir."

Kane had learned those from the estate manager Will Gardener the other day. "I thank you for bringing those. But I know that is not enough to pay for the other debts. I know we have no ready cash. I don't wish any staff here or at the house in Ashbrook to do without their salary or their share. Simply tell me what we can do, Roberts, to be a bit more solvent."

Roberts sat forward, his small eyes bright as a two-year-old's. "We've an opportunity, sir. We can sell the unentailed land in Sussex. I understand there is a cry to build houses in Brighton. So many wish to go to be seen when the regent goes, and there is poor availability. I have it on good authority we can sell our acreage to two men—architects, they are—and they wish to build."

The best and most unexpected news he'd had in weeks. "Excellent. Sell the land. Pay the debts."

The man beamed. "Well, sir. My partner and I have another suggestion. Different. If we keep that land in Brighton and allow the architects to build upon it, we can allow them to sell the structures. It is good seafront property, sir, and we could earn good money in perpetuity."

"Forever?" That might be wonderful in the long run. "But what would I do in the meantime for money?"

Roberts licked his lips. "Sell a portion of your land along the Thames. It is ten acres and navigable by small boat, too, especially in springtime. The town of Richmond grows, sir. People wish to put up shops, and the access to the river allows for transport of supplies!"

Kane frowned. "Why can we not do the same there as in Brighton? Keep the land. Ask for rents in perpetuity?"

"The demand is not as great, sir."

"Very well. Sell. What of my brothers' investments? How do they fare?"

"Only one is left, sir, and it profits." Roberts winced.

Kane had a suspicion which it was. "The sale of Africans? The support of the sugar trade?"

"Yes, sir."

"Apply half the profits of the Brighton venture and the Richmond sale to savings. Then sell those shipping shares. I want nothing to do with them."

The little man sat with his mouth open.

"I know, Roberts. Not done. But I will do it." He hadn't fought against the disasters wrought by the French Terror and the Directory only to support and profit from the sale of humans as slaves. "I leave town. I know not for how long. I trust you and your partner to do all this and bank the profits, pay off my brothers' gambling debts. See that their mistresses and babies have pensions we can afford that prohibit them from begging in the streets."

"I will, sir."

"I will ask for an accounting when I return." *Whenever that may be. If that may be.* He lifted his pocket watch on his fob. "I must go. Thank you for all of this. I applaud your work. Keep a good supply of scotch in the house for the day I come home." *If I do.* "I know we will need a stiff drink."

Kane waited while the little fellow scurried away. He felt lighter than air at the results of that interview. Whatever Scarlett had in store for him, Kane would strive to come home to a family name that had more integrity, morally and financially, than ever before. And if perchance he did not return home, he had seen to it that the next Earl of Ashley, whoever that wretched idiot was, would be in better straits than he had ever been.

*Hawthorne Trading Company*
*1 Clements Lane, Lombard Street, London*

SCARLETT HAWTHORNE SNAPPED shut her father's old porcelain timepiece and dropped it into the hollow of her gown between her breasts. Perturbed, she scowled at Todd Carlton, her head clerk. "You told Ashley two o'clock? And to be on time?"

Carlton gave a tolerant sigh. "I did, ma'am. He promised to be prompt."

She swung to face three of the four men she'd invited to her office. All were seated before her massive mahogany desk, filling up her company's offices with their celebrated good looks, their imperious *savoir faire*, and their chuckles. She gave them what they called her evil eye. "You are not permitted to giggle."

The three cleared their throats and attempted to appear somber.

"Ashley is not now a man of leisure, ma'am." The dashing, dark-haired Godfrey DuClare, Lord Ramsey, regarded her with feigned conviction. "He's too oppressed with details of his new responsibilities to be anywhere on time."

"Come now, Ram." Scarlett was having none of their excuses for their colleague. "I had hopes of his reform, at least in this! But the new Earl of Ashley has not been on time to anything in his life."

"A month late being born, too," added Fournier with the assurance of one who was not only Ashley's older cousin, but also one who caroused with him. "I saw him last night at White's. He returned home early."

"For an appointment?" asked the third gentleman, Yves Pelletier, with a twinkle in his dark eyes. "I understand he has given up frivolous things."

"He did. Long ago. Now he has all the business to take care of," Fournier put in. "The deaths of his father and two brothers within the past year have been a shock. Now he has the whole burden he was never prepared to assume."

Scarlett hated to look indifferent, but her attitude kept these men in line. "For the next few years, he will have to do it from afar, Fournier."

"Years? Surely not!"

Scarlett gave him a withering glance.

Fournier grinned and sat taller in his chair. "This is no review? All of us are on assignment?"

"All of you are on assignment together. Do you have your stories ready for anyone in town?"

"As ever, yes, ma'am, I planned only to be away to my hunting box." He winked at her, his hazel eyes as appealing as any dashing devil's.

Scarlett chuckled at how Fournier, like the others, was so debonair. "Scoundrel," she teased him. "It's a marvel none of your ladybirds has managed to catch you in her nest."

"Most of my 'ladies' are figments of my imagination," Fournier said with a meaningful stare into her eyes. "Well you know it."

She glanced away, brushing him off as she always did. Dirk Fournier, a French-English-German mongrel in possession of an old, rich barony in Kent, had tried for years to tempt her to his charms, but she'd eluded him. The sensuality of Dirk's white-blond hair and rugged complexion could appeal to some. To her, too, in truth, he had, but she'd never succumb. He worked for her, for one thing. Second, the affair Scarlett craved would come one fine day from another sort of man. A patient creature who knew how to charm her and keep her enthralled. If, indeed, such a man walked the earth.

Pelletier sighed. "I am eager to meet your favored man, Miss Hawthorne."

"He will meet your standards, *monsieur*," she assured him with the hint of a smile.

"You will like Kane, Pelletier." Ramsey leaned toward the Frenchman who'd become a part of their London team only four months ago. But Kane had been in Dover, Ostend, or Amsterdam all that time. Scarlett had told them that as cover for Kane's activities there. "He is the smoothest infiltrator—"

"Smooth but always—" began Scarlett.

The door to her inner office burst open and bounced against the wall.

Scarlett stared at the swarthy, towering figure of the man she sought. "—late."

## Chapter Two

" AH." KANE WINCED in rueful apology and understood immediately by their impudent gazes that he was the topic of conversation. "I heard you intoning my name."

"Where've you been?" asked Ramsey, more curious than irritated.

"I have things to do, old man," said Ramsey as he held up his own pocket watch and snapped shut the case.

"One day you'll be on time," Scarlett groused, and indicated the empty chair before her.

"I know, I know. To my funeral." With a dose of his most dashing grin and flourish of his hand, Kane brushed off the criticism. He strode into the room with Scarlett's one-eyed guard dog Todd Carlton glaring at him. Yanking off his leather gloves, Kane shrugged from his greatcoat and flung it over the offered chair. "My apologies. Devil of a storm. My carriage kept slipping in the sleet. Need new wheels." *Can't afford them.* "I am truly sorry, ma'am. I promise to reform. My apologies to you gentlemen, too."

His three colleagues offered up varying degrees of skepticism.

"Do have a seat, Ashley," Scarlett said with a tone that told Kane she accepted his apology even though she feigned impatience with him. But she'd called him by his new title, which spoke of her concern and regard at his new role. With his inheritance still only two weeks old, he wasn't used to his servants bowing and scraping to him with "Lord" this and "my lord" that. He preferred his first name, Kane, or his old moniker, Whit, short for the family name Whittington. For now, he'd just allow Scarlett to call him whatever she wished to call him. She was his director. He'd be a good boy, sit down, and shut up.

With a forced smile, Kane settled into the chair next to his cousin, Dirk Fournier. "This is a rare gathering of us, ma'am. Do tell us the details."

"For each of you, we have a new assignment," said the tall, red-headed beauty who'd inherited this business from her father two years ago upon his demise. She had doubled the profits of the import-export company since she took over, but now, she wanted to extend her reach into the Italian coast, Constantinople, Joppa, and Egypt. Britain controlled the seas. Alas, the Little Corporal, Bonaparte, kept winning battles that had him obstructing many of those ports like a Colossus of Rhodes. "But you will cooperate with each other."

Kane frowned. Never had he worked with Pelletier. Only once had he worked with Ram and once with Dirk, each separately. Successfully. They had not been complex missions. Not dire criminal objectives, like the assassination attempt at Malmaison two years ago. Since then, Kane had preferred to work alone. Usually he won his point with Scarlett. He'd try again.

He opened his mouth, but she arched both elegant red brows at him. "No. You cannot appeal this one. The conditions are ripe for our exploitation, and I will not hear objections. Unless, of course, any of you wish to resign."

A chorus of "hell no" and grunts mingled with silent consideration of her lovely person.

*All right.* Kane folded his hands. He was not in charge. Plus, at the start of any assignment, she gave an advance of cash. He might have Roberts working on sales and investments, but Kane still needed money now. New stone fences at Ashbrook. A new roof on the London townhouse. His two dead brothers' debts to a gaming hell and their mistresses. The expenses never ended. No wonder his siblings died early. It was the cheapest way out of debtors' prison.

Scarlett gathered herself, squaring her shoulders and training her forest-green eyes on each of them. Though she wore skirts—and had the fashion sense of a duchess—she was a rigid taskmaster. Her organization was one fine thing, her due diligence an animal of incomparable ferocity. Her instincts about her agents were wise beyond her years. She had studied their resumés—most of them were once based in Continental towns as tradesmen of fabrics or laces, woods or gems. Kane had established himself in Ostend and Amsterdam with Dirk as exporters of French and German wines and laces.

So if Scarlett Hawthorne had a private life, if she hungered for a man in her bed or children in her house in St. James, she shared no hint of her desires to anyone. If she had, Dirk had always vowed he would be first in line to undo the pins from her flame-red hair and spread her voluptuous body across fine linen sheets.

But she hadn't indicated she wished to romp with Dirk or anyone, including Kane. His long-abandoned reputation in bedrooms was too risqué for her, and she had told him so. He hadn't dared to break the precious bond between director and agent, especially since he had lost his taste for mindless affairs after that day in the road to Malmaison.

Sighing, Kane unbuttoned his frock coat. This was the third time he'd been in this room. Each time had been an occasion of great import, as Scarlett Hawthorne, the head of Britain's second largest trading company, performed her other duty for His Majesty's government and directed the most extensive private espionage network on the Continent.

Scarlett frowned at him. "Kind of you to join us."

Kane inclined his head. The waves of her anger rolled away. Silent and congenial, he knew how to chill her ire.

She signaled to her man Carlton, who promptly stepped toward the door and closed it. With shrewd eyes, she scrutinized each of Kane's friends. A woman of few words, she folded her arms and strolled to her window overlooking the bustling crowd on the street in the city's trade district. When she faced them again, her sultry features were fierce as Athena off to war. "I assume you've seen yesterday morning's newspapers."

Each of the four gave an indication he had.

"And noted the stipulations of the treaty?"

"Quite a piece of work," said Ram. "What in hell is Lord Cornwallis thinking to give Boney all that territory?" The fellow who had surrendered at Yorktown Virginia to the Americans still got important diplomatic positions, such as this one negotiating with the French.

"Exchanging all the prisoners was a fine idea," noted Pelletier of the new treaty of peace between the British and the French signed at Amiens. "Many have been locked away in the filth of those prison hulks for nearly ten years."

"Half the total are long since dead, Pelletier." Dirk ran two hands down his finely tailored wool breeches. "Ram and I had two friends among them. Good men, gone."

"Much," declared Scarlett, "is wrong with this new treaty. But we are not here to debate its value."

Kane crossed one long leg over another. He was eager to get on with this. He needed an assignment, a diversion, an enter-tainment. Hopefully, it would not be too far from London. He had to pay attention to more, he was certain, but he had little time, expertise, or funds to address. Yes, he needed money. A lot of it. Thousands. And quickly, too. Scarlett paid damn well, and he was one of the men she counted on to deliver any object worthy of her good gold coin. The last assignment Kane did for her was retrieve love letters for an MP who was being black-mailed by his wife's lover. "What is it we're after this time, ma'am?"

Scarlett went to pull out her massive upholstered chair, and

Carlton sprang to do it for her. She gave him an arch look that dismissed the presumption of his courtesy, then proceeded to access the chair herself. She sat with a grace that told of her many years of lessons in deportment. Her father had insisted that his only child have a superb education as a lady. Even though she was a cit. "You will each go to Paris."

*Hell.*

Dirk grumbled.

Kane had less desire to go to Paris than his cousin. Dirk had just left that city two weeks ago with one woman sobbing that he was going and another thrilled he had to leave.

"You have all been instrumental in helping us secure the health of the government here. But now you will each do the Crown a greater service."

*Oh, here it comes.* Kane winced. The Crown. A bad sign. He hated diplomacy. Finesse was wasted on men. With it, women could be won in a heartbeat. "We're assigned to the ambassador's staff?"

"Yes."

"The most boring job on earth," said Dirk. "Is there nothing else—?"

She arched a long red brow. "Pelletier will aid you. He will send you help for any mission."

"Anonymously, I assume?" Kane eyed the tall, lean Frenchman, who nodded in reply. Kane knew him only from the dossier Scarlett had sent him that morning. Yves Pelletier, the Comte de Valery whose family had fled the Terror here to England, had endeared himself to Bonaparte's foreign minister, Talleyrand. So far, Talleyrand did not suspect that Pelletier ran his own nest of French spies, all of whom worked for the benefit of Britain.

Pelletier kept it that way. Few in number, rabid in dedication, no one agent knowing another. In many ways, Pelletier had copied his operation on the workings of Scarlett's. Indeed, only the four men in this room knew the others here by background, education, sight, and proclivity.

"Each of you will have a special assignment," she said. "I have carefully selected your goals. In some instances, you will have a partner. But Kane leads on this. He has the background and contacts. You each assist him."

Kane preferred to be assigned with Dirk. And why not? They were second cousins who'd grown up together in the same house, with the same nannies, tutors, and dance instructors in London, later in their Aunt Justine's chateau in Amboise. Then he went off to school in Bordeaux. Dirk had gone to his mother's family in Durlach outside Karlsruhe in the duchy of Baden. Since the start of the Directory in France in '99, the two of them had returned to England and aided Scarlett. During the past three years, Kane and Dirk had renewed their fond friendship, drunk together. Older and wiser, lately they had given up sinning together.

"What do we do?" Kane brushed his palm over his buckskin breeches. He didn't like complex assignments, but he would accept this and appear as if he could manage it. "Steal from Bonaparte's new bank?"

Dirk laughed. "Seduce Napoleon's new mistress?"

Ram chuckled. "Loosen Josephine's corset? Or wet it down!"

Dirk sat back and pointed at Scarlett. "I'll take that job. The first consul's wife may have bad teeth, but she does have a luscious figure worthy of two hands."

"You'll have to work within Josephine's court," said Scarlett without a nod to the sarcasm. "All of it is sensitive."

Kane was tired of this lengthy introduction. At home, he had a pile of documents to sign for his solicitor. "Court one of her ladies, is it?"

"You decide." Scarlett stared at him. "We need a careful touch on this one. You have two goals, Ashley."

*Never simple, is it?* "When do I start?"

"I want you to leave as soon as possible. Tomorrow is best."

Kane frowned. He'd hoped to spend a quiet evening in his library with a good book. "What is the rush?"

"A lady-in-waiting to Josephine has disappeared. We know not where she is. And we must find her."

"I see." Kane liked a good hunt. "She's usually at court. But missing. A fever, perhaps?"

Ram snorted. "Is she nauseated? Or ridding herself of a certain unplanned malady?"

Scarlett fixed him with her dark, inscrutable eyes. "Whatever the reason, she's vital to Josephine." She stared at Kane. "And to us."

At that news, Ram whistled softly. "She's our agent?"

Scarlett set her delicate jaw.

"*Gott im Himmel.*" Dirk reverted to his fondness for his native German. "Scarlett, how did you manage that one?"

Kane definitely didn't like the sounds of this. Aunt Justine had known the new first lady of France years ago when she was married to her first husband, Beauharnais. "Josephine changes friends when she changes her garters."

"Not this one, she doesn't," Scarlett told him.

Kane was not convinced. "You mean to tell me this woman could be so important?"

"Kane has that right," said Ram to Scarlett. "Plus Bonaparte is not known to share all his state secrets with Josephine. After all, he scooped her from a virtual brothel."

Kane shook his head. "Josephine seems to have reformed when she met Napoleon, Ram. She may have a few morsels we could use to our benefit. But we don't know if she shares them with this lady you seek, ma'am."

Kane was not happy with the coils of this. His cousin Fabien Lamartine had been close friends with Paul Barras. Fabien had been working in Paris as a supporter of the Directory, and Josephine had shown more than a special interest in him. Three years ago, Fabien had been tortured and killed by Fouché and his men. The family knew not how or why.

Scarlett eyed him. "True. You told me your cousin Lamartine knew her, Kane. I want you to avoid staying too long in her presence. We cannot afford to have her notice your resemblance to Fabien."

Kane frowned. Fabien had not been as tall or muscular as he. But between them was a facial resemblance, mostly in the arch of the cheek and the slope of the nose. Kane had not been in Society the last time he worked in Paris two years ago for the failed Malmaison incident. "I can do that. However, to work among the consul's Parisian court, I hope I am a prosperous member of the staff."

"You're certainly prettier!" Dirk elbowed him.

Pelletier barked with laughter. "That helps with Josephine and her ladies."

"You will be taken care of," Scarlett said as she stared into Kane's eyes with a determination he had often seen in her. She slid a watercolor sketch of the lady across the expanse of her desktop. "First, find Madame St. Antoine."

Kane knew well Maurice St. Antoine. Having met the man more than ten years ago, Kane respected the older gentleman and was shocked the fellow had wed after the death of his beloved first wife. The man was over fifty, rich as Midas for producing on his Reims vineyards the finest *vin blanc*. A generous employer who paid his farmers well, he had never been attacked during the uprisings of the revolution. He had kept his head, his land, and his good wine production—and amazingly, he had decided to marry a second time.

Kane leaned forward and picked up the drawing. The portrait was on thick paper to hold the fine applications of French *peintures*. The picture had been folded, carried in someone's pocket, the edges frayed in the journey.

The portrait had been done four or five years ago, when the fashion for women's hair was extravagantly long ringlets and the style of gowns was a surplus of flowing fabric worn with dangerously low décolleté. The young woman sat facing forward, staring out at the world with the conceit so redolent of those among the courtiers of the *ancien regime*. The young Madame St.

Antoine was attractive, with a heart-shaped face, dark, almond-shaped eyes, a riot of red curls, and a lush mouth, ripe for a man's aspirations of hours in a bed with her.

"She disappeared two weeks ago Tuesday from court," Scarlett continued. "She was last seen in her traveling coach, leaving the Tuileries at approximately noon. She told her friends she was retiring to her estate in Reims in the Champagne. When last we had word two days ago from a runner from Calais, she had not yet arrived in Reims or back in Paris."

"What do you know about her?" Kane passed the sketch to his friends. Over the years as a youth, and later as a saboteur, Kane had met many lovely young women of the demimonde and lesser aristocracy. This lady's portrait spoke of a certain licentiousness, but struck no chords in him. Was she, then, from an aristocratic family? "And when did Monsieur St. Antoine marry her?"

Scarlett pressed her lips together, her hesitation a warning to him, though he knew not why. "A year and a half ago. She is British."

Kane narrowed his gaze on Scarlett, connecting the missing woman's usefulness to those Scarlett would know well. But she paused, as if she would say more but suddenly chose otherwise.

The corners of Scarlett's lips twitched. "Valuable to us. I know that since she has gone missing, I do not get my reports promptly. I had hoped you might have met her. When last you were in France, perhaps?"

Kane's mind jolted. He fingered the portrait of St. Antoine. Her hair was bright red. She looked fashionably slender. But he could not say this was the lady on the road to Malmaison. The one he remembered all too well was his Raven with the lush mouth and the gall to bite him when he kissed her. "I have not met her, no."

"Well," said Scarlett with concern marring her brow, "we proceed, in any case. She's twenty-four, a dear friend of Josephine, and has been since she was in prison with her in Carmes."

*So we know St. Antoine's age. The same age as Scarlett. We know her tribulations in prison. We also know enough about her to fear her safety may be at stake, as well as what and whom she knows.*

Ram grunted. "Carmes? The Parisian prison where they slaughtered hundreds in a few days?"

"The same," said Kane with stones sinking in his stomach. Friends made in prison were especially ruthless.

Ram tsked. "Extraordinary that Josephine survived. And this St. Antoine as well."

"Few did," said Scarlett. "There are reasons she and the others were not taken."

Kane frowned. *Really?* Scarlett knew that too. "Did we have anything to do with that?"

"With Madame St. Antoine, yes." Scarlett answered that without a moment's pause. "Not with Josephine or their other friend from the cells in Carmes, Cecily, Countess Nugent."

"The mistress of the old Duc d'Orleans still survives." Kane knew all about Nugent. Infamous, once the mistress of the prince regent, the Englishwoman had been personally recommended by him to his friend, the French duke who was so supportive of the revolution that they killed him for his service.

"Nugent lives with Josephine," Scarlett confirmed. "She's very amusing to Josephine. Likes her silks and feathers. Advises on fashion, which scarf to wear today."

Kane took the sketch of St. Antoine from Dirk and placed it in his waistcoat's inner pocket. Many women took up residence with Josephine. Thérésa Tallien, the wife of a former revolutionary, who slept with Paul Barras and wore transparent silk to the opera. Nugent, the Englishwoman, and this St. Antoine.

Kane again recalled the delicious young creature he'd kissed on the road that morning at Malmaison. Was she also in residence in the Tuileries? A friend of Josephine or her servant? Was any other man kissing her now?

No matter. He had other things to consider. "Any idea who might harm St. Antoine?"

Scarlett cocked an elegant auburn brow. "Pick a name. Any name."

He smacked his lips. "Fouché?" Kane hated the man.

Scarlett did not blink.

"Vaillancourt?" *Fouché's deputy?* Kane hated him more. A vicious blackguard who had murdered his cousin Fabien and his friend on the Malmaison road, Brussard.

Scarlett conceded, her face pale.

"I see," he said. "She is central to our operation. Since when?"

"Three years ago."

He scoffed. Scarlett's admission proved he'd been right that she knew St. Antoine very well. Had the two girls played together when Scarlett lived in France as a young child? "How did St. Antoine manage that? A woman so young? Twenty-one when she began to give information to her country's foremost enemy? She must be the most…ingenious woman."

He cleared his throat. One did not disparage the likes of women, friend or foe, in the presence of their supremely savvy spymaster. Miss Scarlett Hawthorne, wealthy, wise, and welcome in many Society homes, was the fiercest Amazon a man could encounter. She brooked no foolish ridicule of the fairer sex. He inhaled, regrouped his thoughts. "What else do we need to know?"

Scarlett frowned at him. "This job requires more than a few days. Weeks—months, most likely. I recommend to all of you to put your estates in order. Including your wills."

The three Englishmen stared at her.

"No, surely not," said Ram, recovering his shock first and giving a false laugh.

But no one dared to do the same.

"*Monsieurs*, not to worry." Pelletier lifted a hand, nonchalant. "I am there to assist."

Carlton stepped forward, grim as ever. Scarlett's man had never smiled a day in his life. The scar that ran from his left cheek up to his black leather eye patch had long ago cut the muscle beneath. "Today, post a few thousand in your accounts with Rothschild. Tomorrow to each, I will add another twenty thousand. More follows."

Dirk whistled. "*Mein Freund*, what are you funding? The rest of our lives?"

But Kane liked the idea of more money than he'd had in his lifetime. "Carlton, hear me, I don't have thousands. I'll take whatever you give me, of course. I could not be more pleased at the donation. I need every penny. But do know, I have at most a hundred. Still, I'll gladly take your twenty thousand, and be prudent. But I don't even have a court wardrobe. I'll need time to have it sewn." He stared at Scarlett.

"Find a good tailor in Paris." She brushed off his concern with a flip of her hand. "Spend what you must."

Ram was dubious. "You are too generous, Scarlett. You give me the impression we are expected to die."

"Of that," said Dirk, who had sat still as a corpse since the money was announced, "I am not interested unless you tell me I am killing Fouché with my bare hands."

Kane licked his lips as the thought of the demise of the French minister of police or his deputy. But he too had no taste for blood. Not since he'd seen how Fouché's deputy had brutally gutted his friend Brussard in the forest that bright June day in Malmaison.

Scarlett inhaled and glanced up at Carlton. When he nodded, she pursed her lips. "With the disappearance of St. Antoine, we have lost more than one person useful to our cause. She was our key in the north of France. My crux. I must have her back, in place, or I must know to what extent her work has been compromised."

She stared at her hands, then at Kane. "Since long before the tumbrel rolled to the guillotine, we had information from our agents. But my problem, my father's problem, always was lack of ability to organize all details in a timely fashion. It takes so damn long to travel with news, and you cannot tell if the gossip in a café cancels the word of a chevalier in a port. But at least we had information. Plenty of it. Now with this lack of one person who had coordinated so much in France—Kane, God help me—I am blind."

Kane had no idea Scarlett was so crippled these past few years. He had refused so many of her missions. He had not volunteered to help her more. He should have.

She licked her lips. "Know, Kane, that there is to be no killing. There is no planning to take a life. Only planning, organizing, to save one life and millions more. If St. Antoine is gone, then we will establish a new center. If she has revealed all our friends, you three with Pelletier and a few more whom I send will create a new network. Fouché may have destroyed our web. Him, however, you will leave to Bonaparte and God. That is your challenge. Above all, you will keep patience as your watchword and prudence as your guide."

Ram sat forward. "Not to fear. We keep our brains in our heads."

Scarlett placed both of her elegant fingers to the gleaming mahogany of her desk. "We begin."

"Do I have a contact? A correspondent? Anyone left in Paris you trust?" Kane wanted the name of a collaborator so he could finish here, then go home and have old Friendly pack a trunk for him.

"Not our friend, but St. Antoine's. Miss Augustine Bolton."

Another woman. The name meant nothing to him. "I do not know her."

"She is Nugent's niece. Close to Josephine and her ladies. She also speaks excellent French."

Kane snorted. The famous mistress's niece was better than no contact at all. "How well do you trust her?"

Scarlett Hawthorne, who was not one to hedge, did it once more today. She pursed her lips, formulating her answer. "She is our best source."

Which told him to be cautious with Miss Bolton. *What a stew!* Well, he had once planned coups on less. He would have to summon the wherewithal to navigate the lady's reliability.

"Kane?" Scarlett caught his attention with her summons. "Bolton is attractive, the court's darling…entertaining."

His brows shot upward. Gone were the days when he bedded every woman who appealed to him. "She is loose?"

"Men like her, but she does not succumb to easy charms." Scarlett was adamant. "Become friends with Bolton. But find Madame St. Antoine or…"

"I know." For the fortune he was being paid, he would find God. "Or bury her." He winced.

Scarlett held out documents to him. "Memorize this list and burn it afterward. And this is the address of your apartment off the Champs-Élysées. It is temporary. You have a *majordom*, who is one of ours. His family works with us out of Pisa. Magnus Corsini. He finds you a suitable house and hires staff."

Kane was surprised at how thoroughly she had prepared for him that he had an Italian in his operation. Did Corsini deal in poison and the *garrotte*?

She must have read his mind, because she lifted her shoulders in a pose of a woman thrilled by her thoughts. "He is from a famous family, yes, with many useful skills."

*As I thought.* "I won't ask what they are." Kane put up a palm, but looked toward his friends. "Am I to know the missions of these three?"

She was quick to respond. "Each has his own assignment, but first and foremost, they assist you. Our temporary minister in Paris is Anthony Merry. Leave him to his diplomacy. He knows only what each of you do for the government, but not what you do for me."

To Kane, she was pointed: "As for you, sir, you become the suave British host of exclusive receptions and balls. You are signing trade deals for silks, china. Especially grain—if you can get it. Fournier assists with diplomats. Ramsey is not far away in a house near the Tuileries."

"No dinner parties for me?" Ram appeared to take umbrage

at that.

But Scarlett had his answer. "If you need it, do. But right away, you are busy implementing the release of our English from French prisons."

"Ah," Ram said. "So then I am looking at numbers of soldiers in French forts, am I?"

Scarlett let her lips lift in an appreciative smile. "And supplies going into them. But remember, all of you work together. What you don't know, you learn. What you know, you share."

Kane scanned the attitudes of each man before him. They were silent. Imbibing their struggles to come. Calm as ever. Intent as always. And deadly.

"The four of you," she said, "are there to ensure a proper, functioning system. Repair it or rebuild it. Feed and complement what we have here." She tipped her head and smiled at them with the consolation of the damned. "Do not fail."

# Chapter Three

April 27, 1802
Tuileries Palace
Paris

THIS EVENING'S GATHERING was much the same as last night's here. Kane had presented himself to tonight's hostess for Josephine, Madame Tallien, one of Madame Bonaparte's ladies, and made his way through the crowd to the supper buffet. Satisfied by his own *maison d'chef*'s creations, he rarely wasted time to eat at these soirees.

He had priorities. Track Josephine's movements. Ask discreet questions about one or two of her unmarried ladies. Appear affable and interested in today's gossip. Who slept with whom last night. Where Fouché's madman deputy Vaillancourt was. Did Ramsey keep his hands to himself tonight? And what happened to Dirk Fournier that he was suddenly enraptured with a little chit from the Vendee?

His cousin should stay clear of those types. Revolutionaries like that were still causing trouble in Brittany and in Bordeaux. Look what had happened to Kane when he worked with that rebel Juvenot. The man had failed, with all conspirators caught and killed. Only Kane had escaped that day...and probably only because he kissed a black-haired beauty too many times.

"*Bon soir, Monsieur le Comte.*" The lady who stood in his way to the table was Madame Julie Averdeau. Her husband, an aide-de-camp to Bonaparte, was a young bit of fluff who managed to find her way into many of her husband's comrades' beds.

"Forgive me, *madame.*" He executed his superb Parisian French, smiled like a smitten beau, and bowed like a prince. "I have not had the pleasure."

"Nor have I, *Monsieur le Comte,* which is why I stand before you. The best way to make friends is to start without all the rules that hold others in chains. Don't you agree?" She touched her open fan to his wrist, her good English his encouragement to get this tête-à-tête over with soon. He did not speak often in English. In French, he could prevaricate.

"I do, *madame.*" He stuck to his French. "Allow me. I am your humble servant. The Earl of Ashley, Viscount Marl, Baron Dayton."

"A lovely recitation," she replied with dainty pronunciation. "I heard you speak French before. How do you speak our language so well, *monsieur* of the many titles?"

"I have family who are from Aquitaine, *madame.* When a child, I had the privilege to live with my mother's family in Bordeaux and later in the Loire."

"*C'est vrai?* How charming. Whom do you have in the Loire? Perhaps I know them?"

Why did Kane have the impression that she knew who his relatives were and only asked to keep him amused? "My family are wine producers."

"Ancient vintners?"

"Indeed, *madame.* Since fifteen-ten."

"And the name of your people?"

He grew bored with this recitation of blood and responsibilities. His Aunt Justine and her family would hate that they were the topic of conversation of these rascals who had usurped power. "The family Lamartine."

"They produce good *vin blanc*."

"Indeed they do."

She sidled nearer, her perfume of roses the most delicate thing about her. Indeed, it was her breasts, her round nipples bursting from their thin confinement, that brushed his forearm. Her invitation was crude. As for her expertise in bed, he could say with certainty that he had no desire to learn. He preferred a lady with subtlety to her charms.

"I have a good cask of the Lamartine vintage from two years ago in my cellar." She gave him a moue of delight.

"How marvelous," he said. "Good taste."

"I give a luncheon tomorrow in my home. Do come, *monsieur*. I will serve the Chenin blanc '00 with the excellent veal."

"*Je regrette*, Madame Averdeau. I have a previous engagement."

"Ah, but I understand you seek a friend of mine who will be in attendance."

He would not take the bait and look like a fool. The lady did not know he sought Augustine Bolton. Only his team knew that. "Sadly, I do regret this, *madame*. Perhaps another time, I might have the honor."

"She will be sorry you cannot attend."

*Damn.* Who was this woman she alluded to? "I am afraid she must be."

She gave him one of her long-lashed dismissals and, with a few polite words, faded from his presence.

He turned away, refusing to see her go and take with her any remnant of his frustration. He had been invited to this supper party by Madame Tallien, who told him he must attend to watch the midnight entertainment of the members of the ballet troupe of Versailles. He couldn't, frankly, give a rat's arse about ballet, but if this errant Mademoiselle Bolton would show her reputedly pretty face, he'd count the evening's boring hours well spent.

Across the room, even Dirk agreed with him. His cousin yawned and tried to cover his boredom with a quick lift of his cuff to his nose.

Kane took the few steps across the marble floor to his side. Footmen bent to them to offer refreshments from trays. Then he and Dirk were blessedly alone in the so-called "conversation" double chairs, which each faced the opposite way. "Past your bedtime, old man?"

"One year more makes a perfect man." Dirk always got a hit making fun of their age difference, since he could do nothing to compare their sizes. They were in many ways the same, save complexion, the tallest and broadest of shoulder in any room. "Not here again, is your certain lady?"

They both took a long draw of their wine and surveyed the room filled with women more naked in their transparent fabrics than Kane had ever seen a woman sans clothes. "Rumor has it she has the ague."

Dirk smirked. "If she dresses like these do, it is no wonder. However, I have it on good authority she is indisposed."

"What authority?" Kane had to assess everything.

"Her aunt." Dirk lifted his crystal flute in a small salute to none other than himself, of course.

Kane honored him with a laugh. "Ah. A point to you. Met her, did you?"

"I was introduced this morning, riding in the park."

"You get up too early for me," Kane observed, as he always had at his cousin's regimented nature. Kane taunted Dirk for his strict training at Heidelberg University. "Too many worms out at that time of day."

Dirk glanced around. "If you got up to go with me, you might benefit."

"To meet the ladies? I do well enough on my own. Besides, I need only one on this trip. I am on good behavior, remember?"

"One can still look...for later, you know?" Dirk flourished his empty glass. "I have talked you up. Everyone is eager to meet the English cousin of the maternal cadet branch of *der kleine Prinz von Bergenhaven*."

"*Jawohl.* I am a bore this trip, Diederich. *Meine fraulein ist nicht herein.*"

"No reason for you to live the life of a monk while you wait to meet her."

"I have no time or energy for *amour.*"

"You've had little since your brush with a certain fellow two years ago."

Kane snorted at the reference to his particular nemesis, Rene Vaillancourt. "He did change my life. I admit it." The deputy chief of Paris police had killed his friend, and in a prolonged, gruesome manner that was unnecessary, too.

"But tonight you are lucky. Look to the far door. The countess and, I do believe, her niece." Dirk inclined his head ever so slightly toward the lady who appeared there.

Striking a pose, one long leg toward the front, her chin up at a mischievous tilt, her lips rouged and glistening, the older woman with cropped coal-black hair and generous bosoms influenced those in the room to fall silent. With her firm, rounded breasts leading the way, the countess strode about the yellow and lilac salon in her flowing pale pink gown, greeting everyone. Unlike many other ladies here, the Countess Nugent revealed only her rosy areoles through her silk. The rest of her was discreetly concealed. Her appetizer definitely amused him so much that Kane fought his grin.

"Come," said Dirk in triumph. "I will introduce you."

Kane stood, at the ready. Relief flooding his system, he argued with his prudent choice to focus on her pleasing face. Every woman had breasts, and heaven knew there were enough of them jiggling around this ballroom tonight that he needn't consider Lady Nugent's worthy of a unique study.

But then his view shifted to a frothy cloud of elegance that appeared behind the countess. His step halted. His pulse leapt—and his cock stirred in hot homage at the vision who strolled behind the countess.

This one was no more than an inch taller. Decades younger.

More lithe. Virginal in a liquid, creamy silk no one could see through. Jade ribbons were tied beneath her full, pointed breasts. A jade ribbon wound through her Grecian cap of black curls.

Kane's hands flexed. His fingers tingled, remembering the feel of her firm flesh captured by his own. Her lips parted for others as, once in a forest in the early morning, they had opened beneath his own. He could feel them now. Supple, giving. A sensation he must rid himself of.

But she smiled at her companion, and his guts stirred. Her smile, one he hadn't enjoyed that dreadful day, was wide and infectious. He must have that smile from her for *him*. Inspire her to it. Lure it from her as she drew it from him now. He knew not how nor when that would be. But the certitude of it filled his surging blood. He would have her—and soon.

*Raven.*

"You know her?" Dirk had stopped at Kane's side.

"I do." She was his contact. His objective. Raven was—

"Augustine Bolton," Dirk whispered. "Let's have ourselves introduced."

GUS REJOICED AT her return to the Tuileries. Her tendency to catch her death from changes in the weather were the bane of her existence. This was what she was trained to do. Socialize. Converse. Learn what she could and share it with her aunt. The dazzle of conversation, the intrigue of each exchange, her rejection of men who thought her head filled with feathers. Her Aunt Cecily was her *entree* to Society that her parents could not give her. Or would not. But from an early age—five, to be exact—Aunt Cecily had brought her here to Paris. She'd sent her home to escape the Terror, then brought her back in her own carriage after Bonaparte conquered the mobs and secured her aunt's safety.

She surveyed the dozens before her, dressed to the teeth with fabrics and jewels and honors that their small little lives had precluded, long before their ambitions joined with another fellow who would have once amounted to little more than a lieutenant. Now his skills as an organizer and a propagandist had united to make him the leader of these whom he had scooped from the underside of many a trough.

"Good evening, *Mademoiselle* Bolton." The man before her had hurried to greet her. It was not the first time the suave captain of the Paris sector had swept toward her with speed. "I am delighted to see you are recovered."

"*Merci beaucoup, Monsieur le Capitaine.* I am relieved to be well again. The weather, it is too variable." She gave him her breathiest contralto. "I am sensitive."

He took her hand to lead it to his thin lips. "You must always have warm fires to soothe you, *mademoiselle.*"

"You are most kind, captain. I choose my locales carefully." *As well as my admirers.*

"Perhaps I might be of assistance?"

*I doubt it.* "Perhaps." She'd lead him on. One never knew when a man would become useful.

"Tomorrow night." He was quick to take up the chance. "I could appear at your door and take you to the theater. I have a box."

*I'm sure you do.* "*Merci, Monsieur le Capitaine.* But I do not yet venture out often. My poor lungs," she cooed, and placed her hand to her heart. His eager eyes followed, looking for a peek at something the silk did not reveal. "I cannot bear to ride in anything but an overheated coach. You understand, I'm sure."

Poor man, he did try to look less than crestfallen. *Quel dommage!*

Her reputation led many to try to lure her to their cocoons. She had lived among these opportunists for too long to take each at all seriously. She was not giving away her virtue for a man who wished to prattle that he had broken the lock on the Bolt's virginity.

"Augustine?" Her aunt swung round and beckoned her onward. "Come here, please."

She did her aunt's bidding, spun, and faced none other than the man of the Malmaison road. She caught her breath. He lived! She had thought him captured, dead with the others who attempted to take Bonaparte that morning. But he'd survived. And my, my, he was captivating. Big. Huge. She had felt his power when he'd taken her in his arms. But she had not recalled the details, only the impression of his magnificence.

Now he stood before her and she could absorb all of his grandeur. Six feet six, at least, towering over her and looking like a giant animal about to eat her for breakfast. She swallowed hard on the pool of desire in her mouth. Her body remembered his lips, his kiss. As if...as if the rest of him were not a feast for a female's fantasies.

His shoulders were a wall. His ice-gray eyes absorbed every tiny feature of her face. He remembered her, and she could do naught but give him a small wink to warn him against revealing all about her that he recalled of that morning.

So she smiled prettily. Why not? She would have *him* for breakfast. The rake.

Aunt Cecily did the honors, the lady's green eyes flashing when she noticed Gus appreciating him. "Do allow me to introduce to you the gentleman who heads the trade negotiations for the British. The Earl of Ashley. Newly dubbed, is that not so, my lord?" Her aunt batted her long, painted lashes at the giant who had once held Gus—handled her, to be precise—and then kissed her. Twice. The scoundrel. Now he was here, his cologne a smooth blend of good soap and lime. The fragrance filled her nostrils and had her pressing her thighs together at his intoxicating proximity.

"How do you do, my Lord Ashley?" She did her demure bow, offering her hand, her expression as placid as her years of practice allowed.

The delicious giant bowed over her fingertips, not quite as

elegantly as he had two years ago in the forest, but he would do. His height would certainly enthrall. He could protect a woman from heaven's wrath. His hair would also do. Pure onyx. Gleaming in the golden candlelight, his mane was worthy of her caress. If he were lucky. Which he was not. Although to be honest, the frosty hue of his eyes enticed her to wager against herself how long it would take her to melt the ice she saw there.

"I am very well, Miss Bolton."

"Refreshing to hear good English, sir." She could compliment him on something so innocuous as his pronunciation of their mother tongue.

"Lord Ashley"—Aunt Cecily addressed him in English as well—"do tell us about your duties here."

He went on about his charge and how he wished to sell many luxury French products to wealthy Britons. "I'd like to ship grain, if Citizen Bonaparte will ease the tariff."

Gus listened with half an ear. Ashley was a devastatingly handsome puzzle. She'd need to learn everything about a creature who could negotiate the trade of French goods to the British shores and, in the next breath, plot to kill Bonaparte on public roads. Such boldness should be applauded—before, of course, being sent to *la Force* for attempted assassination.

"Don't you agree, Miss Bolton?"

She'd been lost to his rich bass voice and the contradiction of his past to present. But she had to nod, didn't she? And discuss…what? Wine? "I agree that wine is vital to any discussion. So much in diplomacy depends on fine wine, does it not? The world will destruct without a good vintage."

Her aunt was focused on the business of trade. "Have you met with *Monsieur* LaGrange yet, Lord Ashley?"

LaGrange, LaGrange. Gus worked her brain. He was the lead financier in Paris for the vintners who sold wine in Paris.

"No," Ashley said. "I have not yet had the pleasure of meeting him. I arrived a few weeks ago, but I have been setting up my household."

"You are alone in Paris, my lord?" Aunt Cecily asked him with keen interest in her green eyes.

Gus covered her amusement. Her aunt was digging to learn if the Monsieur of the Malmaison Road had a wife. Or a mistress he'd brought with him for convenience.

"Yes, my lady. It is only I, my friends working as attachés to the embassy, and my servants."

"It is difficult to find good help."

"My *majordom* seems to have that in hand. Although my chef needs assistants worthy of the many engagements I will host."

"Well, sir!" She tipped her head toward him with glee. "I should be happy to recommend to you two whom I know are available and worthy of your station."

"Thank you, my lady. I should like to have your suggestions. You have been here, I understand, for quite a while."

*Oh, please.* Gus bit the inside of her lip to keep from barking at him. He, like his entire assemblage, had dossiers on everyone long before they had set foot on French soil. He was no green lad in any way, shape, or form. One did not become an assassin in a foreign country without prior investigation of all whom they would meet.

"Come to our salon tomorrow, Lord Ashley." Her aunt had intentions to cultivate the giant in their midst. Why? She liked his looks? Or did she speculate as to his potential as her lover?

Gus's nerves prickled. Was that jealousy? *Absurd!* Her aunt would not want to bed one so young. Cecily Ann Struthers-Sumner had a long history of bedding only the most important men. The Prince of Wales. The old Duc d'Orleans. Paul Barras. Besides…

*Ashley is not a man I want. Why would I? He offers me nothing I need.*

"Thank you, madam. I happily accept your invitation."

"Shall we say two o'clock?"

He bowed. "We shall."

"Do give him our address, *ma petite. Bon soir,* my lord."

Her aunt sailed off and left Gus staring up at him.

"You did that prettily, sir."

He cocked a long black brow. On his lips was a dashing smile. "I am a diplomat."

"Your previous career had less to do with diplomacy and more to do with the opposite."

"That day," he said as suavely as if he were one of Foreign Secretary Talleyrand's men, "I regret more than you know."

She huffed. "Because you failed."

"Because a friend of mine died, quite brutally."

She glared at him—and hated herself for her public display of such a raw emotion. "Be careful whom you play with." She began to turn away.

He caught her wrist. "I saw. I hated the result. I vowed never to involve myself in such heinous acts again. Please don't go."

His words were soft and sweet. She narrowed her gaze on him. "Why? You find my conversation appealing?"

"I would like to, yes."

She wanted to scoff at him, but she was attracting attention from a few. She did not want that. Ever. It was vital to her peace of mind to remain inconspicuous. "If I try to leave, you will haul me against you?"

"Why not? It was quite glorious that morning to hold you in my arms."

"Intent as you were on...other things?" She realized she had raised her voice. Such was not done in the salon of Josephine.

"I don't wish to argue with you, Miss Bolton. In fact, I want to apologize."

She sniffed at him. Out of necessity to keep her emotions in check, she inched toward a corner where no one else was in attendance. No one should overhear the anger she harbored for him—or view the fascination he held for her. "Apologies are now the means of soothing those you have harmed?"

"They always were. I am no longer that man you met in the forest."

"You no longer haul ladies off their horses or catch mice in sacks?"

"No. I talk like a civilized man with those who produce silk and make good wine. I am here to build friendships and business relationships."

She liked his mouth. His articulateness. His bass voice that stirred her insides to warm eddies of desire. He was an infatuation that she must deny. "Are you here to kiss people, too?"

"I am." He grinned. The dash of his charm, the gleam of his white teeth, set her pulse pounding. "And you, *mademoiselle*, do you still bite people who kiss you?"

"Only those who hold my breast without my permission."

He arched a brow. "But when I kissed you a second time, you did not bite. One would wonder why."

"Ah. Simple. You had hold of my arm, and I could not draw my dagger."

He gave her a side glance. "Do you make a practice of stabbing those who steal a kiss?"

"I make a practice of stabbing anyone who steals what I do not freely give."

"I will remember that."

She had to grin at his repartee. "Do you plan to steal from me again?"

"Do you keep your dagger on you always?" His hot—yet still icy—regard did not sweep down her body, yet his finesse triumphed over his lust.

She tingled. Her nipples hardened to points. Her reaction shamed her. She was immune to men like him—smooth, deliberate liars. "Luckily for you tonight, I do not take daggers to receptions."

He inclined his head, his small smile full of regret. "Sadly for me tonight, I have not touched you."

"Do not try."

His starry gaze challenged her. "I never simply *try*."

## Chapter Four

B Y THE TIME Kane had drunk enough wine to cover his
monitoring of Augustine's movements the rest of the night,
he was drained. Moreover, he was angry at himself for not being
suaver. She would mark him off as rude and unworthy of her. He
cursed his ready desire to amuse her. Fed up with himself, he had
his carriage brought round and cursed his folly for the five-minute
ride home.

He got down from his carriage, nodding his thanks to his
groom. He still was not used to having all these people wait upon
him—and he had fourteen of them, God preserve him. He
needed every one for such an establishment as his grand mansion
on Rue Saint-Honoré. Though he certainly wished he had fewer,
he would have desired to have investigated each himself. For
whatever good that would do him, which would be none. In
France since the Terror, everyone told you what they thought
you wanted to hear. Alas, fourteen servants would tell him
fantasies he had no time to pursue.

The *hôtel particulier* his *majordom* Corsini had rented for him
was a four-story, century-old marvel near the Champs-Élysées.
Fronted by the buttery stone of the quarries to the north of Paris,
the house was in the shape of a U, with gardens of evergreens and
roses in the courtyard. The house, once the abode of the Rohan

aristocracy of Britanny and Strasbourg, had lain empty until two years ago, when the Committee of Safety had appropriated it. The last family member who had lived in the house was a Rohan who had gone to the guillotine weeks after Marie Antoinette. Before the man had departed the house, he had ordered all the furniture covered, the china stored, and the Rohan jewels hidden. Four years later, when the committee opened it up, lo and behold, the mobs had not destroyed it. The furniture was intact. The china, too. But the jewels were nowhere to be found.

"You may wish to look for them, *si, conte*? They could be of great worth." His olive-skinned Italian butler had told Kane much that first day they'd opened the house to the air and its future as the property of a British lord. "Rubies big as eggs, I have heard, *conte*." The little Florentine did not address Kane often by his full title, as his lips could not, for some reason, deal with the pronunciation of Ash-leigh. Corsini's articulation reminded him of Friendly's, making Kane ponder the need for all butlers to enunciate precisely.

"I believe if I found the gems, Corsini, they would be the natural property of the consulate."

"A shame." The slender, elegantly attired man caught his wrists behind his back and rose on his toes. He refused to mourn much about rules and regulations of the French. He flourished a hand. "We Corsinis have no such tendency."

"Or they might well belong to any Rohan family member still alive."

The fellow had muttered his compliance, but as to how long he would comply, Kane feared the term was short.

"*Bona sera, conte*." Corsini welcomed him home this evening from the Tuileries and took his hat and gloves.

Kane unbuttoned his frock coat and headed for the grand staircase to his suite.

"*Uno momento, conte*—you have a visitor."

Kane spun. After one o'clock in the morning?

"I took the liberty to place him in the small salon with a fine cognac from Bordeaux."

"His name?" Corsini knew his friends, Ramsey and Dirk. Since Kane took residence last week, the men had visited individually, and both had also been guests to dinner the night before last.

"Citizen Bechard. Is he not from the family of the old Comte de Brissac?"

Kane widened his eyes at the scope of what this *majordom* knew about the world of Paris. The Rohans, servants, wine distributors, linen drapers, men who might claim an old aristocratic title but demurred. "You are well versed in so much, Corsini. Indeed, you are right. Bechard could be the *conte*, if he wished."

*But, smart man, Luc Bechard doesn't.*

Kane took the grand marble stairs two at a time.

Luc Bechard was one of the few from *ancien* families who had survived the convulsions of the revolution these past eleven years. He owed that good fortune to the fact that when Robespierre ruled in the Reign of Terror, Luc had been a mere second cousin to the more famous Brissac counts. When the last count had gone bravely to the guillotine, he left the title vacant. Luc was the only male left in line. He eschewed the title, but took the duties along with the land in the Loire, which added to his abilities to produce good *chenin blanc*. Kane had met Luc many years ago when he visited his Aunt Justine and her family in Amboise.

"Citizen!" Kane hailed his old friend from the open doors of his quaint salon. "I would ask what has taken you so long, but I am so pleased I have quite forgotten to be surly."

The dark, exquisitely tailored man in the leather chair rose to his feet with a grin. "I came, *Monsieur le Comte d'Ashley*, as soon as my grapes allowed."

The two men grasped each other with the hearty clasp only childhood memories induced. At arm's length, they each contemplated the other.

"Taller," said Luc with wide umber eyes. "More man," he added with hands wide, measuring Kane's shoulders.

"You are my match and always were," Kane said. "You look well. No more problems with your lungs." Luc had battled with pneumonia often as a boy.

"I eat better now and worry less."

"You have a few more acres to broaden your yield and decrease your headaches."

"I do. For that land, I am grateful. That it also puts me in the sights of the tax collectors and Fouché, I am not so delighted."

Kane offered the chair once more. "Please sit, and let us not speak of that man until we must. Tell me instead how your family is."

Luc sucked in air. "*Ma mère* is ailing. My mother took to her bed many years ago after my sister and her husband were taken in the tumbrels to the guillotine. *Mon père* died last spring. My younger sister, Inès, at age twenty, is now the terror of the family. She is, to put it finely, beautiful. She knows it and seeks to use it to find a wealthy man. We tell her to find only a good one, but she flirts with anything that looks wealthy."

"And you?" Kane topped up his friend's snifter and poured a generous dollop for himself. "Have you married?"

Luc shook his head and took his time to respond. "I am a widower. My wife died in childbirth two years ago, and I think I may never find another her equal. She was my everything."

Kane took the chair opposite his friend and sipped the cognac. He did not dare to ask if the baby had lived. "My condolences, Luc."

"I survive. My mother tells me I must marry again before I lose my ability to create fine babies, but I see no one who appeals to me. I go on. I have my mother and my sister to care for, twenty-two tenants in the vineyards, and an ancient chateau of...I don't know, perhaps forty rooms. I have not counted. I have no time."

"Are you in Paris often?"

"No. I am currently here in residence in the Brissac house. I paid the fines and the taxes on it, so *voila*! I get to use it when I come to town to sell in the city."

"I want to talk to you about your production, and hope we can arrange export to Britain of your wine."

"Now that times are less chaotic, we produce double what we did in the last decade. Plus people wish to live and forget what we did to each other. We have a great demand for wine here in France. So I don't know if I can give you the quantity you would wish. But we can talk."

"That is the future."

"Agreed. But we must speak of other issues now," Luc said with serious eyes. "It is why I am here."

Kane took a drink. "Tell me."

"I am in the city to talk with those who make barrels for us. I was in a café this afternoon and saw Diederich Fournier. I had no idea he was in Paris. He said he works with you and told me where you are." Luc put down his glass. "I would have come earlier in the evening and been more appropriate, but I had an invitation to a dinner party that I could not refuse. It is fortunate I did not cancel."

"Why?"

"I understand you seek to increase the exports from France and imports from Britain. Many in wine have learned of your mission. They spoke of it at tonight's dinner. It is why I am here. And you must know it. There is a faction in the government—clerks, they are—who do not wish to export anything to Britain. They wish to see the Germans have it, or the Dutch. Even the Russians."

Kane snorted. "If God can help them make it safe to travel so far."

"Exactly."

"Who does not wish to see us make a decent trade volume?"

"Vaillancourt."

"I have met him."

"He and his friends will stop the trade, they say, in any way they can."

Kane was not surprised Vaillancourt was involved in illegal activities. Plus he was glad to have his friend's input on it. Yet he had to appear surprised. "But what is the deputy of police doing mixing in trade issues?"

Luc gave a shrug. "Money, I hear. Is that not the usual motive?"

"I was under the impression that Bonaparte had ordered all graft and corruption to end. The man walks a fine line if he extorts or even influences others."

"It is my understanding that Vaillancourt is involved in many schemes. Gossip only. But I knew you would want to know of his involvement."

With a few more notes of warning about Fouché's men as well as others, Luc left soon after via the back staircase. Kane had ordered Corsini to hail a public carriage from a back street.

Upstairs in his chambers, Kane considered his challenges.

To effect trade deals, he had to worry not only about corruption but also about the French police breathing down his neck. At the moment, the easiest of his assignments was to strike good agreements with suppliers of French goods. Getting them contracted and past the machinations of the police was his next most difficult. But his first, most vital need was to get Augustine Bolton to help him find her friend, Amber St. Antoine.

If St. Antoine was still alive, he'd need to relay news to Scarlett Hawthorne of who remained of her network of informants. If St. Antoine was not alive, he had to note who was newly missing and rebuild a team of agents who could learn enough about productions of goods and grains and weaponry to keep Britain informed of her enemy's strengths.

Which, of course, meant he had to discover as soon as possible the sympathies of Augustine Bolton. Which she was not inclined to freely discuss. To her, he was an assassin. An enemy. One who killed and took and ravaged. No diplomat in fine clothing, but a wolf wrapped in lies. Why would she help him?

*Only if I can help her.*

He snorted.

*Only if she even cares that her friend has disappeared? Only if, to Raven, Amber St. Antoine has, in fact, vanished.*

But a lady who kissed like an angel and fought like a devil would give up few truths without strong inducements.

*And what in hell might those be?*

FITFUL ALL NIGHT, Kane gave up and rose at dawn. He rang Corsini to get a bath ready. A hot scrub could help him focus on Augustine Bolton. What she inspired in him in the dark of night in his bed had occupied him far more than it should.

Persuading himself that she was a woman of intellect, who survived in a vipers' nest of intrigues, he concluded logic was what would sway her. Not flirting. Or raw seduction. Besides, he was not here to dally in a boudoir. He doubted he would be invited into hers. That was a good thing, because he had the premonition he would not wish to leave.

*And I have no time for it.*

He climbed into his tub and submerged himself to the roots of his hair.

He was not a fool for women. Years ago when he was more randy than wise, he took, if they were willing to give. He enjoyed, if they were the type to delight. But he did not tarry. And he did not obsess.

His Raven seemed sophisticated, a creature of this court. Still she possessed an air of wistful exuberance—and independence. As if he were a creature to be monitored for good behavior, she had searched for his purpose—and she could have a few reasons for that. Which meant she might work for Fouché. Or for Talleyrand. For herself or no one. Heaven knew, she certainly did not converse with Kane to establish a relationship and create a liaison.

That, she had made clear.

Whatever her reason, Kane needed her beside him again. To spar, to test, to discuss, to learn from her. About her aunt and that woman's relationship with Josephine. All of it would be useful...and he would treat Raven as a means to an end. Except for the allure of her lips.

He squeezed his eyes shut. No matter. He still saw their lush contours. Her full lower lip. Her plump upper. Their pink that needed no rouge. The corners that lifted without a smile. The way her lips formed words. As if she wrapped her whole self around the contours of each syllable. As if she enticed each word forth to complement the husky voice that had rubbed his desires all through the night.

*Merde.*

There he was again. His hand suppressing his rising member. Rhapsodizing like a schoolboy over the curve of her jaw and her breast...

*Enough!*

He rose with a whoosh of hot water to the tiles.

He needed her knowledge of St. Antoine. And he needed it quickly. But that relationship took time and finesse.

Until he was near her again, he had best throw himself into his own tasks. He had memorized Scarlett's list of current agents. A few were men—and two women—he had known years ago. A few were those whom he'd only heard of. He would send out a few of his footmen to locate them. See if they still lived in the surrounding *faubourgs*. Then he would investigate their actions himself.

In between those searches, he would begin to negotiate for products manufactured in and around the city. The Sèvres china and Gobelin tapestries and rugs were items that wealthy British would eagerly snatch up. To those who could not afford such luxuries, the lace handkerchiefs and fichus from the artisans of Chantilly would bring a smile to many ladies. Later, he'd go to Lyon to buy silks in quantities. Those negotiations should be quick and easy. Then he'd hunt for his scarcest need. Grain. Barley. Wheat.

He would plan to go to the Champagne region to Reims. He'd say he went to visit with a few vintners to buy up their wines to ship to British shores. But he'd say he would go to the St. Antoine vineyards last. He could not claim he went to visit Madame St. Antoine, because he had not met her when he was in France before.

To go to St. Antoine's estates, he'd need a good alibi.

His Raven could give him that if she came as Amber's friend—and his.

THE SUN WAS bright in the late morning sky as Kane left his carriage and approached the *Halle aux blés*. The granary for the city of Paris was a circular building, topped by a dome. It stood in a circular courtyard in front of a pillar erected by Catherine de Medici. Once a palace of hers had stood here, too, but was gone long ago, demolished for this necessary storage facility. Here on the Rue de Viarmes near the Seine, those who wished all kinds of grain came to supply their households, cafés, beer breweries, and shops.

He entered the grain market and inhaled the aromas of fresh grasses. An old *vendeur* sat tallying his morning sales to the *boulangers* and *pâtissiers* who made the city's baguettes and pastries.

Kane came alone. His French was good enough to haggle and authentic enough to inspire confidence in Parisians who regarded the British with critical eyes.

"*Bonjour, monsieur,*" he bade the *vendeur* who worked on his long, worn leather ledgers. Two muscular fellows sat on each side of him. The cash from the day's sales must be in the papier-mâché boxes strapped to the poles behind the three. "I am here to ask this morning's price for barley."

"Gone." The accountant took one look at Kane and scowled. "Come back tomorrow."

"Whom do I speak with if I wish to buy more than a day's supply?"

He turned up his head, his eyes small and unforgiving. "Why?"

"I am *Monsieur* Whittington, and I wish—"

"*Anglais?*" he asked with a smirk.

"*Oui, monsieur.* I am with the British—"

"Thieves."

Kane was not insulted, but even more pleasant. "*Je suis désolé, monsieur.* I assure you, I am here to buy and pay a good price."

"Why?" asked one of the husky bodyguards, rising to his feet, his hands coming out of his pockets at the ready.

"We British like to eat and drink, just like you."

"Not selling you a thing. We need our own."

Kane had predicted a wise *vendeur* would not allow him to buy wheat. But this was the season for spring barley. "I understand. But do you have barley today you have not yet sold?"

The *vendeur* pursed his lips. "You have coin?"

Money always spoke loudly. Kane contained his grin. "I do."

"How much?"

"How much do you have for sale?"

"Are you buying large amounts through the financiers?"

"I am," Kane assured him. The man really wished to know if Kane was buying for the clandestine market. Caught, the man would lose his position. He appeared old and wise enough not to wish that. Besides, Bonaparte had called for an end to the corruption by the previous directors that had destroyed distribution of grain and driven up the price to absurd levels. The French financiers had come to heel, seeing Bonaparte's wisdom to keep prices reasonable. No one wanted a return to the mobs and the guillotine because people were starving. "I wish to buy tons to put on barges to sail up river to the Channel, *monsieur*. And legally, too."

"The tax, *monsieur*, is twenty-two percent."

"I know." Kane would pay even more, if this fellow had his way.

The *vendeur* glanced at his comrades. The two nodded at him.

Kane saw his advantage. "Perhaps we four could go to the café just there and share a glass of wine?"

That was when Kane saw a flash of brilliant black curls beneath a tiny, fashionable bonnet of apple green. The woman who hurried onward had breasts that bounced beautifully in time with her hurried step. The lady's self-satisfied smile was defined by the pout of her luscious lips.

Those lips were the ones he had dreamt of for more than two years.

He curved his own in a grin and murmured to himself, "I have you."

## Chapter Five

COUNTESS NUGENT LIVED on Île Saint-Louis, the tiny island in the middle of the Seine. The sumptuous house, five stories tall, was once owned by her lover, the old Duc d'Orleans.

Kane's hostess and he had enjoyed a few minutes of greeting and useless chatter, then Kane moved on to the footmen who offered a selection of wines from the Champagne. The English-woman's salons were renowned for the buffet, the conversation, and the assignations that many attested occurred in her tiny back garden. However, last week, Paris was regaled with one observer's detailed description of three guests enjoying a *ménage à trois* in the *majordom*'s wine cellar.

Kane usually was not interested in such tales. This afternoon he gazed across the crowded room, interested only in finding one person. Josephine Bonaparte, whom he hoped to avoid, per Scarlett's warnings, was in attendance, and he sought to be anywhere she was not. Madame Averdeau, who had pursued him last night, was here, but so was Augustine Bolton.

This afternoon, Augustine stood across the room talking with a gentleman who bent to her every word, gallant and animated. Was the man a suitor, perhaps? Whatever his relationship to her, she gave her polite words of excuse and took up a position at the elaborate pianoforte a few steps away. She put her fan down and sat upon the bench with a brush of her violet silk skirts.

With no regard to gathering admirers to her, she sat with her hands in her lap for a long moment. Slowly, her head turned and her marvelous dark green eyes met Kane's and slid away. She put her long fingers to the keys and, smiling to herself, began a Mozart piece Kane knew well. He played it often himself. Sweet and short, it fit the mood of the salon. It pleased her too, for she did it with a smile, then replayed it. That second time, she drew polite applause, including his, even from so far away. She clearly felt his acclamation, because once more her gaze traveled to his and locked. For only a second, she lavished him with her attention. At once, she was gone, up and away from the instrument, her fan in hand as she strolled among the throng...away from him.

Alas, patience was his watchword. To drown his need to rush to her side and swoop her away to his carriage and his purpose, Kane diverted his attentions and went in search of a good wine.

He would work his way toward her. Slowly. This was her aunt's house, and her residence, too. It would do him no good to look too eager.

He strolled on, surveying the two hundred or more guests. Dressed in the finest satins and silks in colors of the rainbow, the ladies appeared in the *haute couture*. The flowing styles that resembled the gowns of Roman and Greek ladies were dictated by the leadership of the stunning brunette, Madame Bonaparte. Some said she wore a gown only once and discarded it. Gossip had it she took three hours to bathe and dress, changing her clothes four and five times a day. Her husband, it was told, demanded she look her best, before and after he ravished her.

Today Josephine had chosen a demure muslin with intricate embroidery. The delicate white fabric fell over her supple curves as if a breeze caressed her. She moved among the throng as if she were a queen. She was restrained, modest, and polite. Her friends worked hard to emulate her in manners and style. Few equaled her brilliance, but paraded, down to their painted toes, every asset they possessed so others would notice their own beauty.

Kane smiled to himself. A man in such feline company could quickly grow hard and foolish. But he had only one desire. And as he conversed with this one and that, drank and dined and sat for a hand of cards, he tracked the one woman he sought. Meanwhile, he listened for any indications of who might discuss the whereabouts of Madame St. Antoine.

One claimed she had gone to oversee this year's vines. Another mocked that idea and speculated she was in hiding in her own cellars in her house here in Paris. A woman took umbrage at that and proclaimed that the poor girl had gone south to Aix for the sun for the warm months.

Kane made note to investigate the likelihood of each of those possibilities. But finished with his hand of cards, he pocketed his winnings, then strode toward a footman offering delicacies. The tray offered silver spoons filled with two tiny balls of crab, between which stood erect one pink, steamed shrimp. Two ladies partook and giggled over its similarity to a certain part of male anatomy.

Smiling at their comparison of the bright crustaceans to something that could never curve like that, Kane liked the taste better than their humor. He wiped his fingers on a hot napkin offered by the accompanying footman and moved around to the billiard room.

There, at two in the afternoon, stood three ladies and four men with their cues. The gentlemen were swathed to their ears in elaborate cravats, their shoes off, stockings on, their breeches firmly buttoned. That last was particularly intriguing, and their prowess owed much to it, given that the three ladies who played cards with them also played with the men's self-control.

The ladies wore silks of such translucence that they might better have worn nothing at all. In the most ethereal shades of shells from the sea, they had donned gowns that exposed charms best meant for their lovers. When they bent to their shot, their breasts hung forward. When they sank a good point or failed, they chuckled or brayed like fishwives. None of the women had much else to recommend them but their audacity—and the men took advantage of their displays, admiring but not advancing.

Kane monitored how he directed his attention away from the players. Derision of others was not the finest attitude to display in public, no matter how louche any of them appeared. And the bets stacked high in coin and promissory notes. A veritable fortune was here to be won.

A woman's grassy *verveine* perfume enveloped him. "You have a fine discretion."

*Raven.* His blood rushed to his head at the fragrance. He was at once attentive—and hard. Her rough whisky voice captured him. He turned to her. The sight of her, so close and smiling, filled him with more need and more respect than he had dared to admit till now. "I appreciate finesse."

"Good to be a man of many talents." She sounded less like a critic and more like an ally. "I also disapprove of the display."

For him, the atmosphere grew sweeter. He was at once at comfort in a room of strangers. "Is this normal?"

"The exhibit?" She faced him, her smile wide and enchanting. Her lips were plump and pink. "Oh, yes. The winnings? Today's are particularly large."

"Is there a reason for it?" he asked like a boy just wanting to hear the lady he liked speak to him.

She tipped her head in speculation—and she let her gaze speak volumes. Her eyes enthralled him. They were not simply green. Or simply dark as a wooded glen. Or simply anything at all. They were large, round orbs with golden flecks that sparkled in the sunshine flooding through the windows. If he were a younger man and a virgin, he would have melted at her radiance. But he was practiced in the arts of seduction, even jaded, he could say.

"Ah, well." She sniffed and handed him another glass of wine from a footman. Then she nodded toward a window. Kane fell in beside her as she led them toward a private corner. "The reason those three gamble? They are in need of money. Always. For their modiste, and their husbands, and their household, yes. They need the money. And exposure is the way to get it."

Why did she tell him so easily? Why was she here at his side? He was wary of her motives. He took a drink. "Do many gamble away their virtue so easily?"

"By showing a little bit of skin?"

"That is more than a little skin."

She gave a laugh. "A little nipple, then?"

"Are people so lax, truly?"

As she considered that, she opened her lips, and he wanted to trace them. Such beauty deserved homage.

She spread her mouth wide in a smile. And he was undone. His own lips were open, needy.

"Yes, lax," she purred. "Eager. You would be, too."

He was already.

"Needy and urgent to have all the pleasures of life." She made a moue of such charm, his cock stood straight up. "To have them now without delay, because tomorrow you may be gone to the darkest hell."

He flinched.

She saw it. "I know. You English do not torture each other. Not like we do." She took a long drink of her wine and gazed out upon the partiers with a disdain he knew they should not see in her. Wisely, she shook it off.

"Do you think of yourself as French?" he asked her for diversion from his raging need to capture her words as they left her tongue. Damn, he was grateful that this frock coat covered his flies. That she did not notice was his blessing.

She waved her crystal flute before her. "Half. I am a bastard."

He startled. "I'm sorry, I don't—"

"I shocked you. I do apologize. Tell me you do not know my life story."

As a challenge, it was a good one. He would not lie. It would not benefit him one iota. "I do know you are twenty-one. You came to Paris when you were five."

"Very good. Your British informants are accurate. I am honored to be among those who matter to the government. Do you know more?"

"You returned to your home and your parents in '92."

"Hmmm." She sipped her own wine. "Aunt Cecily sent me to London at the start of Robespierre's Terror. Do you know my parents?"

"No." That was the truth. He'd never met any of the Boltons who were related to the dukes of Wharton. Infamous rakes, all.

"Keep it that way, do. You will be better for it. They were— they *are* no better than many of Robespierre's ghouls. To answer your question, I like to think of myself as French. But, of course, my birth certificate says I belong in the parish of St. George's in Mayfair. I am a creature of my surroundings. I belong to no one but myself. I belong wherever I am. A creature of every place and no place. Of everyone's and no one's." She whirled toward him. "Tell me you don't know this."

"I learned the facts, not your feelings...until now."

"You are bold to be honest," she said.

He knew she said it as truth and as praise. "I should like to be bolder. Will you be honest?"

"Try me," she said in that mellow tone, her lips caressing the words that could lure a villain to surrender to her charms.

"Why are you here?"

With the arch of one dark brow, she said, "It is my aunt's house."

*Point avoided.* "And talking to me?"

Her gaze grew warm, and the charm was as real as her evasion. "Because you are my aunt's guest."

*Point deflected.* "Of course." He lifted his glass, done with the direct approach. "Tell me about the group there. The men." He indicated those who played with the saucy female trio.

"Men of the Bourse. Would you like to meet them?"

The bankers. "Should I do that here?"

"I think it would behoove you."

"Why?"

"Don't you need to know everyone to better understand your chances of success? After all, in your previous endeavors, were you not...shall we say, focused on privacy? Now you need to count on your sociability."

He gave a laugh. "I hope you do not think I am sent here with my so-called previous endeavor as my blank paper to do as I will?"

"That would be shortsighted of your government." She was smiling at him.

Suddenly what he had wanted last night in his bed was *all* he wanted. To taste her. *Foolish.* "Indeed."

"Unless..."

He surveyed the room. Their conversation was noted by her aunt, a footman, and Vaillancourt. Why *him*?

Pins pricked his nerves. He did not know her, only her pedigree. Only her aunt's oddly mixed background. Only her friendship, reputedly, with St. Antoine, whose sympathies were with Britain. He could only attack what he knew and do it as it happened. "Are you a friend of Monsieur Vaillancourt?"

She cursed, but did not look around. "I hope never. I assume you ask because he observes our conversation?"

"Like a lover."

"He could be so lucky."

Relief gave Kane a joy he dared not show her. "Are there others with similar aspirations?"

She faced him. "A few."

That gave him pause. In this atmosphere, among these people, she had no man to defend her or uphold her. "With similar results?"

"Oh, yes."

"None appeal to you?"

She tipped up her chin, defiant and ravishingly lovely. "Exactly."

He was tongue-tied while his mind shouted in glee.

"Are there ladies you might be interested in?" she asked, and he was shocked—and pleased, too.

"Only one," he said with such fervor that she blushed to the roots of her short, lustrous black hair. Once more, he was struck mute.

She was not. "She is not available."

"Why not?"

"Her aspirations do not include"—she waved a hand—"the obvious."

He inhaled with relief. "Is that not the preoccupation of this court?"

"It is. That does not mean I must include myself."

"Thank heaven."

She held his gaze. "You are a pretty talker. No wonder they want you to negotiate treaties."

"Not treaties. Goods. Merchandise."

At the implication of that last word, she arched her chin higher and considered him as if he were her fondest desire. "Some things are not for sale."

Did she imply she was above the fray? He had to know. "When all else seems to be, again I ask, what is the real reason you decline?"

"I want more than to be exhibited. Or used." She was fervent. "Or sold."

"Exceptional. *Brava*. But how do you do hold to that in this atmosphere?"

She smacked her lips. "Carefully."

"I admire that."

"Do you?" she shot back, as if it were a challenge.

"A woman must be revered for her individual talents and aspirations."

Her face lost all hauteur. Drained of every pride and artifice, she looked at him as she was, simply a young woman alone in a jungle filled with predators. "I hope she can be praised for her honor and her integrity."

"She can be," he whispered. "By the right people."

She regained some of her composure. "If she can discern them."

"I know she can."

She inhaled and drained the wine in her glass. "It must be wonderful to be so sure of other people. Have you not ever been disappointed that your assessment of someone was entirely false?"

"Oh, yes. Horribly wrong."

"What was the result?"

"He died." *So did I, in many ways.*

She squinted her lovely, luminous green eyes in a survey of the guests in the salon. "I don't wish to die."

The severity of her tone shook him. But in this crowd of grasping opportunists, he could only appear blithe. "Be careful, then."

She lifted her chin in a stance that told of courage. "I will. You must be, too. After all, you do not want to see another man die."

"Nor you."

"Nor me." She nodded, trying to curve up her lips in a smile and failing. *"Merci, Monsieur le Comte. A bientôt."*

## Chapter Six

"**I** SAW YOU talking to that British attaché, Ashley, last night." Her aunt sipped her apple and pear concoction from her crystal goblet. Her pale green eyes ran over Gus with deliberate concentration. She wore a morning gown to come down to sit with her niece and eat breakfast. Unusual, but pointed of her to do so. "He is quite devastating."

"Do you think so?" Gus spread her little serviette out upon her lap. She waited as her aunt's footman served her coffee—and while her aunt got to the point she came to breakfast to make. Aunt Cecily was assessing how well Gus liked the new man in their midst, no doubt about it. "I like his looks."

"A very impressive figure. Norse heritage, perhaps. Rollo's offspring, I would say." Her aunt put down her glass and took up her fork and knife. "It is good he has refinement in his features. And in his manners."

"I do agree, *Tante*. It is difficult for a big man to appear at ease in a salon if he lacks poise. This one, I am happy to say, seems at home here."

"I hear he has relatives in the Loire."

Gus wondered who had told that tidbit to her aunt. "That I did not know. Good for him. Are there many?"

"A large family. His mother's brood live near Amboise. Wine

growers of many generations."

"Perhaps that is why his French is so good."

"It may also be why he is a negotiator for trade." Her aunt looked her over much too closely as she dallied over her *petit déjeuner*. "You find him attractive, don't you, *ma cherie?*"

"I do." Lying never succeeded with her aunt. The woman was much too discerning. It was how and why she had survived the cruelest moments of her life. Still, Gus inwardly shivered at her perception. She thought she'd given a strong impression that she was wary of Ashley. Who else had detected such emotion beneath her façade? Ashley himself, perhaps?

"I understand, my sweet girl." Her aunt sighed. "Were I younger, I might find myself entranced. However, I do caution you about him."

"*Tante*, I decided long ago that I will not allow my heart to meddle in politics or foreign affairs."

Her aunt sat quietly staring at her. "Fine to say. Hard to do. Why? Hmm? I say he is different. Only you can say why he appeals to you. But to your conflict with him, I did see that you clashed with him. Why?"

Gus would not reveal to Cecily that Ashley had been one of the conspirators on the Malmaison road two years ago. Her aunt was a woman with complex friendships and multiple loyalties. Once the mistress of George, the prince regent, she was handed off by him to his dear friend the Duc d'Orleans. For many years, the two had lived together in his house in Paris and in his seats in Chantilly and north of the river Oise. For her aunt's relationship with the royal Bourbon, she had been carted off to Carmes prison and suffered the inquisition of the mobs. Through it all, Cecily had never said a word against her lover. Nor had he implicated her in any of his doings with the Revolutionary Committees.

They had guillotined him anyway. The very day Cecily was to die in the same manner, Robespierre had been killed by his own supporters. Cecily and her new friend and cellmate, a young woman, a widow of great charm, Madame Josephine Beauharnais, had been set free. The two remained fast friends, enjoying the fruits of Josephine's second husband's success.

Gus had not mentioned that she had been waylaid by one of the men who attempted to kill Bonaparte that day on the Malmaison road. Amber had said nothing, either, to protect Gus and herself. Gus had been ashamed she'd been caught by rogues. Worse, she feared if she told the details that the police might turn what she said against her. It was possible. It had happened to others. She had vowed not to be so naïve. She had kept her silence. And would now too. Today, she had other reasons to be discreet...and her aunt knew them not. Gus wanted that to remain true.

She met Aunt Cecily's curious gaze. "The Earl of Ashley is an argumentative man. He needs time to adjust himself to his diplomatic role."

"I thought he showed a spark of romantic interest." Her aunt cast her a sharp eye.

"He did. I dissuaded him."

Aunt Cecily inhaled and glanced to the far end of the room at the doors to the breakfast kitchen. That was all that was necessary for the footman to lift his porcelain carafe and come forward to pour her cup full of coffee.

"*Merci beaucoup,*" she said in dismissal of the man after he poured. When he had disappeared to the kitchens, she lifted her cup but paused to say, "You still feel the same about all the men at this court?"

Her words had Gus tracing the rim of her plate with a finger. "I do, *Tante*. I still do not have your skills at perception of a good man. I know not whom to trust. You have given me my inheritance, and with that independence. I will use it."

"Money is cold comfort when the joys of life and its recriminations come to call."

"I feel...nothing." Which was not true in regard to Ashley. He intrigued her, confused her. Her breasts swelled at the memory of his touch. At the sight of his large, dark hands, her nipples hardened. Her mouth watered at the sight of his lips. All of those places on her body where he had once touched, she still felt his impression. But she had been childish once. She would not succumb to a fantasy of *amour* again. She would not have him, would not take him for her lover. "I will remain free."

Her aunt knitted her brows. "*Ma cherie*, love does not leave room for freedom."

Gus found that statement odd coming from her aunt. The woman had never once voiced concern for Amber's sudden departure from town. Nor her continued absence. That meant she knew Amber's reasoning and/or her destination, or she simply cared not an iota. All of that was either a secret, or a simple disregard of the other person in their lives who had been part of their little family.

Irritated about all of that, Gus took a path to discuss her aunt's regard for her. "Your love has never restrained me. Yours has always been the only love I have ever needed."

"My affections, Augustine, are no comparison to that of a lover."

Gus shook her head.

"No, Augustine, you have been well loved as a baby and youth. To know bliss, you will one day take a man to your bed and to your heart. In fact, I recommend it, sweetheart. Greatly. And soon. While your youth allows you the—shall we say?—dexterity to enjoy the arts."

That had Gus choking on her coffee.

"Forgive me, my sweet girl. But I have a warning. When you choose, you must take care to ensure the consequences are not yours alone. I have taught you how to avoid that, and I mean for you to employ those means. My other stipulation is, if your choice is to be this Ashley or one of his colleagues, that you marry him."

"No! Aunt, I will not put myself in service to—"

"Augustine, it is the only way to secure your reputation. You have spent most of your life here with me. In this new regime, we see that a mistress may have a certain *je ne sais quoi*. A certain prestige. She may have her own household, her own court, her friends about her. She may gain a living from her lover and secure a house and land. That, never to be retaken by her benefactor if society is stable. Here in France, society is a volcano. Still. Take my word on it.

"But British law and British society are different. Precise and ruthless. A mistress is of no import. She merits no wealth and all ridicule. Her children are bastards from birth, never to be legitimate and never to inherit a penny. You have the forty thousand I have given you, my dear girl, but if you use it in Britain to secure your life beyond any *affair de coeur*, you will not have all that secures your freedom."

Her aunt pushed back her chair and rose. "Have your affair, my dear, with whomever takes your fancy. Enjoy him. But if your lover is British, by all that's holy, girl, marry him."

"I HAVE NOT seen you about town lately." Gus scooted up to Ashley's side three weeks later. The afternoon was a hot May day and the party was a celebration of a financier's birthday. His wife, who was painfully drunk, danced solo in her wet muslin and golden sandals that showed her very large toes with very big bunions.

Gus had seen Ashley arrive and waited for more than an hour to approach him. She could not appear eager, after all. But in a spectacular frock coat of plum and a complementary waistcoat of embroidered lavender, he cut a most riveting figure. He was coming up to snuff, looking like a diplomat of the first water. She recalled his clean, crisp fragrance and needed to inhale it...and inhale him again.

Even as he took her hand to his lips, he chided her with a glance. "Is that so? I thought you missed my company."

"I worried you were ill," she offered with pluck, "and I never missed you."

He arched a brow at her. His jaw, that chiseled, square perfection that gave him power, flexed in one of his devastating grins. "I do believe, however, I have seen you everywhere."

She had not been discreet enough. *Not good.* "Impossible. Many Frenchwomen look like me. The dark hair, the eyes."

"Believe that, do you? You also believe in Monsieur Perrault's fairy tales?"

"*Oui*, I do!" She grinned that he knew the famous author who had penned the tale of the orphaned girl who had to work for her horrid stepmother.

He bent near, his voice low and intimate. "I saw you in the *Halle aux blés* and outside the manufactory of the Gobelin."

She took a sip of her wine and fought for an attitude that was not flirtatious. Others would see. They always did. "Ah, but I have been here with my aunt, bored and needing your prickly self to amuse me."

"Prickly? Not I." He looked out over the assembled eighty or so. "I am the soul of diplomacy. That is why I've been successful with so many."

She was proud of him. "Tell me how many contracts you have signed?"

"Why? Do you need to go tell others? Don't bother. I am certain they already know, just as you do."

"Eight?"

"Nine, as of this morning."

"You do yourself proud." She shook her head, wishing to move to the crux of her needs. "I hear you move on to the Loire soon."

He gave a laugh. "You have excellent information."

"Thank you."

"How do you manage that?" he asked quite merrily.

She covered her truth in a flutter of lashes. "Friends."

"Ah. Always in a pinch, visit a friend."

"Or write."

He lifted his glass in a toast. "Send a carrier pigeon."

"Or a dog."

"No!" He stared down at her. "That I have never heard of! Do you have a pet who can do that?"

"No. But it sounds possible!" she told him.

One of her aunt's friends approached them and doused their repartee. The lady had spoken to Gus of her desire to meet the impressive man who negotiated for the British. She was a mistress of one man who, it was said, beat her. If the woman searched for a new admirer, Gus rebelled at the prospect the lady would take Ashley to her bed. But she was talkative, and when Ashley's fellow attaché Lord Ramsey joined their discussion, Gus hoped the woman would train her eyes on that man.

But soon another of Ashley's team, Lord Fournier, an English baron who was also part German, joined them and conversation shifted to politics. The lady lost her chance to enchant anyone. She moved on.

"Forgive me, gentlemen," Gus told them minutes later, hating the topic of who was most influential today, and not wishing to show her own disinterest in their views. "I see a friend of mine from years past."

RAMSEY GAVE KANE a wicked eye. "You have made a conquest."

Dirk grunted. "I'll say."

"Not quickly enough, I tell you." Kane fought the urge to bring Augustine back. He needed to keep her with him and become friendlier. He was losing advantage. Few had said any word of St. Antoine's whereabouts, and he was losing hope of finding her, alive or dead.

Last week, he'd gone north to Chantilly to investigate a trade contract. He'd asked vintners there if they had seen St. Antoine lately or talked business with her. No one had, and they questioned her disappearance. They said she was very attentive to the wine market and others' production. Their lack of knowledge made him testy. He'd investigated a few contacts in Scarlett's list and found three intact. Fearing two departures from St. Antoine's agent network, he'd established a few preliminary inquiries about several men whom he might enlist as new agents for Scarlett. Then he returned to Paris, unable to be away for long without an excuse.

"No matter," Ramsey put in, cool as January in his demeanor. "I have news. You will like it."

"As do I," Dirk added.

Kane's hope stirred to life. "What? Quickly, tell me."

Ramsey took a drink and poked Kane's arm, giving the impression he spoke about something hilarious. "This special person visited a certain friend, you see, recently in Compiègne."

"However," Fournier added with a nod, "I have it on authority the one we want is in Varennes."

*Varennes?* "The little town in the east?" Kane was stumped. This was where Louis and his wife and family were discovered during their escape from Robespierre on their way to Vienna.

"Near German states." Fournier, whose mother came from a small German principality that bordered France, had a twinkle in his eye. *"Javohl, mein Herr."*

Kane's mind whirled. Why would Madame St. Antoine go so far east? If she were afraid of someone, she would seek friends in a small town. Varennes was small. Did she know anyone there? "Good news, then. Fortunate that we are about to see certain people here begin their summer holiday. I say we are each traveling, too."

"I should visit my grandmother in Durlach." Dirk took a long draw on his wine. His maternal family lived in a section of Karlsruhe, the capital of the German state of Baden. The margrave had taken a liking lately to the First Consul of France. "The Black Forest calls to me."

"Will you hunt a few boar?" Ramsey chuckled.

"I have hunted a few *bores* here, and I'm ready to down others in my mother's land," Dirk said. "I understand a few in this town become dangerous to them."

"A problem for us there?" Kane asked Dirk.

"A big one. New treaties that affect one important family. My friends are," Dirk said, surreptitiously glancing around, "missing."

"Go quickly, then." Kane turned to Ramsey. "And you, sir?"

"Official duties. I will tell it abroad that I travel with Dirk as far as Verdun. I understand the citadel there has a few British prisoners whom Fouché denies exist. Against the treaty and all our new friendship, wouldn't you say?"

"But you pause in Varennes?" Kane asked Ram.

"I do." Ramsey's gaze drifted to Augustine as he spoke to Kane. "And you have plans to travel soon?"

"I do. To go north, I need a traveling companion to help me with details. I am anxious to get started. Plus, time grows short."

*And my enchantment with my alibi greater.*

# Chapter Seven

G US HAD WANTED to talk with Ashley more, but she had her social duties to perform. She sped away to do them.

Her aunt hosted a unique blend of her enduring friends today, and Gus had not yet greeted each one. Cecily was a stickler for protocol. It was another of her moves that had helped her survive and prosper. Gus would follow her footsteps. It was wise to do so.

Her aunt, who had come to France long before the revolution to be introduced to the old Duc d'Orleans—or Philippe Égalité, as he was later known before he was guillotined—was well received in many social circles, old and new. All were formidable. Most were here today. Madame Bonaparte had not yet arrived, but she was expected.

Talleyrand, minister of foreign affairs, was here already. He had lived in London for many years, and had known the Bourbons and the revolutionaries. He had worked in various capacities for both. While he did pretty things, Talleyrand was not in any sense of the word a pretty man. Nor was his archenemy, Joseph Fouché, the chief of police.

Fouché was another who kept his head and his sense, making him a good choice to ferret out rebels and suppress undesirables. That man was absent today. The sly fox had ingratiated himself with many in different political circles so that, at any given time, he could be called upon to round up any segment of the population on the whimsy of one of his supporters.

Gus allowed her gaze to wander in the direction of Fouché's second-in-command. She glimpsed Vaillancourt in conversation with a woman, but she did not catch his eye, lest he consider it an invitation to join her. He had done so far too often since Amber had disappeared. If he sought to pump Gus to discover Amber's location, he would lose. And if he sought to replace Amber with Gus in his affections, he would also lose at that too.

Oh, true, Deputy Rene Vaillancourt was a handsome man, tall and lean, superbly attired in the finest fabrics and colors that brought his sun-kissed Provençale complexion to best light. Dark of eye and enchanting of manner, he'd been said to seduce many women with his sapphire eyes and silken tone. Word was he was an attentive lover, leaving no inch of a lady's skin untouched, no desire unquenched. Gus had this on the authority of one of her friends who had succumbed to the man's persuasions. Her friend was now in the country near Compiègne recovering from his refusal to marry her—and from her visit to the local midwife, who rid her of her pregnancy.

Such disregard for a woman riled Gus. To prohibit similar disrespect of her own reputation, she guarded her words—and her body. Especially since Vaillancourt had increased his attentions on her, she would continue to be cautious.

Except today. With the Englishman. She had failed. Her instincts had leaned toward him, sparked by the magnetic lure of his person. In physique, he was huge. In demeanor, he was serene. In attitude, he belied the first impression she had of him as a terrorist. That he had even taken time that day on the Malmaison road to subdue her with kisses spoke of his expedient approach to life. And his rogue's magic ways. Both were the thrust of his appeal to her now.

He was quick to think, impelled to act to attain his goal. Was it any wonder, then, that to achieve her own goal, she had sought the aura of his words and the shelter of his regard? The few minutes with him had been comforting.

And yet so naïve. She was foolish to want anything from him. She bit her lower lip.

Why had she given so much of herself away? She never did that. It was dangerous to do that in these perilous waters. With Amber gone to heaven-knew-where, how could Gus herself succumb to the lure of a man she knew to be a spy? An assassin?

She found him alluring—against her own desire to remain celibate. Against logic to take him when there were so many handsome men here for the asking. So many ugly men here available at the crook of her little finger. She could so easily get a rich man with friends, a poor man with brains, or a political beast with charmingly vile skills. She did not need to attract the Englishman. The suave fellow with the glossy hell-black hair that drew her fingers to stroke him. Her lips to sip him. Her tongue to explore him and find...*what*?

That the Earl of Ashley was no better, perhaps worse, than those parading before her. That he was not interested in her as a person but as an *entree* to those in power here. That like others, including Vaillancourt, he desired only to use her. To seduce her to working for him. Or waiting for him in his bed.

Well, too bad—she needed no lover. Wanted none of the complications. The late-night visits. The impromptu rendezvous and heartache. The money, the guilt. The illegitimate child or the deadly diseases. She definitely did not want the British man. The dashing creature who kissed like a satyr. The diplomat in sheep's clothing. The friend, foe, murderer.

She drained her glass, her gaze straying to him as he laughed with one of Josephine's ladies. The woman flirted with him, and he feigned interest with politesse and a furrowed brow.

Jealousy pricked her.

Just as a spark of inspiration flooded her with excitement.

Could she use him?

When she smiled at him, he did not fake anything. He was

lured, drawn to her. And though she was as pulled by him to naughtiness, she would not reciprocate in kind, but ask for something different.

If only she were adventurous. If she were as confident of her skills to evade as her friend Amber was. If she could live the charade and pretend she knew little and wished only for the drama, the escapade of life.

*What would it hurt to try?*

She covered her surprise at her extraordinary thoughts with a sweep of those in the room. They were avid gossips. Looking for the simple explanations of every glance, every sigh. Of women, most thought everything was possible. Especially if they opened their legs and gave satisfactions.

On the contrary, Gus had no simple explanations for what she had chosen to do. Two years into this and she was happy she had to report to only one. Her identity was secure. No one suspected her of any dubious act. No one had asked her to explain a thing. Only to deliver.

At that moment, in the corner of her eye, she perceived that Vaillancourt studied her—and she ignored him with a quick turn toward a friend.

In her view was Ashley, who now sat across the room, in deep conversation with Madame Tallien. He was in her path. Delicious, devastating, persistent. Here in the very function that she might use to her own purposes.

*If* she trusted him.

*If* she could deny herself the lure of him.

That conundrum had her turning toward the window to the gardens. Might Ashley be useful to help her find Amber? If he wanted relationships with vintners, silk weavers, and dyers, she could lead him to them. She could introduce him to farmers. Though she knew many estate owners who grew barley, potatoes, sugar beets, and wheat, not all of those crops could be sent along the Seine west to Britain. The potatoes could be shipped most easily without spoilage. Less easily could the barely and wheat be sent. For those estates north of Paris where dairy products were the major produce, he could not want the milk and cheeses. Rich and flavorful as they were, they would spoil before they got to any port along the Channel.

Yes, she could help him. Not simply as one who would introduce him, but as his friend. His dear friend who traveled with him. It would be a mutually beneficial agreement between them. She would argue that she built a business of her own to complement his. A network of suppliers of goods for the British Isles. She could argue she needed to make money for the service she rendered him. In the land of shopkeepers, everyone knew the value of making money from an enterprise. A woman could do that. *Should* do that.

Ashley would be her colleague. Though, as her traveling companion, he would also be her camouflage and her security against undue advances from men.

She would ponder it. Sketch her chart of positives and negatives.

She smiled to herself.

Proud of her novel solution, she headed for a group of her aunt's friends who sat together in the far corner. They had been here for a few hours, and their consumption of wine and cognac showed. Their slurred words and relaxed bodies told stories quite a few in this room would love to hear so that they could use the knowledge against them.

She stopped. Such tales would anger her.

"Don't bother with them, Mademoiselle Bolton. Come talk with me."

The thin baritone voice of Vaillancourt climbed up her spine. She set her teeth, unwilling to let him see her revulsion.

"Monsieur Vaillancourt." She did the gracious thing and gave him a small curtsy. "How are you today?"

"*Tres bien, mademoiselle.* Allow me to fill your hand with... What is it you adore?"

*Slick viper. Not you.* "White wine."

With the arch of a thin brow, he beckoned a footman. "I have not seen you lately. I missed you. Word has it you were ill."

"I was. I do not do well when the weather changes quickly from warm to cold and back again. I had to rest."

"You recuperated at your aunt's country house, *oui?*"

"In Compiègne, I did." Alarm that he knew this shot through her veins. Why would he bother to learn this? If he thought this endeared him to her, he was wrong. She would not ever succumb to his charms. "When my chest is full, I am laid low. I must rest without distractions."

*Curse it.* His gaze followed her hand to her bosom.

"But when in Compiègne, I understand you attended a soiree of the Ladies of Joan of Arc."

A footman responded to Vaillancourt's summons, and with one hand he took the crystal, and with the other he took her gloved one. With a flash of damnably beautiful dark blue eyes, he placed the glass in her hand.

She steeled herself against his arrogance. "*Merci.* Yes, when I was well enough, I met with them. I like stories of Joan of Arc. She was there before the British took her to Rouen and burned her at the stake. I approve of the ladies in Compiègne who do such good charity work for the orphans of that city. Far too many children pay for the greed of officials. The new government changes nothing for starving children."

"Careful, *ma cherie.* What you say can be overheard."

"I am English, *monsieur.* Under the new treaty it would be a sad strategy of the consulate to take me away and intimidate me." Her chin went up with her dislike of him and all he represented. "Don't you agree?"

"There is such a thing as teasing the lion, Augustine."

She sucked in air, surprised that he would be so bold as to use her given name—and ignore her jab at the inequalities and inefficiencies of the new consulate. "Do I pull your tail, *monsieur?*"

His dark sapphire eyes flashed with sexual overtones. "You interest me—and you know it, Augustine."

*No, you play at it. It is Amber you want.* "Monsieur, surely a man of your skills and friends knows that I have no interests in attachments."

"So I have heard. But then, you are much too lovely to remain alone. A lady of your beauty and education is a lure to many men. Including me."

"I thank you for the compliment, *monsieur*. But I am not in the market for a husband. Not yet."

"Then it is a good time to have experience before one claims a husband." He raised his dark brows.

"I find the concept of a husband useful. One need worry only about one person's whereabouts, one person's liaisons, one person's diseases."

"You are too direct, *mademoiselle*."

Suddenly she was no longer Augustine? *Well and good.* "I will have no lovers, *monsieur*. Only a husband. When I am ready."

He leaned close, much too intimate for the hour and her tolerance. Indeed, he even grasped her upper arm. This was very uncouth of him. Desperation was not a good plan.

She glared at him. "Please, sir, remove your hand."

"I think the lady has a very good suggestion, Monsieur Vaillancourt."

Gus breathed in relief and moved in such a way that the point of her shoulder fell against Ashley's broad chest.

"The lady and I were talking," Vaillancourt said, tilting his head up to confront her champion.

"It appeared that you were harassing her, *monsieur*. She is not to be abused." Ashley arched both brows. "I suggest you take your hand from her arm, before I must do it for you."

The deputy complied.

Others noticed.

The comfort of Ashley's chest beneath her shoulder was all that kept her from shuddering.

"Come with me," Ashley urged her in that smooth way that sank beneath her skin. His hand on her forearm led her to twine her arm in his. "Head high. Smile. They look," he said, and all the while he led her away toward the hall and privacy.

Her knees threatened to buckle, but she kept pace with him and plastered what she hoped was a normal expression on her face. She smiled and gazed up at him, chattering about whatever in hell it was he decided was the topic to amuse them.

At the far end of the hall, where the grand marble stairs could lead one down into the gardens that bloomed in a thousand colors of the rainbow, he opened a door, led her inside, and shut the damn thing.

Then she fell into his open arms, her fingertips to her lips, her body shaking, her gasps small, guttural sounds that tiny animals and children made when monsters came to call.

His fingers splayed up her throat into her coiffure. He held her as if she were porcelain, rare and delicate. His lips were nestled in her hair, and she felt kisses, small and dear, imparted there.

She clutched him closer, though she shouldn't, and made to stand apart from him.

"You've no need to push me away," he murmured. "When one wishes comfort, why deny yourself when it is given without need for repayment?"

She leaned back against the wall, her view of him amid the shadows of the unlit room a realization of the sculpted power of his face. He was a big man with large features. But each was in proportion with the others. The broad forehead and the black shock that fell over it when he was earnest. The strong, straight nose, nostrils that flared in his exertions. The eyes, large, brilliant as lightning. Cheeks that arched, high and wide, giving him the look of constant curiosity. She had lain awake, drawing him in her reverie. Never attempting in daylight.

Her skills were sharp and honed. She did not sketch those irrelevant to her. Only those whom she must. Only when they were in question.

"I thank you for that rescue."

"No need," he assured her. He caught strands of hair at her cheek as he pulled on the curl. His fingers teased her skin. She rolled her lips together to avoid the impulse to close her eyes and drift in the euphoria he created. "Does he do that often? Come to you and press his attentions?"

"No. Only since one of my friends is missing."

He flinched. "Was he enamored of her?"

"He was. She did not return the affection."

"Smart of her, I would say. And from what I saw in there, you do not care for him."

She shivered. "But there are consequences to deny him."

"Oh?" He cupped her chin and raised her face. His gaze grew fierce and frosty. "What are they?"

She gulped and considered the intricate fold of his cravat.

"Tell me, Augustine. I will help if I can."

"No, you cannot. Though I thank you for the offer."

"What does he do for these consequences?" he persisted.

"He orders his team of guards to call upon a lady who refuses."

Ashley balked, his eyes hard, bright fury. "How? What do they do?"

"He inspects the house. Looks for...anything he might use as example of a crime."

"Who has he done this to?"

"Two friends of mine." She feared Vaillancourt. She did. Badly. He was as insane as Robespierre had been. Many said it. Many who knew him better than she.

Ashley caressed her cheeks with his thumbs. "Can your aunt not keep him at bay?"

"Cecily is careful what to ask as favors of those in power. Even Madame Bonaparte has her limits."

Her eyes closed again. He was all comfort and safety, and she had never had that from a man. Not her father. Not her aunt's lover, the Duc d'Orleans.

Gus twined her arms around his waist and leaned against

him. He was solid, hard muscle, a wall of certitude. But she had no right to hold him, and she looked up. "We must return. He could make life difficult for you, too."

"He cannot touch me," he breathed.

She shook her head. "He dares much. I would hate to be responsible for him harassing you."

"There is a way to prevent him from hurting you."

She adored his positivity and tipped her head, a wistful but vain hope at lightening her burden, if only for a moment. "I know none."

"As of minutes ago in the salon, I became your champion. Now I can become more."

She swallowed loudly. Temptation shimmered through her bloodstream. She ran her fingertips down the supple silk and satin of his waistcoat and frock coat. "We are friends. I never do more."

"We can pretend—"

Dazed by his offer, she stilled—and thrilled to the temptation. He stared at her lips. "We could give the world a fine act."

"Kisses are dangerous." *Yours would be devastating.*

"Not as dangerous as that man's attentions."

"How do I know you will remain true to your word?"

"I would never harm you. In any way. I have my own reputation to uphold."

"You once were a rogue. Aside from your actions on the Malmaison road two years ago." She swallowed, having given him more information than she should.

He snorted. "You have a dossier on me, do you, Augustine?"

"I have word of your past on good authority."

"I would have to know why you have such information." He arched a brow, his gray eyes glittering. "Or we could agree you have purpose of your own. Then, to foil that man, we would play at being lovers."

Her heart told her to accept. Her old fear told her to reject him. "I—I must think on it."

He stepped backward, his palms in the air in the manner of surrender. "Do that. But decide quickly. Vaillancourt's pride has been pricked. A man like that never waits too long to take revenge."

## Chapter Eight

T HE BATHHOUSE WAS a reputable establishment near the church of St. Denis to the north of Paris. Gus took hired carriages and, as ever, changed twice to ensure her secrecy. Her aunt did not like her going there and had railed against it. But this was the twenty-fifth of the month—time to collect what information came to her from her source in Amboise.

The bathhouse was for men and women, so it seemed normal for her to wait outside there to search for her contact each month. She went on the same date each month, but because she had been ill in April, she had not appeared then. She worried that her associate had feared for her survival—or her sudden duplicity. Such was always a possibility in the work she did. But each month, she altered the conditions just enough to lessen the chance someone would capture her colleague and try to substitute himself for her man.

She took her second carriage around the remains of the medieval Peripherique wall. She changed clothes in the alley of a small village *faubourg* where no one cared if a woman in old shoes and moth-eaten bonnet appeared and hailed a carriage from the square. That lady was a stranger. She had no similarity to the female who had appeared across the square on the same day in March. In fact, that woman who had appeared had been attired in clothes fit for a poor shopgirl. This one who alighted from the rickety fiacre looked like a prosperous barmaid.

Gus strolled the plaza toward the old basilica and bought bread from the patisserie, careful to examine those around for any who followed her. The church, built in the second century, was where all French monarchs and their families were buried. Or to be precise, it had been where they had rested in peace until the early '90s, when terrorist mobs attacked the church, pillaged the fine statues, and rummaged through the bones of royals in their graves.

Finishing her bread, she wiped the crumbs from her mouth with the back of her hand. A vision of handsome, dashing Ashley popped into her head. If Ashley knew she was here, he would scream at her for lack of brains. But he did not know what she did or with whom or how or why. Even if he suspected, he would need ever so much more information to put together the puzzle of her actions. She might debate the necessity of revealing some of that to him, but after this interview she would decide. After all, he was too delicious to learn he died for knowing her secrets.

The square was clear, and she hurried toward the door to the bathhouse. She loitered, per the plan. But no one appeared. Fearing she had the hour wrong—or her associate did—she paid her coin with thanks to the proprietor.

With no other way to wile away the time until the next stroke of the hour, she took the hall to the women's room. The men's and women's steam rooms were separate from each other. The women's part of the house was always clean. No one was about. She quickly disrobed, folded her clothes and tucked them in the cubbyhole, grabbed some toweling, then turned toward the steam room.

The heat through the tiled floors was torrid this spring day. Gus didn't mind. The heat warmed her as little else ever could, and for days after a visit, her breathing would be easier. Inside, two other women sat, towels around them, their eyes closed. She knew neither of them—nor did she expect to.

After about ten minutes, Gus rose and headed through the far door to the sunken bath. She'd spend only a few minutes here, then dry, dress, and return to the entrance to await her contact.

She strolled along one side of the oblong pool. Inside, one young woman sat by the edge of the water on the stone bench. Gus took one hard look, then another. She blinked. Recognizing her was a shock. The fact that this young lady was here in the baths was either too much coincidence or none at all. Gus feared the latter, and it boded no good.

She put her towel on a stone bench and stepped naked into the warm water. Today, the presence of the lovely golden blonde with expressive umber eyes spiked Gus's nerves. But she schooled herself to casually float on her back for a few minutes. She did not wish to approach her too quickly, assuming the girl knew that Gus and her brother met to transfer all sorts of information that could get them imprisoned and even killed. After a few minutes, Gus let the waters carry her toward the sister of her aunt's vintner from Amboise.

"*Bonjour*, my friend. I am surprised to find you here." Gus had to know more before any other women entered the baths.

"My brother could not," the girl said. "He was watched when he came to meet you here in April."

"I was ill in April," Gus whispered, wondering how much the young woman knew of her brother's association with her.

"I come instead to tell you to beware as you leave."

Inès Bechard's older brother Luc ran his own estate and produced fine Chenin blanc, which Aunt Cecily bought by the barrel. Luc Bechard also sent his wines—and information for Gus—along the Loire River to the Atlantic coastal ports. "What happened to him?"

"He was followed from the square outside. After much diversion, he lost them. An ugly, slender man with a long nose."

"Anything of use from the Loire?"

"My brother says to tell you all is quiet for the swallows." Code for military increases in the forts to the sea near St. Nazaire.

"Any other news?" Gus raised her brows. The entire network knew that Amber St. Antoine was missing and everyone searched for her.

"None."

Gus nodded. *"A bientôt."*

Inès gave her a small smile as she scrambled to her feet and picked up her towel. "I accompanied your aunt's order north. This vintage is superb. Stay well."

GUS TOOK HER time leaving the bath. No one else had entered, and at that, she took heart. Still, she was on guard and made much of drying her short hair and donning her clothes.

Outside, the sunlight hit her hard. She squinted into the brilliance. The maple trees were taking on new buds. A few birds chirped somewhere nearby. The refuse dumps at the far corner stank. The night soil man had not come on his rounds last night as he was supposed to do. That was not new. Paris was filled with filth, and the outlying *faubourgs* were worse. No one wanted to pay the taxes. The Bourbons had put too high a price on each citizen's contributions to the monarch's wealth. So now the kings and queens of France were not missed. Only the chaos that erupted without them in charge was. Bonaparte had a plan to cover the open sewers and clean the streets. But many thought he was as dangerous to the health of the French as the blood that ran in the streets and the offal that sat in the gutters.

Despite the stench, standing across from Gus, lingering as they ate baguettes, were two men. They were far too well dressed. Neither as servants at the baths or for the local citizenry could they be taken. They conversed with each other in solemn tones, but their roving eyes betrayed their mission. Every person who emerged from the baths was their favorite subject. Including her.

Gus knew at once who and what they were. Vaillancourt's men. One of the two was a short, ugly, pockmarked fellow with the longest nose Gus had ever seen.

They sought someone. If it was she, they would not get her.

Not today.

*Please not today.*

Gus strolled along, not in any hurry to give the two reason to follow her. She speculated that Inès had been treated to their scrutiny, too. Did these men have associates who had followed her friend?

Gus would not know. Not until next month on the twenty-fifth. Not unless Luc Bechard came, or if he concluded it safe to send his sister once more.

Gus continued her walk south through narrow streets, where she ducked into alcoves and darted out into an alley. She kept a pace that was brisk and purposeful but, she hoped, not indicative of flight. Through more prosperous thoroughfares, she walked and bought produce or haggled with *vendeurs*.

Nearing the hills of Montmartre, she picked up her pace. Her nose twitched. The refuse she had smelled before was fragrant compared to the rank odor that drifted toward her now. She had to lose the two men, and had hope they'd hate her choice of a path. She scrambled to get away, even as her feet slid on the grime and guts and urine. Her eyes began to water, and she choked on the foul smells. She hurried onward and ducked quickly among the animal pens of the abattoir of Montmartre. The poor creatures rattled their cages. Cows and pigs and chickens raised a wild hue and cry, smelling the blood of their brothers being slaughtered.

Gus picked up her pace through the pens and headed for the tallow vats. Weaving among the large tanks, she lifted her scarf to cover her nose and mouth to kill the odor. When she emerged from the stink and dallied in front of a blacksmith's stall, she stopped, gasping for good air and coughing.

Casually, she glanced over her shoulder.

They were gone.

And so were her hopes that she could operate alone.

She had to find a new technique to continue her mission and collect her information.

She sighed. She knew what that must be.

She was a fool to go on as she had. From inaction, she gained nothing. She would change.

She needed to find Amber—and she needed help.

If she had nerve to ask for it.

"YES, IF YOU could sign here…and here." Kane breathed a sigh of relief as the sales agent for Sèvres china signed the invoices and shipping agreements. Kane had concluded the sales for the manufacture of a dinner service for one hundred for the Duke of Abingdon. The hard paste porcelain service of gold and jade with the duke's insignia totaled twelve hundred and two pieces. The order was to be completed within the next year at the porcelain company's manufactory south of Paris and shipped up the Seine and across the Channel swaddled in enormous sheets of muslin.

Kane eyed the man who had guaranteed the transfer of money, French financier Armand Vernon. He appeared pleased with the sale, the largest going to a private citizen. Much of Sèvres's recent purchases were by the three consuls for use in their official capacities. While that brought money in the door, it did nothing for the continued health or reputation of the porcelain manufacturer.

Monsieur Vernon rose to shake hands with the *vendeur*, Jules Lavigne. "*Merci beaucoup, monsieur.* We are happy to see your product receive such fine reception abroad."

The little fellow beamed. "I am most pleased, Monsieur Vernon. This has been a happy experience. Especially because *Monsieur le Comte d'Ashley* is so accommodating."

"I assure you," Kane said with his own hand out, "the entire experience has been a joy. Thanks to you, sir, an educational one, too. I now know the differences between hard and soft pastes."

Kane cocked an ear. The tinkle of piano drifted through the closed doors of his study. The tune was familiar. Mozart, no less. Corsini did not play. No servant would dare. So then, a visitor with skills had come to call. And do what else?

His pulse jumped.

"We like to offer the world the best in brilliantly colored and durable porcelain." Monsieur Lavigne smiled up at Kane. No more than five feet tall and very round, the Sèvres salesman was a jolly fellow who knew well his wares, but bartered the final price like a braying donkey. Just now, he lifted his head like one, too. "I say, *Monsieur le Comte*, that is an accomplished pianist to give us the Mozart so very well."

Kane knew much of Mozart's works. Had played them often himself. He had heard only one woman in Paris who played with such expertise, and that was at a party weeks ago.

He had not seen Augustine much lately. Briefly yesterday, he spied her outside a modiste shop on the Champs-Élysées. They had not talked, as she was with her maid. He had worried if Augustine were ill again…or she had decided he was not worth her time.

But now was she his pianist? Who else could it be? Would she come here? Unannounced?

He hoped. He feared the reason—and he could not get away from his guests fast enough.

"Is that your wife, perhaps?"

Kane offered up a look of pride. "A friend who visits."

"Ah. A talented friend." His brows quirking, Monsieur Lavigne tucked his sales papers inside his portfolio and latched it with a flourish. "Very fine, indeed."

Kane nodded. "Thank you for everything. My *majordom* will show you to the door."

Vernon was right behind him. "I will see you soon, I wager. A

Gobelin contract, I hear?"

"I do hope so," Kane said with a fresh urgency, the chords of music flowing into his bloodstream with a desire hot for so sweet a June afternoon. "*A bientôt*, Monsieur Vernon."

Kane counted to twenty, assured that by then his two visitors had followed Corsini down the marble stairs and out to the courtyard. With a restraint born of the need for a serene façade, he took the stairs down to his conservatory at the back of the manse.

The room, a pale blue with gilded molding of acanthus leaves and smiling cherubs, was stuffed with violins, one cello, a harp, cymbals, drums, and a fine old pianoforte painted in pink with decoupage along the base. Kane had passed through the small room when first he'd inspected the house.

Corsini had informed him that he could fit three rows of ten inside. "If you wish to host a musical evening." His butler had grinned like a child with a sugar cake.

"Do I need reasons to entertain in Paris, Corsini?"

"*Si, conte.* You are a man alone. Dream of ways to invite the court to favor you."

Kane took the hall toward the back of the house, knowing he had just discovered a reason to invite Society to his home.

He thrust open the double doors and smiled at his gorgeous pianist. "Mozart?"

"Do you like him?" she asked Kane without missing a note or even looking up at him.

"I like him more now."

She chuckled and played on. He closed the double doors and paused as the click of the latch permeated the room. They'd have privacy for this conversation, as she clearly needed. She had come to him in the middle of the afternoon, and he'd ask if she'd arrived in full view of all in the courtyard or come through the servants' entrance at the back alley. However she had come, he rejoiced that she had come to him.

He strolled toward her. He was so pleased she was here. She

wore a gown of silk the color of water, iridescent blue and greens that swirled like eddies over her breasts and the tops of her shapely shoulders and arms. He itched to feel the beauty of her body's synchrony, but then, to put his hands on her, he'd stop the music. And he had rules. With her for this now, he remained a gentleman.

He'd not talked with her since the financier's party. It was as if she had disappeared like a sylph. A spirit of air and his imagination. Until yesterday along the avenue as he sat in a street-side café lunching with a wine *vendeur* and she was once more flesh and blood and beauty. "I worried you were ill once more. I asked about for you."

"So I have heard."

He stood at the edge of the keyboard. She looked healthy and played with a devotion and an expertise he marveled at. "You are well?"

"I am."

He sat down beside her. Her fresh spring cologne wafted over him. He clasped his hands together to keep from gathering her close. "I saw you yesterday. You should have come and spoken to me."

"AUGUSTINE," HE SAID so low she nearly did hear him over her rendition. "Have you stopped following me?"

She continued to play and knew not how she managed. She wished to throw herself into Ashley's arms, but that would be so rash. So she executed the bars perfectly, though her mind ran to the two men who had tracked her from the baths of St. Denis south to Montmartre.

"Augustine, I've missed you."

Ashley's words were ambrosia to her, a plea to stop and talk to him, but she used the music as her barricade. She'd rehearsed what she needed to say, but knew not how to trust that she would speak without sputtering with fear.

"Will you stop to talk to me?" he asked in that voice that poured solace on her fear like sweet honey. "It is why you are here, and I don't wish to fight for the floor."

She took the piece to *pianissimo*, forcing her mind to reason—and him as he inched toward her. Him, as he put his hands to the keyboard and accompanied her little Mozart song...until she stopped playing. He went on for a few bars. She smiled at him in thanks and praise, but her expression was a pitiful, helpless thing. "You did not tell me you played."

He put his hands in his lap. "If you talked to me more, you would know much about me. I am thrilled you have come to visit me, Raven."

She tipped her face up higher to more fully consider his handsome one. His eyes were that hot ice she adored, hooded and needy. His face much too handsome. The proportions of forehead to cheek to jaw, the wide arches of his brows, the straight line of his nose, his lips. Oh, God, his lips were the wide, firm, manly form that sculptors would envy and emulate. He was too striking for this proposition she had for him. Too kind and much too dangerous to even approach. But she would. "Am I Raven?"

"You are," he told her with a look that spoke of his fond remembrance and regard. "My beauty from the road."

He was much too devastating to her reason, as well. She grinned, but it was all pretense. "You mean the one with the breadcrumbs in her mouth?"

"Yes. The one who bit me."

She rolled her eyes. And began to play again.

He put his hands on hers. "Why are you here? Eh? In the middle of the afternoon?"

She met his gaze. He appeared so cool, so collected, and she was so distraught. She had an urgent need to capture all she could from the moment, if only she had means. And he...he was her means. "Time ticks by."

He waited, his beautiful ice-gray eyes languid with the sweep of his thick black lashes.

She went back to her keyboard, the music, distraction. He let her play alone. "I need a favor."

"I see. What is it?"

She began her rehearsed appeal. "If you will help me, I can help you. I have friends, associates, connections who would be useful to you in your trade negotiations."

"I am certain you would open many doors for me and my mission." He studied her, searching and finding with his haunting eyes her anxiety. She knew the moment he saw it because he paled. "You bargain with me, Augustine? Why? You needn't. If it is something I can do, I will."

She seized her courage. To accomplish what she had to do, she would be safer with him than she was now alone. She paused her play, but did not face him. "I need you to pretend we are lovers."

She heard him catch his breath.

"Augustine, look at me. Does Vaillancourt threaten you?"

She gazed up at him. *He has me followed.*

"Does he?"

She shook her head. "I have a friend whom he threatened."

He sat quite still. "And?"

She pressed her lips together. "She left court. The city." She turned to face him more fully on the bench. She could not help herself and kneaded her hands. "She is missing. I have not had any word from her. Not that she would send me letters. She was too afraid. I have looked for her for weeks."

He frowned. "How?"

"I pretended to be ill and recovering in Compiègne in my aunt's house. Then to be visiting friends. But those were ruses." Tears burned her eyes. "I have looked for her in Compiègne and Chantilly and Meaux."

He drew her against him, her face to the curve of his throat.

This was where she'd longed to return since that time when they ran to the small salon and he took her in his embrace. This felt so wonderful, so peaceful.

"Why those towns?" he asked, sinking his fingers into her curls.

"It was as far as I could reasonably travel from Paris and not raise suspicion. Plus," she said, wincing, "I was alone and feared who would tell others I had gone so far."

"Augustine!" He pulled back, dark with concern. "You went alone?"

"My aunt's two grooms went with me. They thought I arranged assignations. They are trustworthy. Aunt Cecily pays them well not to divulge anything about our household to others."

He cupped her cheeks. "My darling woman, you could be betrayed at any time!"

"I know," she admitted with hateful resignation. "I know, and yet I had to trust. But I cannot continue to do it. That tempts the odds. Oh, don't you see? I cannot continue, but I must! I must!"

He caught her close. His arms were the vises of security. The promise of safety. "Where else do you wish to go to find her?"

She shuddered in his embrace. If he knew anything at all about her actions, he would know more once she told him this. "Reims. I seek Amber St. Antoine."

A spark of recognition had him blinking. "The widow of the vintner?"

"The same," she blurted. "You know her?"

He shook his head. "No. I knew her husband, Maurice."

"She is my dear friend. If I go there openly and Vaillancourt or his men learn of it or follow me, Amber is in danger. I cannot let that happen. Yet I must know where she's gone. She is my very best friend, my sister in all but blood, and I am so angry that I cannot find her that I—"

He put a finger to her lips. "Darling, don't. You upset yourself."

She wrapped her arms around his torso. "I have tried to find her. I sent out pigeons. She...she did not answer."

"Pigeons?"

"Five! To her home. They returned without word. I even sent out—" And she stopped, horrified. Her mouth dropped open. What she had been about to tell him would only make him vulnerable—and angry. He might even refuse her his help.

He caressed her cheek. His eyes were consoling, his expression sweet. "What did you send out?"

She scrambled to find a way to dissemble. To tell him the truth but cover her real actions. "A message through friends of mine that she was missing."

"And? Did you receive responses?"

"All were negative."

"I see." He drew her to him again, her head against his warm, muscular chest. "Why go to her home, then?"

"Because she may have gone and left a message for me there."

"Has she done that before?"

"Yes." She drew back. "I must go. If you won't help me, I go alone. I must. It has been weeks since she disappeared. I cannot fail her. And I must tell you one more thing. You will be surprised."

"Out with it now, then. What is it?"

"Amber was my friend with me on the Malmaison road that morning."

His mouth fell open. "Is that so?" He paused, frowning as if he were trying to recall Amber's looks. "She did not see me that day. How will she react to a British fellow looking for her?"

"She won't object."

He nodded. "Good, then. I will help you. We will tell others we go in the next few days."

"Why not tomorrow? We must go soon."

"Because you worry so much about her, and because...why?"

She had to tell him more. "Her life depends on it."

He stared at her as he imbibed that. "I see. However, to create the impression that you and I are intimate takes time and exposure."

"Do you come to Madame Tallien's salon tonight?"

"I do. I accepted." He kept stroking her cheeks, his thumbs big and warm, making her insides quiver.

"Wonderful," she said, grinning. "Thank you." And at that, she made to rise.

A hand to her wrist, he waylaid her. He threw her a sidelong look, his magnificent eyes laughing. "You wish to wait to start this act?"

Her body warmed at the prospect of having him hold her again. Her nipples hardened, and in her stomach, desire stirred. She clamped her thighs together and hated the fact that after all these years of abstinence, she was succumbing to the lure of a charming man. "It will be exciting if we build the anticipation, don't you think?"

"I anticipate enough now." He wound his arms around her back. "If you don't, a small sample might help you."

"No. I—"

But he stood and swept her up off the bench into his arms. With stern determination on his face, he strode with her to a settee. There he set her down and put her on her back to the arm of the plush furniture.

She was thrilled. She was flummoxed. She summoned her gumption and lied like a murderer without hope at his hanging. "I don't want to do this."

"Ha! Is that so?" He came over her, his long, strong legs twined with her thighs. He tipped up her chin and brushed his fingers over the swell of her lips.

"It is."

"Really? Or do you tell me tales with your lips"—he widened his eyes at her, then sent them down her bodice—"while your body tells me other stories?"

"I am not yours to have. Not now—and not during our bargain."

He threw back his head to laugh, but it was short. And his anger was not pretty. "You offer me only help with my negotiations for the service I render you?"

She bit her lower lip.

He stared at it. "I see. I get short-changed, don't you think?" Was he joking or serious? She could not decide. "Not completely. I will be an entertaining companion and give you good recommendations."

He snorted. "I should be honored."

"You should."

He came down, his nose nuzzling hers, his lips ever so near, his voice breathy with hot promise. "But if you wish to convince Vaillancourt of our affection for each other, then you must allow yourself to enjoy this experience."

She gave him her best bit of gumption. "I am a good actress."

"Darling," he ground out, and cupped her cheek. "You are the worst."

"You don't know. You have not seen me in action."

One of his hands came up, and with the tips of his fingers, he grazed across the hard, aching points of her nipples.

She shivered to life but shut her eyes and clenched her jaw, suppressing the groan that rose in her throat.

"You fail your audition, Mademoiselle Bolton."

Her eyes flew open as he grabbed her hands and pulled her to her feet. "Go home. Forget the act. Just show what you feel when I touch you, and we will succeed."

## Chapter Nine

T HAT NIGHT HE appeared at Madame Tallien's salon, filled to the brim with this bowing and scraping. He needed to be off with Augustine.

He searched the crowds and found her with her aunt. The countess appeared strained, unlike her usual self. So too did Augustine appear stiff. He hoped to God she had not changed her mind. If she had been frightened enough to come to him for aid, then she would not back down now. Would she?

Cursing the need to work the room like a friendly hound, he took his time. Such was always beneficial. Tonight he learned that Bonaparte debated his appearance. How any of it mattered, he had no idea at the moment. But everything was worth the hearing. Paris might have put away most of its guillotines, but similar "beheadings" occurred each day by word and simple deed.

At last, he came upon Augustine. He took her hand to his mouth. The feel of her skin on his lips was a delight that his body appreciated all too well. *"Bon soir, mademoiselle.* I trust you are well."

"I am. I am," she repeated in an uncharacteristic manner.

"You are nervous. Don't be."

"I have never begun a charade like this. I know not what to do."

That surprised him. He expected that her aunt, with all her experience navigating the shoals of the prince regent's world, and then that of the late Bourbon Duke of Orleans, would have educated her niece in the art of the affair. But he had detected her reluctance. Was there some incident in Augustine's past that made her shy away from intimacy with a man? He could change that, if he were to revert to the rogue of his former self. But he would not. This man wished to be a finer one for her. "There is not much to it."

"No?" She gave a sharp little laugh. "How is that?"

"First, you relax." He offered his arm so that they might stroll about the room together. Patting her hand on his forearm, he noted how she suppressed a quiver. "As I said earlier, it is important to appear to have fun."

"Make it fun, Ashley." Her plea went right to his head—and his groin.

He maneuvered her so that she faced outward to the throng. He had to conceal his physical admiration for her request. "That's easy. I will tell you about my day."

"Oh, do." She squeezed her eyes shut a moment and swayed a bit toward him. "All I've been treated to this evening is who sleeps with whom—and why."

"Ah. Drivel." He winked at her. "I will tell you tales of four thousand gold louis that have gone into the bank as payment for Sèvres. Another two go in a few days for the sale of Gobelin rugs."

"The English have money to burn," she said with a look of pleasure at the news. "French do not. We must write promissory notes to purchase such goods. Some simply steal goods from their former owners and call it theirs."

"Theft inspires revenge in those left without their goods."

"Of course it does. Others counterfeit coin. Did you hear that some in the assembly run a ring of fraudsters? Bonaparte swears he will catch them. Some say they will go to the guillotine." She shuddered.

"Darling, look at me. Really," he said, and lifted her face to see his dashing smile. "Look at me."

"Did you know that the home of the new Bank of France is a *hôtel particulier* that once belonged to members of the royal family?" She looked lost, betrayed. "The Molyneaux of Normandy fled, all sixteen of them."

His heart turned over for her compassion. "Friends of yours?"

"Yes. A special family with many girls. Friends of mine. The Molyneaux of counts of Normandy. They live in poverty in England."

"Yes. Many do." He knew so many French émigrés.

"No homes. No money." She clasped her hands tightly together. "Many left with the clothes on their backs."

"I am not surprised. Their choices were few, and death did not appeal. And as they fled, they left so many homes and chateaux vacant."

She nodded. "Or burned or looted."

"Committees of government confiscated so many of the former owners' property. I suppose in many ways it is wise to put the facilities to use. Otherwise, they will deteriorate...or not be available when the owners return."

"You think they will?" She was stunned.

"It may be possible. The world turns every day. People forgive each other."

"They should, shouldn't they?" she asked with a sigh.

"My house I rent is spectacular. I would love to meet the family who once owned it. They had good taste."

"It was the property of the famous Rohan family. I knew the last owner," she said with a wistful sigh. "I was very young, but I have distinct memories of him. He was always ready to take me on his knee, tell me little fairy tales, and give me a hard sugar from his pocket. He liked candy—and me. Unique, he was, always kind to me. Few here were. I was the odd child, the English niece of the Duke of Orleans' favorite. An oddity."

Kane reached out to take her hand. "Yet you are here, an

adult and very well received."

"I am," she said with acceptance in her tone. "Here is where I am loved."

He stared at her, noting the yearning in her voice was as powerful a note as the appreciation. "Your aunt has been good to you."

"She has. You can never know how much. There is so little love in the world. Especially here." Her sad green eyes circled the room.

"I understand," he said, and he did, quite well. "Many do not show affection for others."

"They have not learned. They do not know how."

He sorrowed with her, but ventured the reasons for it. "In the past decade, they have been too afraid to show much. Self-preservation is the first need. All else must fade to second place."

She tilted her head to regard him, and her hand, still in his, tightened as she drifted toward him. "You sound as if you know this yourself."

"I do."

"Will you tell me?" she asked with the same innocent desire as a child who wishes a bedtime story.

"I can. It is a long tale, I'm afraid. Fit for our journeys soon to come."

Her almond-shaped eyes widened in delight. "Tell me all of that, please."

"Shall we try the veranda?"

"In the moonlight?" She grinned, all eager naiveté to hear his story. Drat his vain rogue's hopes, but she was not inviting his advances.

"We dare not allow others to overhear," he said, providing reason for his move. With a nod toward the far archway to the grand salon, she went with him toward the French doors to the soft night air.

They strode to the banister. By the light of the moon and stars, they could see the outlines of the small, trim parterre, elaborate and meant for silent contemplation.

"Do you like gardens?" she asked him, and he was surprised at the turn of her thoughts. He'd anticipated she'd want answers about their coming days together and where they'd go.

"I do, as a matter of fact." He stood, facing her, the profile she cut against the navy velvet sky enticing him to put his hands on her. Instead, he leaned an elbow on the stone. "I often helped our gardeners when I was a child. My parents had no use for me. A third boy is so irrelevant. A phantom to them. I was out to the stables and the gardens, dining often with the tenants because I didn't want to go home to the big, cold, dark house."

She showed her sorrow at that by placing her hand on his. "You suffered from their inattention. How sad."

"On the contrary," he said as he watched strands of her hair lift in the gentle breezes. He indulged himself...or rather, he ignored the voice that yelled at him to keep his hands to himself. He traced the curls along her temple and her cheek. Everywhere he touched, she was silk and satin. "I had a very happy time of it. Our tenants are good, solid folk who took me in when they needn't. They fed me, bathed me, allowed me the joy of their children as my playmates, and I, in turn, learned how to plow a field, turn a calf in the womb, and shoe a horse."

She gasped. "What fun. I wish I'd had the same."

"But you have lived here. With your aunt. You have learned so much that others could not duplicate."

She set her teeth and frowned into the cloak of night. "It is worth...many things. But I think at this moment what I have learned does not match your fabulous, enriching list of a life well lived."

"What you do, Augustine, to find your friend, shows you have learned one thing well."

She turned to him, a serene acceptance in her gaze. "Tolerance for those who hurt others?"

He inched closer, cupping her throat. "Love of your friend. The need to find her."

Her lashes fluttered. "She has been my boon companion for so many years. We have learned how to survive this life together. Even when she married, and she said at first that she did it for security, she shared with me her thoughts and fears. In my life here, no friend compares to her, and I fear that Vaillancourt has hurt her." She sniffed, and suddenly could not hold back her tears.

Then she came into his arms. The feel of her, the wealth of her love and her fear for her friend seeping into his body, was more than he had ever thought he might know of her. That she trusted him for that overjoyed him.

He drew her solidly against him. Stroking her back, he curved his other arm up so that he could cup her nape. She was the most lithesome woman he had ever held. He had known it on the Malmaison road that morning. Tonight he embraced a greater truth about who and what she was—a person with heartaches and triumphs. A young lady who wished for companionship and affection. One who gave it as well. But more than that, she was soon to be his unwitting aide. His companion to find her friend. And his lover, by pretense only.

But with the knowledge that that was all she could ever be— for her sake and for his—he clasped her close and whispered words of comfort. She would be his darling friend, a compatriot in the search for the woman they both must find or save or mourn.

When she raised her tear-stained face to him, he had to brush away her sorrows. He had to smile and say she was the finest friend to do what she embarked upon now to find her. He had to raise her chin and say, "Augustine, you will not cry again for the loss of your friend. We will find her."

She clutched his frock coat. "I have been so lost. I could not find more ways to look for her. You are my champion to do this for me, and I will never be able to repay you."

"Friends do not give recompense for the help they give each other."

"We are friends?" she asked with hope in her lovely, sad eyes.

"We are."

She sniffed and gave him the ghost of a smile. "Like no others."

He nodded and brought her closer. "Like no others."

"And friends," she said with wide eyes, "kiss each other."

"They do." He settled her firmly into the curves and hollows of his body. If he struck a match, he would have gone up in flame.

"Despite," she whispered as she frowned, "any charade."

For all that she was and all that was yet unknown to him about her, he had to search and he had to proceed with their plan. They had to move toward their pretense here and now. "They kiss to seal their belief in each other."

She rose on her toes. "I want that from you."

"Do you, darling?" He could not help the endearment that slipped out. She was his sweet conspirator, soon to be more. "Come kiss me, then. We'll work for the best of each other."

Her gaze was on his lips.

He closed his eyes. If she did not kiss him soon, he would dissolve. Her lips were all he had ever wanted, the part of her that drove him to tormented memories at night.

He felt her thighs and belly and breasts slide along his body. She was supple, her thighs strong, her loins elegant, her breasts lush. And then the part of her that had lived in his reverie for two long years brushed his.

He was gone to some bliss he'd only sampled on the Malmaison road. He opened his mouth, and she came with a moist and tender press to his flesh. She jerked away. He stilled, paralyzed by what he'd had of her, what more he needed of her.

If it was a second he waited or an eternity, he could not say. But she moved upon him, her hands to his shoulders, her lips slanting on his. Shy as she was, untutored, unpracticed at this art, she put her mouth to his open one with an urgency that took his breath and gave him blithe and rapturous reward. She sank her fingertips into the hair at his nape and moved her lips upon him in a demand he gladly rewarded.

He lifted her up against him, the fullness of her all his.

She broke away. Her eyes wide and startled in the moonlight, she searched for answers, he supposed, to her enchantment. Letting her decide again how far they would go with this kiss, he set her to the stone railing of the veranda.

"Ashley," she called, her hand behind his head drawing him near. Then she opened her legs in raw invitation for more. He went, drawn, fool that he was, lost to her spontaneity and pressed between her thighs. She was at the right height to squeeze her legs together and lock him in. But she was too far back along the stone to feel the power of his cock, rigid and full of his delight in her.

He tore his mouth from hers. Breathless, he put his lips to the hollow below her ear. He would absorb her, all of her, inside him and never have to leave her to others and the uncertainties of their world.

"WE MUST STOP," she murmured, though like a besotted girl, she arched her neck to give him greater access. She could not wish him gone—and oh, how she wanted him to stay and give her more of his lips and his arms and the stories of his childhood. Through those brief tales, he had become a boy, a solemn and vital person whom she could trust for the moment, for the task, for her needs. *But no more. Not a bit more...*

He lingered, his lips on her throat and her shoulder as he seemed to inhale every essence of her. With a small blessing of his open mouth to the hollow of her throat, he drew back.

He took his time, his enchanting eyes examining her. With deft moves, he fluffed the ruffle at her bodice and pulled down her skirts over her knees.

"Thank you," she said with a true smile, though she breathed rapidly, in no way recovered from his thrall. "We have done a good job of displaying our interest."

"Have we?" His bass voice was gruff, the question asking a thousand more things than the obvious.

She nodded, hiding her gulp. "Yes, just now, two have come to the doors and left."

"Polite of them," he said, and cupped her cheek. "We cannot go in yet."

"No?" Her mind was too full of him, her question too whimsical.

"You are flushed. And I am not fit to face anyone." His brows rose by little degrees to reach the black shock of hair that had fallen—with her help, she was sure—over his broad brow.

She giggled.

He rolled his eyes and, hands on his hips, considered the stars.

"How long do you need?" Lured, she glanced down. *My, my.* She flashed him a wicked pout.

"Hours, if you keep that up! You may not have had lovers, darling, but you've learned how to entice a man!"

She smarted, sobered. "I—I didn't mean..." She waved a hand.

He caught it midair. "I know. What I meant to do was make you laugh more. Not imply that you are loose."

"Thank you. Again. I am grateful for you. For this agreement we have."

He lifted her hand to his lips and, turning it up, dropped a kiss into her palm.

That too set her insides gushing with a new, wild need. His affection could become a habit.

"I should go in," she said with regret.

"Yes." He straightened a few tendrils of her hair from her temples to hang along her cheeks. "Otherwise, they will say we did more than kiss."

She slid to her feet. "I am no longer pink?"

"No, my darling. You are simply stunning." He breathed slowly, deeply, while he seemed to memorize every aspect of her face. He turned to one side and extended his arm. "Go in. Leave me."

She shook out her skirts, avoiding looking at him, hating to leave him. "We must discuss our plan. You will come to call on me tomorrow, I hope?"

"What time will do?"

*Any. Come home with me. Or I will go home with you.* "Oh, I don't know!" She had a hand to her cheek, blushing and confused. How could she want him to linger? To kiss her and... "Ugh! What hour does a lover call?"

"An eager man calls at dawn."

"Well, that won't do. If this party drags on, I won't be home until three."

"Noon, then?" He reached out his hands.

She took them, needing every minute with him she could grab. "Come for breakfast."

He snorted. "Twelve it is."

"When you come tomorrow, will you have details on what we do? How? When we go?"

"I will try. I promise nothing. This is complicated, Augustine."

"Gus." With what they had shared here, he must call her as she was best known to herself. It was the mark of friendship, yes? "Those who are my friends and family call me Gus."

"Gus," he uttered as if it were the most delightful thing he'd committed to memory since his own name. "Tomorrow."

By his very regard of her, she stood bedazzled. "You'll tell me."

"Anything you wish to know."

"Because we are friends."

"Above all."

## Chapter Ten

KISSING ASHLEY LAST night was not what she had expected. Gus rolled to her back, arms out like a human sacrifice on her massive bed, and grinned. Certainly, kissing him was not what she had wanted to do.

But then the feel of his lips on hers had brought an explosion that felt like lava. Fierce, uncontrollable. She narrowed her eyes on the view of the *trompe l'oeil* painting on her ceiling. Hades absconding with Persephone.

*Hmmm.*

The Earl of Ashley was not chasing her. The difference between him and most men at this court had struck her from the start. True to his calling, a man of delicate sensibilities, even if he appeared to be as formidable as a fortress, he was a man she could admire, even cling to. And if she were not careful, when she kissed him again—for she had to—she could get lost in him. A man of finesse and diplomacy with lips that laughed and bewitched.

She would be careful. Rational.

Their kisses on the Malmaison road were that of desperation on his part and shock on hers. Even desire. No wonder she had felt compelled to sink her teeth into him.

She slapped a hand over her mouth and chuckled. Love at

first bite, it was not. More like fascination at first taste.

And then, because she told herself to forget the saboteur on the road, she had parted with him but had, in truth, never erased him from her reverie. Then he reappeared like a genie from a magic lamp.

Ashley. An earl. A diplomat. An exquisitely built mountain of a man who kissed like a lover.

"As if I know what that is!" she whispered to herself.

Her only kisses had been the barbarous press of Pascal Moreau's wet lips to her that night he'd tried to rape her.

She curled up into a ball and buried her face in her pillow.

Ashley's kisses were no comparison to that brute's. "Even in the road, his lips were…"

Tender. His of last night were the stuff of—could she dare name it?—rapport. More, actually. Camaraderie.

*Ah! Like a military pal.*

*How complimentary, Gus!*

She threw back her covers and sat up, disturbed but rejoicing in the results. All evening long, she had avoided—but relished— the sidelong glances sent her by those at the salon. Ashley and she—by those kisses and minutes on the veranda—were officially entangled. Those who mattered here knew it. Even Vaillancourt had absorbed her with his dark, malicious eyes as if he had always known she could be seduced.

She shook off her negativity. Ashley and she had done a good thing last night. Their ruse had worked.

What had not worked was her behavior. She had kissed *him*.

A natural act. A foolish girl's.

She squeezed shut her eyes. Since she'd been thirteen, she'd told herself she would have no ordinary man. She would one day choose a man who would be totally hers. Disciplined and docile. Afraid she'd leave him. So afraid, he'd never roam. Never demand. Never need anything other than what she wished to give him.

But she had enjoyed this one, this giant of a man, this exemplary one who definitely belonged to himself. This Englishman with the dubious background. With the legitimate government assignment. With eyes of ice and shoulders of a mythic god. Arms of iron and lashes (she had to grin) that a *femme fatale* would kill for. A body that stood so tall, so broad, so exquisitely sculpted, that she...

She squeezed her thighs together. Years ago, Amber had told her the gush of desire for a man could make her pulse with need. Make her yearn to place her own hands on her body and press and stroke.

But....

*No.* She would not succumb.

She put her feet to the carpet and went to her mirror. What a picture! Her hair stood on end, and her puffy eyes popped. Who would want this woman who wished to be celibate? Her nipples beaded, hard and aching in the silken muslin that abraded her and made her want him more.

She groaned, pulled the fabric from her breasts, and strode to her bellpull. She gave it a yank.

Arms crossed, eyes upon the carriages crisscrossing the streets, she welcomed the sun. Ashley should bring a small cabriolet, open to the world. And, as per their agreement, he would come prepared to kiss her for all to see. This time, she would be good. He would do all the kissing.

He would be the aggressor. For the moment's thrill. To establish the reason to travel. Create a cover. An alibi.

"*Mademoiselle, bonjour.*" Her little French maid scooted before her. "A bath or breakfast first?"

"Bread and coffee, Natalie." *Sustenance for kissing a man.* "I'll have them in the tub."

"CORSINI?" KANE HAD rung for his butler only minutes ago. With

Ram and Dirk gone to the east, Kane had need of a person he could trust to recruit incorruptible men. In such a rush to leave town, he expected that his *majordom* could fill his needs. Scarlett Hawthorne had hired Corsini, and she had excellent skills in the art of selecting aggressive *agents provocateur.*

"*Si, conte?*" His butler appeared at the door to his bedroom.

Kane stopped his assembly of informal frock coats and breeches he wished to take to the country. Corsini had hired a valet for Kane, and young Gaston Clement, a Frenchman, had gone to find Kane's trunk in the attic.

He sat on the edge of his bed. "I need a delicate matter done."

Corsini folded his hands before him as if he were a prince appearing in public. "*Si,* I can help you, sir."

"I do assume, because you were hired for me before I even knew I was to serve here, that you can do me the favor of hiring certain male associates I might trust."

"You have the right of it, sir." Corsini seemed to grow taller in stature.

Kane hid his grin. He had an inkling Corsini had already done him a favor to hire one good man. Kane had never spied the fellow at his work, but he had a sixth sense that someone followed him. And justly so. Kane was second head of mission until the government-appointed ambassador arrived. No one knew when that might be. So an envoy needed protection, didn't he?

Kane strolled to his armoire and took out a few cravats. "My trip to the country is of indefinite duration. I informed Clement a few minutes ago. I trust you will impress upon him the need for secrecy."

"*Si, conte.* I will. Fear not of anyone in the household being indiscreet."

"I will have a guest with me. A special friend."

"I understand, sir. And does this require added security?"

*Good man.* "I need three carriages for three nights from now."

Corsini's dark eyes held his like magnets.

"Each carriage exactly the same."

No word passed his butler's mouth.

"Each set of coachman and groom attired exactly the same. The horses—"

"The same breed and color. *Si, conte*. What time?"

A devilish smile stole over Kane's face. He appreciated his butler's insight. "What would you recommend?"

"Three, sir."

"Three it is." Kane waved a hand. "I will need two more men with similar responsibilities to the man you currently employ as my... Shall we call him...my shadow?"

Corsini merely inclined his head.

"One man to follow each carriage and report to you. Your choice how that is done, of course."

"Naturally." The Florentine was not dazed.

Kane was not surprised.

He frowned at what he now had to tell his butler, hating that this next request was so very necessary. But he would take no chances with Gus's life, her need to find her friend—or his own need to find St. Antoine.

"I wish the three to remain in service well after I return. Twenty-four hours a day. I never wish to be alone, Corsini."

With a few strong Florentine words under his breath, the lanky fellow flashed a confident grin. "The finest I will employ. If you are ready, *conte*, the landau I hired for your ride in the sunshine is waiting in the courtyard."

## Chapter Eleven

B REAKFAST WITH KANE was torture.
    He had arrived on time, looking tired but dashing, eager to get on with their ruse. Dressed in a fashionable morning coat and waistcoat of azure shades of blue, he wore cream breeches that fit him to a fare-thee-well. When he strode toward her, Gus could marvel at the play of his thigh muscles and other accoutrements that made her wiggle in her corset.

He was a fit and healthy dream of a man.

Curse him and his easy laugh.

So he knew she admired his assets. Good. She would continue to eat up his calm and delight in the lush prick of her desire for him. It was not like her to care that he was Adonis come to call. More like Zeus, he was, really, filling up the tiny breakfast room with his massive height and weight. Making her fingers itch to sketch his chiseled cheeks and classic profile.

Meanwhile, she became as silly as a thirteen-year-old again. Gazing at naked statues in her father's gallery. Wondering how long Ashley's cock would be if he were, like last night, attracted to her. Her mind blanked. Her need to find Amber fled. Her madness to taste his lips had her straining to move them in logical conversation.

But she degenerated into a girlish bundle of nerves. Oh, that would not be so very appealing to a man of the world like Ashley. Damn his *savior faire*.

While the butler and a footman bustled about serving them, Kane hit upon the weather. The iced-over Thames had destroyed many ships in December.

*Had it, really?*

The famine that had struck all of Europe was taking a toll.

*Do you think so?*

"Prices of grain," he said with a look of concern for her lack of focus on their topic, "show it."

"The Seine broke its banks in January," she offered, like a town crier.

"Did you flee?"

"Flee?"

"The house? The city?"

She shook herself to attention. "No. No, no. Our cellars were inundated, and the kitchen staff lost their quarters. Only lately have our servants been able to bail out all the water."

"Tragic." He sat, serene as if he were in church, and went on about damages in London from winter storms.

She wished she could measure the length of his black lashes. Why would a man need such lovely things? It was not fair.

"Gus?" He cocked his head. "Does she?"

"What? Hmm. I apologize."

He flicked those lashes downward.

Did he hide a grin?

She had better ideas what to do with those lips.

"Your aunt," he said, and gave her a look that implied she had been miles away, "does not join us?"

*Ah. Well. No.* "She remains abed until at least three. Last night went on and on. She stayed until the very end."

Thank heaven he and Gus were alone. Aunt Cecily, perceptive as that lady was, would see through her bumbling. Gus's assurances to her that she did not care for him would be for naught.

She had to find her footing.

"You slept well last night?" she asked, filling a void with a stupid, stupid subject.

"I did. And you?"

"Not very." She reached for her tea. "I have trouble sleeping occasionally."

"All the late nights add up. They are not good for you. Nor for anyone."

"They cannot be avoided," she bit off.

"I understand." He accepted cheeses and sausages from the tray the footman offered him. "It's good you and I are—"

Wincing, she slid her gaze toward the kitchen door and the threshold to the hall.

His brows shot high. Then he nodded.

The walls did have ears.

"—shall we say?—able to break away better than others." He smiled and went back to his eggs.

The butler hovered over her. Blind with dismay, she took a scoop of eggs that would choke a horse.

Her companion noted it with dubious brow.

She glared at him and jabbed her fork into her mound of food.

"Was last night a success for you?" she ventured in an attempt to cover her petulance and make decent conversation.

He stopped, his fork in midair, and looked at her across the circular table. His brow crinkled in a frown. "With potential offers of sales for England?"

"Of course." She knitted her brows in reprimand.

He sipped his coffee for a minute, all the while examining her as she shoveled her breakfast into her mouth and searched her brain for her reason.

"Why don't you tell me where you wish to ride today, Gus?" He tucked into his omelet and toast, as unperturbed as the cucumbers on the plate.

"Shall we go east to the Louvre, around and back?"

"A fine plan." The click of his silver utensils on his china filled the void. "Should we have our coachman pause before Notre Dame?"

He wanted details of where and when he'd kiss her? "Fine."

He gazed up from beneath the cover of those long, lush lashes. "You prefer another place?"

*Couldn't the act just be...spontaneous?*

He cocked his head.

"No." All planned. Very well. Their scheme demanded he do it in the most crowded public place. She attacked her omelet.

"I have a landau," he said at length after he'd put down his fork and knife. "But I suggest you bring a parasol."

"I can. But we should put the top up anyway."

He stared at her.

She could almost hear him tell her that privacy defeated the purpose of their drive. But the seclusion would give more spice to any gossip's tale.

She smiled at him, hoping he'd go along. "Men wear all those layers of clothing. Wool, even in this weather. Putting up the top will help. I don't want you to get too hot."

He took his time, chewing his food and stifling his laughter. Was he always so controlled, or was it just her who made him quirky?

"I have refreshment in the carriage for us. We won't get overheated." He gathered up his serviette. "If you are done, we should go."

GUS COULD NOT escape their pact. Her nerves were unnecessary. If she thought he was going to push her into an affair, she was wrong. He was no cad.

But he would let her stew. They had been out for at least an hour and the sun was glaring down. He crossed one leg over the other as he sat facing her and trying, mightily as he could, to avoid gazing at her too long.

She sat like a delicacy against the overstuffed autumnal-brown squabs. A cream and pink confection in an apple-green frosting, she should be plucked and eaten.

He swallowed a groan. Her gown was a pale green, festooned with so much lace that she might as well have worn an iron maiden for her protection. But the cotton—he thanked the modiste—betrayed her. The fabric hugged her breasts like frothy *blancmange*. A trickle of perspiration wended down her cleavage and formed a tempting arrow toward her hips.

He could dream, couldn't he?

But they had matters to discuss...before they got to the real business here today.

He told his cock to take a holiday and went to work. "You have not told your aunt we go away together, have you?"

"Not yet."

"Why not?"

"She will object."

"I see. To me? Why?"

Gus threw back her head, and the neat white feathers in her little hat fluttered against her blue-black hair. "She likes you. But she wishes me to remain as I am." Her green eyes danced. "Pure. White. Snow. She only wishes to protect me from rogues."

He smacked his lips. They went around the Louvre and headed toward Notre Dame. He had to pry. His safety and hers depended on his knowing every detail. "She does not know why you truly go away with me, does she?"

"No." She sat forward and skewered him with her gaze. "And before you ask me why she does not know that, I will tell you it is because she likes Amber. Very much, actually. Loves her equally to me. But she will not appreciate that I am compelled to find her."

He wondered on the ramifications of that. "There is more to that. Tell me."

Gus licked her lips, and he had to press his thighs together to quell the urge to gather her up and put her in his lap. "Aunt Cecily does not believe one risks one's life for anyone."

"I suppose I should applaud that. But I don't agree."

"Some things are more important."

He considered her. Beautiful beyond any woman he had ever seen, raised to be a queen of Society, and she valued her friend enough to risk her life to find her.

"When will you tell her?" he asked, because he could see she fought sharing a thousand other things with him.

"The day we leave." She examined his face as if memorizing his every line. "When do we go?"

"Three nights from now. In the early morning. We leave from my house. You should arrive around nine. Say you're going to dinner at a friend's house. But the carriage you take from your aunt's will be one I send for you. He will be at the kitchen entrance at ten minutes before nine. Bring as much as you think you can easily carry in one reticule."

"We're not being fashionable." She smiled at him, haughty and happy and hellishly stunning.

"No. Bring breeches."

She pressed a hand to the wealth of her ripe breasts. "I am shocked, sir, you think I own a pair."

"Of course you do," he said, and got up and moved to sit beside her. "A woman who rides early in the morning with few clothes rides later with only a few more."

She laughed. "She does! I like a good game of chess, too."

"Not this *vingt-et-un* that Bonaparte and Josephine like?"

"No," she said with pride.

"I am sorry." He shook his head. "You do not want to play me."

She was game to fight him. "Think you're good, eh?"

"I am."

She preened. "I, sir, am better."

"How do you know?"

She arched a challenging black brow. "I have proof. I play for money."

He feigned shock. "You gamble. Tsk-tsk. I should have known."

"A woman needs coin for lace and ribbons."

And, he'd wager, for something more precious. He reached for her hand in her lap and put it in his. "I'll play you for money."

Her large green eyes drifted to his mouth. Her fingers tangled with his and skimmed the wool of his flies. She breathed deeply, her eyelids fluttering as she said, "Yes. To pass the time when we are not traveling, let's."

"A deal," he declared, knowing full well her mind went to items that were not coins, but the wealth of his jewels beneath her fingertips.

She shook herself and drew away, though her gaze seemed stuck to his. "Have you any details of where we go?"

"To the northeast. I have not finalized the details. It takes time to prepare such affairs."

"You know France well."

"I do." He toyed with her long fingers and brought them to his lips.

>>>><<<<

ASHLEY RESTED HIS beautiful, iridescent eyes on hers. He was relaxed, almost ebullient.

But Gus would not give herself all the credit. He was here for his own self-interest. He wanted contracts, more than anything.

"When I was a boy," he said, pressing her hand to his cheek, "I was sent by my parents to visit my aunt and uncle in the Loire. They own a vast estate and grow grapes near Amboise."

She watched him caressing her like a lover. Short of breath, with pounding heart, she found some logic. "Will you have them send wine to your buyers in Britain?"

"I will, yes."

"The grape yield has been good this year. Despite the floods and drought."

"You know much about growing grapes." He put his arm around her, and she relaxed into the circle of his embrace.

"A woman should always know facts about her surroundings. As much as she should also make something of her own."

"A mark of preservation as well as helping others respect her."

"Do you wish to make something of your own?"

*I have done. Every day.* "I am a fairly good artist."

"Is that so?" He nodded, impressed. "What is your subject matter?"

"Portraits."

"Excellent. Have you done many?"

"I have." She grinned up at him. "I will bring my sketchbook with me on our holiday and attempt a likeness of you." She would not tell him she already had attempted that. He would not need to be emboldened by her interest. "I think your jutting jaw would be so easy to draw."

He pursed his lips. "You draw me as the man from the Malmaison road, eh?"

"No. That man…" She lifted her hand to caress his cheek. "That man is not here. I do believe you left him at home in England."

He dipped his jaw into the palm of her hand, his pale eyes glittering in the sun. "You are right. He has gone."

"Will you tell me why?"

He stared at her, but it was not her he saw. "He observed what was to have been a dastardly deed that day. He saw instead an even worse event. The death of his friend."

Her heart turned for him. "The one you spoke of before."

"Yes. The one so heinously murdered."

"Tell me." She reached across and put her gloved hand in his.

"It is not fit for a lady to hear."

"Tell me. I will not demand you cover the worst for me. Who

am I? A woman sheltered from the horrors of what men do to other men and other women? I may not have lived the Terror, or seen it, but I hear of it. Your event is part of the mayhem the French have loosed on the world. Tell me, Kane. I may call you, Kane, may I not?" She smiled at him. "You said last night we are friends. Please, let us be. Tell me."

He sat, far away in his grief. "He knew he might die that day. We all did—of course, you do not do acts like that and not count the possible toll. That day, the event turned on us. But on my friend Brussard, it turned brutally." He blinked and turned to her, horror of the past lighting his face with a determination that had him drawing her up to him and her nails digging into his arm.

"I work for peace now. Only that. I want what you want. A life lived with possibilities, not death or subterfuge. Only light and air and freedom."

He was a man who changed and grew. And in that luminous landscape he created, she rose to his lips and kissed them. He was heaven to savor, all masculine power and hungry lover. Eager and insistent. One who took her to him, caressed her throat, and held her there to murmur his praise and kiss her back.

She did not count them. He did not stop. She would not make him.

When their breath was gone and a few in the streets clapped and shouted their approval, she fell back to the squabs and stared at him.

"We have been successful today," he announced as she rearranged her bodice and he shifted in his breeches.

The whole of Paris would have her in his bed tonight.

Oh, that they were right.

How wrong she had been about kissing him. Not torture, but bliss.

She had only two more days in this carriage to do it. Then as they made their way into the country, there would be no more.

The reality of it had her losing sleep that night and the next.

## Chapter Twelve

THREE DAYS LATER, Kane appeared at two o'clock, their agreed-upon time for today, their last day in the city. Shown to a tiny salon at the rear of Countess Nugent's mansion where a pianoforte stood in the sunlight from the window, he awaited Gus.

He stood by the tall windows looking out toward the boulevard. He did not detect anyone following him today. But then, Fouché and Vaillancourt employed the very finest. Kane never underestimated an opponent, certainly not the renowned police of new, bold, unruly France.

He took no chances. The three sets of diversions for the coming trip out of Paris would be an excellent ruse. He wanted no one to hurt Gus or St. Antoine, if they found her. He'd take no chances anyone would interrupt their trip or take Gus from him. Their kisses of the past few days had told him he could wish for more. Even if Gus told him she did not wish to be intimate with any man, he knew men and women changed their minds about such things.

He flexed his shoulders. He wished he had not changed his mind about Gus. But there it was. He liked her. He admired her. He wanted her, but he had not used intimacy as the lure to make her do his will.

He would not crush the opportunity to find St. Antoine. He'd learned much in his youth about women. Gus needed to come to him in all things. And as for him, he was too old to spoil an assignment by seducing a woman who did not wish to be taken.

Still, he thrilled to the touch of Gus's beautiful lips on his. She would kiss him today in the open carriage in the brilliant light of day for all to witness, just as she had the past two. Her kisses were a true and honest event. He would never tell her that. She'd run from him, and that, he could not have. Not now. Not when they were about to embark on the journey to accomplish their goal.

So he would take her away. To his old friend's ancient hunting lodge a twenty-minute ride from the center of Reims, tucked into the rolling hills full of vineyards, they would go. Few would find them. Few could intrude. As he recalled from his youth, the house was huge. It sat atop a small hill and overlooked the nearby vista. There was a library where they could sit and read. A well-stocked smokehouse. A village lady who kindly supplied vegetables. And a small, useful kitchen.

Impatient for Gus to appear for their ride, he strode to the pianoforte in the center of the countess's salon and sat down. The appeal of the open keyboard was too much, and he began the Mozart that he and Gus had played together.

Only a few bars into the music, he paused at the sight of the woman who appeared at the threshold. The lady was not Gus, but her aunt, Countess Nugent.

The woman was a legend in France and England. Perhaps forty years old, she looked a decade younger. Admirable for the changes she'd endured and the horrors she'd survived. Gracious, still a queen of Parisian Society, she had navigated years of associations with notorious men who had rewarded her with a less-than-perfect reputation, large parcels of property, and a fortune in jewels and investments to support it all.

"Good afternoon, Lord Ashley." She sailed toward him in an azure chiffon that billowed as she flowed forward, defining her still superb figure. "I am pleased you are on time."

He bowed with chivalry. "I am pleased to be received."

"Do take your leisure, my lord." She took a chair opposite the sofa she nodded toward. "Augustine will be here shortly. I took the opportunity to come speak with you myself. You and I have met, talked, and established a certain enjoyment of each other, haven't we?"

He took to the sofa done in bold yellow and jade Chinoiserie print, relaxing into the cushions, but his attitude was an act. The lady wanted something. He had an idea what it was, but he would hear her out. He doubted, however, he could comply with her wishes to leave Gus here.

"Augustine tells me she goes away with you."

He lifted his brows in affirmation.

The countess folded her hands in her lap. "I will be bold, sir. This affection you have for each other runs hot and fast. I find your decision to take a holiday together in the country abrupt and dangerous."

"Sometimes one sees in another a reason to act quickly."

"Not in this city, sir. Not with my niece."

He clenched his teeth. Had she dissuaded Gus from going away with him? "I do not wish to cause you pain, my lady."

"It is not my pain I anticipate, sir. But Augustine's."

"Aunt Cecily." Gus stood in the doorway. Her cheeks were red with anger, her head high. "I am of age."

Gus walked in, stuck her parasol against the wall, and headed straight for Kane. Plunking herself without ceremony on the sofa, she stared at Countess Nugent. "We addressed this subject days ago, Aunt."

"My warnings have not changed, Augustine."

"I took note of them. I must go with the earl."

The countess scowled at the two of them in turn. "When do you return?"

*As long as it takes to find St. Antoine.* But Kane could not say that, because whatever the countess's objections, a long period away from Paris and her was definitely not what she wished.

Gus took his hand into hers. "We do not have a time limit."

The countess noted Gus's gesture. Then she rose from her chair and strode toward the tall windows in which she sparkled like the sun. Or a fiery demon. "Ashley, you have been at court approximately one month. You do not know the waters you navigate. I daresay few of us do!"

She strode toward the pianoforte. With a few fingers she hit a melody he knew well but could not place under the tense atmosphere. "We are not so far from the days when the guillotine ruled everyone's life. We are in a period when hard decisions by a very few rule the day. Those in power tread carefully. The women who walk here must tread with delicacy. A lady's reputation is her calling card."

Gus scoffed. "Except for Tallien, the Bonaparte sisters, and a few notable others."

Kane had the distinct impression that she implied Josephine Bonaparte.

The countess took offense. "Yes. They dare, *ma petite*. They can. They are older, more experienced in the art of maintaining their allure...and their power. You are not."

Kane anticipated where the countess led, but he wanted an end to her haranguing of Gus. "What is it you want, *madame?*"

She faced him with thin lips and an eagle's eye. "She is a virgin."

"Aunt!" Gus spat her outrage.

"She has had no lover. At twenty-one, she is an untouched beauty, and she has chosen that because she swore she loved no one."

"I do not love Ashley, Aunt Cecily. But I will choose if I will be his lover, not you."

Kane covered his wince. This was becoming much too intrusive. "I will take care of her, *madame.*"

"Will you?" The woman took him in, head to toe. "You are a supremely handsome rogue. Charming and skilled in diplomacy. Why am I not to assume you are talented as a lover as well, eh?"

Truth now for this woman was best, even if it would confuse the hell out of her. "*Madame*, I did not persuade Augustine to come to me as a lover. But as a friend."

"No?" Cecily scoffed and shot a look at her niece. "Tell me you went to him. Made him a proposal for this scandalous holiday."

"I did, Aunt."

"Why? Why? For all the men who would have fallen at your feet, you choose this Englishman? He is titled. Landed. Well received. An envoy. But he is penniless. A third son who had nothing until his two older, more scandalous brothers fell into their graves!"

Kane moved not a muscle. Cecily knew much about him. How? From French spies in London, most likely. Well, tit for tat. It happened.

Gus stiffened. "I like him. I like him more than I have any other men I've met in this murderous city. I will go with him, Aunt. I will. And you cannot stop me."

The older woman whirled on Kane. "Then hear me. She goes with you. You will not harm a hair on her head, do you hear me? She is a sweet girl, meant for a man who can be tender with her. Kind and considerate of her. Are you that man?"

He nodded. "I assure you, *madame*, I am."

"Prove it to me."

"Stop this!" Gus was on her feet. "I will not be treated like a child."

The countess showed a glimpse of compassion toward her niece. "You are not, Augustine. Sir? What say you to me?"

"Anything you want from me for Gus's safety and happiness, I will gladly do."

Gus glared at him. "She sucks you in."

He reached to take her hand once more and stroked her knuckles. "I will do what she wants, Gus."

"Ah. And will I?" she threw back at him.

"I hope you will agree," he said with equanimity. "I wish to go in peace and with your aunt's blessing."

Gus considered that, for whatever good reason came to her.

Kane had to give her cover and solace. "Darling," he appealed to her in a murmur. "We must be rational. We need to do this with full cooperation from your aunt. She can tell others of her approval and not raise any eyebrows."

He would need the countess to present his and Gus's absence in the best light. They would be gone, and for who knew how long? He needed cover, and so did Gus. If the countess did not provide it, both of them were sure to encounter problems when they returned, no matter how well they succeeded or failed in their search for St. Antoine. "Gus, it is essential that your aunt approve of us."

She heaved a big sigh of acceptance and spun away from him. "Tell him, Aunt, what you want."

"Thank you, sir." The countess, in her element of unimpeachable power, was gracious in her victory.

He waited.

"I ask this of you, sir, because you are a man of integrity. You would not be here with the duty to negotiate these contracts were you a charlatan." She strode near and resumed her chair. "You grow intimate with each other. Enchanting kisses often lead to more. On the verandas, in carriages. Receiving the applause, no less, of passersby. Yet days are too early for you to decide to go away together.

"But I do not debate your timing, only the results of this holiday you share. You may have only kisses now, but we know what they lead to. For a man, it's one thing, a feather in his hat, to say he's claimed a lover. It is even better for his manly reputation if he can say he has enjoyed many women, many affairs. I know not how many you have had, Lord Ashley, and I will not ask. The number is irrelevant to my needs. I simply want the best result for my niece. She can decide to go away with you, sir. It is her right. She is old and wise enough to do this. But I am old enough and wise enough to ask one thing."

"Name it," he declared, eager to be done with this confrontation.

"If Augustine returns a woman educated in the fine arts of intimacy, I have no objections to that. It can be a joy to learn. You appear to be the man, sir, who can enlighten her. If, however, she has asked you to remain celibate with her until such time as she decides if she is infatuated with you, that is better."

The woman pursed her lips and, for a moment, gazed toward the window...and, dare he say, he thought she stared with melancholy into her past.

"Do know, sir, I have taught Augustine the ways to prevent pregnancy. It is up to her and—I hope—up to you to employ them if indeed neither of you wishes to have issue from this escapade. Yet I know, as do you both, those measures often fail. But if Augustine returns here with child, I will press you both to marry."

He could have predicted as much. "Yes. I hear you."

Gus's green eyes grew wide with anger. "Let us go, my lord."

"No need to leave. I shall!" The countess got to her feet. "You will, I assume, Lord Ashley, take appropriate precautions as you leave the city?"

Kane appreciated the woman's thoroughness. "I have protections for us."

The countess put out her hand. Approval was in her stern expression. "Take excellent care of her, sir. I have loved this child since the day she was born. I have saved her from all sorts of terrors from her parents and their inadequacies. I wish my niece to have a joyous life, and that does include the opportunity to fall in love without impediments. But I also wish to see she have a happy life beyond this room, this time, this court. Should you provide any deterrents to that, sir, I warn you, I may look like a shallow woman, but I have my abilities. I will use them."

He took her proffered hand. "I understand. Thank you."

Gus stood, arms crossed, tapping one foot against the glossy marble tiles.

When the countess had retired and the door was closed, Kane braced himself for the torrential storm he'd now navigate.

GUS HEADED TOWARD the door, where she bent and snatched up her parasol. Then she swirled toward him. Her face held all the emotions he expected. Insult, anger—and a staunch determination. "Shall we go?"

Awash in pride for her, Kane stepped forward to offer his arm. "I thought we'd take a drive across to the left bank today."

"Perfect." She bit off the word even while her nails dug into the sleeve of his superfine frock coat. She jabbed her parasol tip into the floor as they strode from the salon to the staircase. "I want to kiss you in broad daylight."

He said nothing. He wanted more than that, more than one kiss today. More than the threat of none ever after.

They had climbed into the landau, he facing her in the seat opposite.

He waited until the coachman directed the horses to walk on before he spoke. "Tonight we leave the city in the still of the night."

Her expression stark, still smarting from her confrontation with her aunt, she turned to face him. "I welcome it. For many reasons."

"I hope you will tell me what they are."

Tears pooled on her lashes. "I will confide in you."

"Thank you. Trust is necessary for what we do." He brushed the wool of his breeches, then told himself *the hell with it* and switched to sit beside her. He drew her to him, and she came, pliant in his embrace. His thigh along hers, she nestled into the crook of his neck. "My darling, we can talk and flirt, or we can be done with this charade and you can kiss me now."

She lifted her face and ran her gaze over him with a desire he only glimpsed. She cupped his jaw and lifted to take his lips. This time was different from those others. This kiss held charm and madness, fear, and a search for rapture.

He gave it. Gave her all he had. Kisses, countless and sweet, lingering and delicious. Her lips were what he had savored from the instant he first tasted her. What she gave him of herself these past few days were morsels of the banquet he wished to share with her. In fact, he would never have enough. But he had to let her reach that reality by herself. And so he let her go.

Dazed, she stared at him. A shadow of regret crossed her lovely face. "Now you don't have to pretend to want me anymore."

He brushed soft black curls from her cheeks and smiled with the same sorrow wrenching his guts. "Now you don't have to kiss me anymore."

He sat back, glancing out at the gawking passersby, then quickly back to her. "But from this moment on, let us be honest. My actions were no pretense. Neither were your kisses."

## Chapter Thirteen

DAWN HAD BROKEN into their carriage and the sun's rays on her face had awakened her. The past few hours in their coach had not been comfortable. She rubbed her eyes. Ashley's sleep was so deep, he snored.

She did not awaken him. He was quite beautiful, really. For a large man, he moved with grace. He also kissed like a satyr. Since yesterday in Paris when he called her bluff, she'd admitted to herself how she wanted more of him than kisses. He was her self-proclaimed protector and confidant, her fellow conspirator. Would not the ultimate expression of union be the mating of his body with hers?

She blinked at that astonishing desire, and writhed at the urgent heat in her body. For two years now she had avoided men. Ignored their advances. Discouraged any signs of sexual interest in her. The brutal Pascal Moreau had set her away from any man.

But this one was unique. Kane had not rushed her, or man-handled her. Had not sweet-talked her or promised erotic fantasies. On the contrary, he had accepted, even welcomed, her friendship—and accepted her own offer to help him.

Friendship in Paris of the French Consulate was a rare flower that grew only in secluded, well-tended soil. Their friendship had budded in need and blossomed in an attraction that held the enticement of more. And with him, she had to confess to herself, she wanted all there was to enjoy. Despite her past, despite her aunt's injunctions. She wanted this man and she would, if he agreed, have all of him. She knew how to avoid pregnancy. Knew how to brave Society's murmurs and ignore them. For once in her life, she would take what she wanted. Him, if he truly desired her. Him.

She grinned to herself and regarded him and his reptilian snores. She was pinned to him, molded to him, breast to belly to groin. She loved it all.

She chuckled and tried to move. But his arm was an iron pillar that pinned her to him. She gave herself over to finding some new position that did not require her to wake him. Beside her, he had reclined as best he could. The stack of pillows did nothing for his large frame—and beneath his embrace, she would not complain about the way he clamped her to him.

She snuffled, quelling her delight at the feel of his very healthy set of male *accoutrements*. Even unaroused, he was formidable—and his proportions conjured fantasies that made her drool.

She had to get away and fidgeted, but how could she move with him draped all over her?

"Stop that," he warned in a growl.

"I can't get comfortable."

"Neither can I. You're rubbing your nipples against my private parts." He rolled her away from him, pulling her back against him with her derriere tucked into his crotch. "Now go to sleep."

"I'm hungry," she whined like a pesky child.

"Later," he said as he dropped a heavy bicep over her and planted a sensuous kiss against her neck.

"And I have to wee." She bit her lips to keep from laughing.

He tightened his grip. But his thumb brushed the swell of her breast—and she wiggled in response. He clamped her close, his whole hand covering her breast. "Witch. One thing we don't have in this coach is a bourdalou."

"But Kane…" she pleaded.

"Weeeeell, hell." He sat up, ran a hand through his tousled hair, and banged on the roof. "The woods it is, my sweet."

"You'll come with me."

"To guard you, yes."

"But…" She winced. "I don't want bugs crawling up my legs."

He feigned horror. "You see me swatting them away, do you?"

She ground her teeth and banged on the roof herself. She had a sudden vision of his fingers sliding up her legs. The scintillating idea made her need to wee more urgent. "Bugs like me."

"I bet they do," he murmured. "Just hike up your skirts. Make it quick."

She cringed as the driver slowed and pulled to the side of the road. "Men!"

"Women," Kane moaned, and had a time of it getting comfortable.

"Something bothering you?" She bit her lip to suppress her chuckle as he arched his spine.

"With all your wiggling and giggling, I'm not in any condition to get out of this carriage."

She was proud of herself. There was *really large* evidence. It was the first time she had gotten him to admit she had any power over him.

"Stop preening," he groused.

But she burst into laughter. He had an erection that certainly made her proud.

The carriage rolled to a stop.

"Out," he barked at her, when he had alighted and offered his hand.

"Are you sure you don't have to relieve yourself?"

He narrowed his eyes at her. "Come." He led her to the edge of a copse of birches, where she waited, arms crossed, until the coachman and groom turned their backs and Kane did the same. Minutes later, all four of them happy, they were off again.

"How long do you think it will take us to get to our first inn?"

"A few hours." He flicked melting gray eyes at her and then at the basket beneath the opposite seat. "Dig us out the flask of water, baguette, and cheese."

THEIR ACCOMMODATIONS IN the inn that evening were much better than the cab of their coach. At least they had a bed. Tiny, it stood against the rough logs of their little room. They began the night in it together, but were apart within an hour. Ashley took to the floor with an eiderdown that left either his feet or his massive arms sticking out.

Whatever showed of him was just fine with Gus, but she would have preferred to have his warmth pervading hers. Practical, she gave in to the current conditions and sighed.

"At least the lamb stew we had for dinner was good," she said, standing over him.

In response, he threw a pillow at her and rolled away.

KANE'S HOPES FOR arriving at his lodge the next day were high. They'd better. The allure to keep Gus's supple body against his was becoming a devil's temptation.

The first morning, the *faubourgs* of Paris had given way to the gentle breezes of the north. The aromas of mustard plants, their bright yellow flowers blooming in the rolling waves across the hills, filled his mind with what he had to accomplish here.

The verdant forests of the countryside shaded their journey in the hot June. They had changed horses at the inn yesterday, midday. Gus and he and their two coachmen ate from the well-stocked wicker baskets. A mild cheese and good white wine, fresh boules of bread, and crocks of butter complemented the salty hunks of ham from the smokehouse.

"I need a nap!" Gus patted her tummy and climbed into the coach the second day. She slept for a few hours, once more cuddled against him amid blankets and squabs.

He gazed at her. Her hair in his fingers, her lithe body curled along his. She was a fiendish temptation, and he was conflicted as to what precisely he was to do with her. But he had told her to be honest. He must be with himself. He could no longer simply befriend her. He wished to stroke her and pet her. *Hell. We* wished to eat her like candy.

But no. He had to keep his hands and his cock to himself. As along as he did, they would be focused each on their pressing goals. *Curse it.*

So their journey of three days north went without incident. The carriage was comfortable, the journey full of their growing need to touch and stroke and kiss. But oh, their friendship was gone. In its place was this chafing arousal that rubbed raw his restraint with a knowledge that whispered, *She's yours to have.*

THE HUNTING LODGE he had retained was close on the road to Reims, owned by a very old friend of his who traveled often to Bruges and Ostend for his chocolate trade. The man was still alive, Kane was pleased to learn.

Henri Montand had been one of those on the list Scarlett had given Kane to investigate whether he still worked their network. Montand and Kane had sent coded messages to each other these past few weeks, and when Kane knew he would need a venue to investigate St. Antoine's whereabouts, he readily asked Henri for use of his lodge.

As their carriage passed a farrier's hut and a wine tavern, Gus perked up. "I know this part of town. You did not tell me we were to be so near the city."

"If we are to travel to St. Antoine vineyards, we must be fairly close."

"Why did you not tell me that?"

He met her gaze with frankness. "I did not tell you much in case you let slip where we headed."

"You did not trust me to be discreet." She did not sound insulted, only stated a fact.

"I had to learn how well I could trust you, Gus."

She squeezed his hand. "I understand. We are well invested in each other."

"We are." He traced the exquisite line of her cheek. "And you will tell me about your relationship with Amber St. Antoine. I need to know what we look for, when and how."

"You are right. Let's have a bath and dinner and then talk, shall we?"

THE THREE-STORY LODGE was a grand affair for a house that sat in a valley among the gentle hills of the Champagne region. On the edge of a thick copse, the small chateau looked like a perfect place for many to enjoy themselves as they went out each day to hunt for deer.

"But that is unusual these days," Kane told her as he poured from a crystal decanter a pretty, pale, buttery *vin blanc*. "Many have cleared the forest. There is so much land under cultivation."

"Mostly wine?" she asked him, so pleased to be sitting in a warm gathering room with a roaring fire, good wine, and excellent company. Her company. He, alone.

She took a sip and thrilled to the smooth flavor—and to the prospect that if she wanted the Earl of Ashley, she would allow herself the pleasure. But after her aunt's pointed warnings, Gus forced herself to focus on her task at hand.

"Some barley, wheat, but mostly wine, yes."

"And who have cooked dinner for us? The aromas are"—she inhaled and closed her eyes—"tempting."

"The gentleman who owns this lodge is on business in Bruges. He had a maid who lives in."

"Patrice. I met her upstairs. She helped me unpack. A very friendly lady."

"He also hires a cook to come in each day. There is a man of all trades who lives in the stables. Our coachmen stay with him in the lofts."

"I hope they are warm. Those men worked extremely hard these past few days to bring us here. I would have them well fed and comfortable."

"As would I," Kane told her with a smile. "It is good to reward those who help you."

"A tenet we all learned from the revolution, isn't it?"

"Indeed." He came to sit beside her on the settee before the fire.

"So am I to understand you know the owner of this chateau?"

"I asked a friend to find a house I might rent for a few days." He looked at the flames as they danced behind the grate. "This is close enough to Reims. I wanted us to be able to duck into town and leave easily."

Why did he not sound totally honest with her? But then, she had not told him all the reasons she sought Amber. "You have been to the St. Antoine vineyards, I imagine."

"I have."

That sounded like the truth, so Gus gave him more of her own. "I am so eager to go into town tomorrow and ask at the house for her. I want to put an end to this worry about Amber."

"I doubt it is wise to do that right away. Tomorrow I propose we go north past the St. Antoine vineyards to a small village I know."

"Why?" she said, with her chin up, disliking the delay.

"A diversion. Also to check that we are not followed." He sent her a compassionate smile. "If we see no one likes us a little too much, we'll go into Reims the next day."

She nodded, her face serene, her manner cool. "Logical."

He put out his hand. "Come. We will eat, and you will tell me about Amber and your friendship."

"There is not much to tell. My Aunt Cecily took her in the same way she did me. I was seven when Aunt Cecily brought her to Paris after Amber's parents died. Amber was nine. Amber's father, James Gaynor, was a minor knight, a former aide to the prince regent's younger brother, the Duke of Kent. Her mother had been a close childhood friend of Aunt Cecily."

"I have not heard of the Gaynors. It is an extraordinary act of generosity for your aunt to take in two young girls and treat them as her own."

"Exactly. She has been the best mother. Better than mine, certainly. I remember the woman only screaming at everyone."

"No way to live. I know. My parents married for money and position. It was the death of them both. No one should marry for that." He paused and looked her in the eye. "Did Amber care for her husband?"

"Very much. It was a love match. At first Amber denied it, but it was true. After his death, she grieved so long that it affected her health. Even her work and her attitude toward those whom she opposed. You liked Monsieur St. Antoine? You said you knew him."

"A fine gentleman, yes. I met him years ago through another friend of mine. A vintner from the Loire."

"Do you know many in the Loire?"

"My cousins, the Lamartines from Amboise. And the family Bechard, who also produce good grapes."

She dared not freeze.

Yet Kane looked at her oddly. "What? You know them?"

How much should she give away here? Her gaze locked on his. He saw the answer, and she could not deny the truth she now must reveal to him. "Monsieur Bechard, *oui*, I know him." She got up from the settee and walked toward the fire. "He has come to Paris to sell his wines. Aunt Cecily buys from him regularly. Barrels of his vintages."

"Gus?" he prompted when she did not turn.

"He does not like the new regime." She could venture that.

"No, he does not," Kane responded quickly. "Is there more I should know about your association with Luc?"

She set her teeth. He called Luc by his first name. Unable to hide all truth from Kane, she faced him with what she could tell— and what might put him off this line of questioning. "He has kissed me."

Jealousy flashed across Kane's strong features, to be replaced by a curiosity that was cautious. "Did you like his kisses?"

Hot tears welled, and she knew they came from tension and the fear of betraying Luc with lies. Oh, she was, at base, a very poor liar. Kane had gotten that right. Thank God she now spoke truth. "No. I have not liked any man's kisses. Only yours."

He raised his glass to her, drank, and sent her a ghost of a smile. "There is more there you do not tell me."

She sniffed back her telltale tears. Only her sorrowful eyes told him the truth.

But he rose, put down his glass, and strode to her.

She bit her lip as he took her own glass from her and wrapped her in his arms. She lifted her face to him, unable to speak lest she say something damaging to her cause.

He stroked the fullness of her lower lip with his thumb. "At the moment, my darling, I cannot care that you leave me in the dark about whatever else I should know about Luc Bechard. I hope that if or when I need to know, you will tell me. For now, I confess I am enthralled that my kisses bring you delight. They do me."

Ecstatic at her release from telling any lies, she flung her arms about him and lifted on her toes. "Oh, please. Kiss me lots."

He sank his fingertips into the cap of her curls. "I must not."

"Then allow me…" She slid her fingertips around the cords of her neck and brought his mouth to hers. She brushed her lips on his.

He groaned, his tongue invaded, and he explored all of her. She let him. Let him have her all. The taste of him, the power of him, the passion of him, was an elixir she'd never had with any man. It broke over her like a tide. She caught her breath, and her gaze sought the same passion in him. "I've never had a man protect me, want me, need me."

His fervent eyes drank her in. "I am thrilled to be all of that for you."

"What can I be for you?"

"Friend. Confidant." His mouth turned down.

Was he sad? How could he be? She wanted him. Did he not reciprocate? "Not lover?"

"That, we must stop to consider, my darling." He crushed her close, his hand against the back of her head, cradling her to him. "We must be mindful of your future."

She pushed him away. "You stop because of my aunt."

"No." He stood, his massive shoulders lax, his fists curling, defeated. "I stop because of you. I will not hurt you."

She gasped. Her heart hurt at his words. "Will you? Hurt me?"

He put up a hand, pointed a finger in the air, and dropped it. Defeated once more, he shook his head. "Never intentionally. Never by plan. But—"

Insult made her want to stomp away. Yell like a harpy. But she caught her tongue, held her wrath. "You have a sweetheart?"

"No."

"You have a wife?"

"No. No one."

"What, then?"

His nostrils flared. His eyes grew grim. "I have a mission. And you are not part of it. What we do here…" He gazed around as if he looked for phantoms. "What we do here is for you. What I

141

must do here is beyond that, and I doubt you would want to aid me."

She took a step forward, his words striking fear through her like a hot arrow. What did he do? More than buy goods, china, rugs, wine? "Why wouldn't I want to aid you?"

"You have a life here. Your aunt, whom you love. Your friends. Your Amber, whom you so desperately wish to find. When I am done here, I will return to England. That is not your home. You do not like it. You said so yourself."

He took a step backward, his hands out, palms up, warding her off. "If we go forward, you could become pregnant. Passion is not a subtle thing. One does not think. One only acts in the throes of all that wanting and—"

"And you do not want me." She was sick with longing. How foolish she must look to him.

He had her in his embrace again, and this time, his hand to her jaw, he kissed her like it was the only thing he wanted to do before he died. His lips were rough, raw with hunger and insistent with need, soft with rapture. "I want you. I do. Open your eyes. Look at me."

Hers were filled with tears.

"Oh, sweetheart. Don't cry. I never mean to make you cry." He thumbed her tears away. "I want you, Gus. Tonight, tomorrow, as many tomorrows as we can take. But if you think we will escape the results of all that wanting, all that caring, you are wrong. I would take care not to give you a child. But even at that, what we would share would tax us in our hearts. I would not have you hurt, darling. I would not have me, either."

"Well then!" She struggled to leave his arms.

"No!" He pulled her back. "Hear me. You must know that if I ever got you with child, I would want him or her as mine. *Mine*. And I would want you to become my wife to make that so. I will have no by-blows in the streets or in anyone else's house to take their name. I am more man than to allow a bastard to walk this earth without my name and claim. Think on that before you ask for my kisses. God knows, I will try to think on it before I am so tempted to taste you again."

He put her from him, a muscle in his jaw working. "Come now. Let's have our supper."

## Chapter Fourteen

$A$ ND WHAT A rotten meal it was, too.

Oh, the cuisine was superb. The company was silent. Angry.

The turmoil gave him indigestion. Plus he had a devil of a time getting to sleep.

He rose early, cursing his fate to find a woman who inspired him to consider marrying her, no less! He must be mad.

He fled to the kitchen, happy the maid had not come this morning to witness his poor attempts at the coffee. But with time, and a little jostling of the utensils and provisions, he had a brew. He'd downed two large cups of coffee so strong that his hair could walk down to the cathedral on its own, push aside the lawyers who had taken up residence a few years ago, and ask for penance. He was about to prepare another pot when he heard Gus pad down the main stairs.

She sailed into the tiny kitchen, humming her delight at the aromas of coffee and bread. If that was what it took to get her to be congenial with him after last night's debacle, he'd cook all day long. And so, without greeting, she came to peer over his arm at his preparations. The feline smile she conferred told him she was not only grateful for his efforts, but also pleased he was doing the work.

*So be it.* He'd play carefree, too. After cutting off chunks of yesterday's boule of bread, he placed them on long forks and stuck them in the fire. The roaring fire, by the way, that he had stoked tremendously high out of frustration at their argument, his lack of sleep—and his desire for her, so close in the next room.

This morning, she wore a heavy robe of forest-green wool, tied with a sash at the waist. Her black curls tousled, her dark eyes drowsy with sleep, she looked delicious. He refused to praise her. She might preen, and he might get caught ogling her. Not a way to continue their friendship.

Spinning away, he busied himself with the coffee. Sad to say, his cock did not get the message that this was only breakfast. He winced, grateful for the concealing folds of his own woolen banyan.

She huddled near the fireplace on a wooden chair, kicking her long, bare legs out to catch the fire's heat.

*Tease.*

Silent, he extracted one hunk of sizzling bread and offered it to her by the tip of the fork.

She grinned and tested the heat of the bread with her fingertips. But she shook her head and gave him a wrinkle of her nose.

*Too hot still?*

Hmmm. That was not the only thing that was. To his regret. And frustration.

No matter. He bent to the small table between them, pushed the crispy bread to a small plate, and slathered a pat of butter on top.

Grunting her approval, she pulled the plate toward her and bit into the toast, licking her lips and making little moans of delight as she crunched the thing. Flakes of the crust gathered on the rise of her plump lower lip, and she swept them off and into her mouth with her tongue.

He could not take his gaze away.

She ate slowly—ignoring him or flashing green eyes at him, the wench. Was she a practiced seductress?

He'd never thought so. But with him, she was flawless.

He shook his head—and poured himself more coffee.

She picked up the knife and slathered more butter on the bread. It melted and slid to the plate. She scooped it up with her forefinger and put it in her mouth. There, she sucked at it, as her gaze locked on his. He could have jumped the table and put her on it to have his way.

She was a temptress.

He was in agony.

He shot to his feet and went to the counter. He'd boiled water and set tea leaves to steep long minutes ago, not knowing if she'd prefer that. No matter. He needed something to do, so he poured tea into two different mugs.

With his cock blinding him, he slammed her cup to the wooden table.

She tsked at him. "You'll break the crockery."

"You break my patience."

"Well, at least it's just that," she said, and got up.

"Don't go." His words stopped her at the stairs. "I'll have our groom go into Reims and pay the local farrier for the use of two horses from his stables. The village we'll visit today is only four miles up the north road. We'll pretend we are out for a diversion. We'll take a towel in our saddlebag filled with bread and cheese and buy a flask-full of *vin blanc* from the local *caviste* for our luncheon."

"We pretend, do we, that we are a couple sharing a rendez-vous?" Her question was full of defiance and irony.

Kane hated what he had refused Gus last night. But he had refused himself, as well. What choice did he have?

She had left him last night, sullen, soon after they'd finished their meager dinner. The maid had made up two bedrooms, as he had requested through his go-between. He had retired to his own room, then tossed and turned in his bed. Yet he was here to do a job. So was she. They would pretend. They had to.

"That's the idea, yes." He dared to hope that, as they went

about their search these next few days, she might act like a woman in love—even if, at the moment, she hated him.

"Do you know anyone in this village we'll go to?" she asked.

"Not a soul."

She gave a nod. "I'll wear my breeches, then. Easier to ride in."

His mouth watered, his lashes fluttered, and he turned aside so she could not see the hunger that surged through him. He picked up their dishes and marched to the counter to wash up.

"Good idea," he bit off. "Do you have a coat to go with that?" How many men would love to see her bounteous breasts bouncing as she galloped? *He* would.

He blew out a breath and turned to face her.

The look on her face told him she understood his thoughts. She was a female who detected when a man savored the mere idea of her. "I do have a riding coat. More of a frock coat, thank you." Her black brows arched elegantly. Her gaze ran down his form to his bulging flies. "Do you?"

He was erect. So high and hard, he hurt. But he'd be drawn and quartered before he'd turn away. "I do."

She smiled, like a cat. "Marvelous." She would have headed for the hall and the stairs.

"One thing."

"Yes?" She was almost purring in delight.

"That first day, on the Malmaison road?"

"What of it?"

"You said you carry a knife."

Her laughing eyes went dead still. "I did."

"Do you still?"

"I can." Her gaze darted to the kitchen window. "Do you wish it today?"

"I recommend it."

"Because we have company?"

"No. Only as a precaution."

"How charming." She whirled away, her back rigid.

"Gus?"

She paused, her hand on the rail. "Yes?"

"Wear it from this day forward."

PUTTING A HORSE between her legs did wonders for her outlook on life. Sour as she was about Kane's refusal to have an affair without marriage, she was no shrew. She had been a royal tart at breakfast. She would not do it again. It did not make her proud of herself, and, heaven knew, she favored liking herself. She'd practiced the silly art of seduction on one man once too often, and he had acted on the invitation. Amber had saved her that night. Although not before Pascal Moreau had frightened her out of her mind, hurt her, made her bleed. His advances were because she had been foolish to flirt with him. That a deputy minister of justice, a friend of Vaillancourt's, had nearly taken her virginity was not a fact she was proud of. Afterward, she promised herself she would be more earnest—and never flirt again. So wanting to be kissed and caressed by the likes of the British Earl of Ashley was not in her favor. Not when she was so intent on finding Amber. And he was so intent on never taking her.

Besides, she told herself, she preferred riding horses to men. While that was true—or she insisted it was—she liked watching Kane Whittington ride a horse. He sat tall and commanding in the saddle, and Gus grew fascinated by the play of his massive thigh muscles. Did he look like so much man naked? Would he crush her? Would she care?

Aah! She gave her mount a command, and the mare trotted ahead.

"Don't rush. Stay with me," Kane told her when he had spurred his horse and caught up with her.

She was back to controlling her views of him as he took in the sun and trees and spring air like a man who lived for the freedom of the ride. But it was true, man and animal flowed as one. Amazing, since the beast, who went by the name of Charlemagne, was a brute.

Their groom had done the very best job of finding an animal capable of holding his master. The horse, a noble ebony Percheron with a long mane and neat, braided tail, had to stand fifteen hands high. More than that, he was an affectionate joker who nibbled the shoulder of Kane's coat when he stood talking overly long to the village *boulanger*. The animal wanted the big carrots Kane had bought from the greengrocer, and the horse did not fancy waiting.

Her own mount was an older, gentle mare by the name of Alyse who responded to Gus's commands with an ease that made Gus smile.

She had to confess that their day out along the country roads, amid the fresh air and bounteous late May sunshine, raised her spirits.

"I apologize for this morning," she told him as they walked their horses home along the road that afternoon. Whipping off her broad-brimmed chip hat, she threw back her head to enjoy the wind through her hair. "I wish to call a truce."

He pointed toward a public wine *vendeur* on the far corner. "I say we buy a good wine to celebrate that."

"Let's." The best wine, young or old, came from barrels closest to the vineyards. "You've come this way to enter town and stroll past St. Antoine's townhome, haven't you?"

He nodded. "I'm reviewing our security."

She discreetly eyed their surroundings. Everyone in the street appeared to be about their own business. "And what do you think of it?"

"Normal."

They turned at the corner house to walk toward the public stables and return their horses.

"Shall I challenge you to a game of chess?" he asked her as he opened the door to the wine shop.

>>>><<<<

THAT WAS THE beginning of an evening filled with a hearty dinner of roast lamb, creamed potatoes and fresh spring asparagus, fierce competition, and speaking of the little things that forged a finer understanding of each other. Through it all her desire to enjoy him burned through her, and she had no resolve to deny it.

Gus held out her wine glass so that Kane could refill it. "You think we are not followed, is that right? So we will go tomorrow to the St. Antoines house?"

"I think we are safe to do so, yes. Am I right that you are well acquainted with the St. Antoines' *majordom*?" he asked her.

"I am." They sat on the carpeted floor before the fire, warm and pleasantly sated. She was grateful the tension had lessened between them. "He is a lovely little man who adores Amber. And she him."

"I too know Monsieur Bonnet."

She liked Kane, his ease and poise to move in any situation among many different strata of people. He was not a prig or a poseur, but genuinely himself. Kind and considerate...even to horses. "I am not surprised. One day, I hope you will tell me why and how you conveniently know ever so many people in this country."

"One day soon, yes. Will you return the favor?"

"I will," she said at length. "But here you are the enemy."

"I am not yours," he declared with compassion in his eyes.

She met his frankness with her own. "No. I see that. Your proof, I mean. I am grateful."

They drank in silence.

She considered the popping flames of the fire. "Do you think Bonnet will be inclined to tell anyone who inquires that we have been here?"

He gazed at her with sorrow and resignation. "Do you?"

"No. But torture has a way of denying anyone of their ethics."

He winced and took a huge swallow of his wine.

She shivered. "Tomorrow, should we go to the front door?"

Kane shook his head. "We will alarm Bonnet if we do otherwise. He is possibly already bewildered by his mistress's disappearance or by Vaillancourt. I hope to God he and his men have not bothered Bonnet."

"Don't you think they have questioned him?" she asked.

"It is most likely."

She bit her lip. "But Bonnet is so sweet. I would hate to think he'll meet a bad end. Or that I brought it upon him."

Kane put his arm around her and kissed the top of her head. "We have to ask him."

She put her head to his shoulder. This affection filled her with awe...and need. She fought to put her mind to the subject at hand. "So we go knock on his door, even if we sign his death decree in doing so." She groaned. "I hate this."

He drew her closer.

She curled against him, taking his tenderness and salving her conscience with it. Wrong though it was.

He got to his feet. "I am not happy either. If he has no idea where she is, then you and I must come to terms with a dilemma."

Gus knew what that was. She stood and pressed her hands against his warm, massive chest. "No, Kane. We can't give up. We can't go back to Paris without her."

He set her away from him and gave her a consoling but sad smile. "I agree. Go to bed. We have much to do to find her."

## Chapter Fifteen

T HE FOLLOWING MORNING, as they made their way toward the center of town and the St. Antoines' manse, he and Gus were friends. Allies. They were avoiding the complications of an affair. While he could not be happy about that, he could be proud of them both. They had problems. She knew things *still* that she was not telling him. He had much he had not revealed to her— not even that occasionally he'd glimpsed one of his own men following them. Kane was simply pleased that he and Gus moved on, united.

Maurice St. Antoine had lived in the old manse in the capital of the canton of Reims since his birth. The house, a four-story-tall beauty with circular dormer windows and a high roofline, was of the French Renaissance. The manse had been in his family since Francis the First had been crowned across the *place* from the Reims Cathedral. The shadows of the twin spires fell over the tiny street as their carriage rolled up to the front door.

Kane climbed down and offered his hand to Gus. She gave it, but with silence and not a little trepidation.

Kane took in her appearance this morning. His beautiful Raven was her brave self this morning. During breakfast, she'd brooded, and he could not coax her from it. Finally, she had given in and shown him her courage with a shake of her head. She had affirmed that they would do what they must, accepting any outcome.

As for their growing ease together, their growing affection for each other, his mind could declare their relationship would be platonic. But his body yearned for her to come to his arms as naturally as she had last night. He enjoyed her company. He admired her courage. He desired her lush, firm body. And she, dear God, wanted him. But that was no reason to go against her own wishes to remain unmarried. Or his own to sire no bastards. Or, heaven forbid, to roil her aunt. Powerful as that woman was in Society, he needed her to accept him and praise his work.

Gus would not be his. He had known it from the start. From the Malmaison road. From the salon the first night he had met her. Gus was a creature of the court. A favorite along with her Aunt Cecily. He was here to pick her brain, to learn where Amber was. Not to seduce her.

How unfair that would be.

And how marvelous that would be. To have her, he increasingly knew, would be more than a thrill. He would want her a second time, a third...and more. He would want her as his own. The jealousy he'd felt when other men looked at her, or when she spoke about them, caused him a little madness. Thus, he suspected that the need to claim her as his own was more than manly pride. But he dare not name it. That fine affection he could not afford. Not here. Not in France.

Not now. Perhaps...not ever.

He assisted Gus up the steps and then rapped the knocker on the polished black door.

The little Frenchman who answered stared at him, then glared at her for a long moment, and finally broke into a smile that showed all his teeth. He welcomed them inside with a wealth of greetings. "Mademoiselle Bolton! Monsieur Whittington! *Bon jour. Bon jour. Merci, allez!* Please come in!"

They entered the small hall, the rays of sun shining golden rays on the golden oak walls and highlighting the red and blue

Turkish carpet that ran down the long hall, where a huge, circular stained-glass window poured all the colors of the rainbow upon them.

"*Bonjour*, Monsieur Bonnet," Gus greeted him with a tender clasp of his hands. "Forgive us our early morning call and without sending any notice." Kane smiled in remembrance of how well the *majordom* had taken care of him years ago when he was young and in such need for secrecy. "I come with my condolences for the passing of your master."

The thin little fellow clasped his hands before him. "*Merci beaucoup, monsieur.* He was a good man. I miss him. We all do. Will you both come into the salon, please?"

Kane followed Bonnet and Gus into the beauty of the three-hundred-year-old house, fragrant with roses and the hint of cinnamon. He took a huge chartreuse silk Louis Quatorze chair near the fireplace. Gus sat in a matching chair opposite him. Having no master or mistress at home, Bonnet had not lit a fire. The beautiful pink and lime room was cold and forbidding.

"Thank you, *monsieur*." Kane regarded Gus with a small smile. "Mademoiselle Bolton and I are here eager to talk with you."

Bonnet's pale visage darkened. "I welcome a talk, *oui*."

"Have you still the one maid?" Gus asked, and turned to Kane to explain. "Monsieur Bonnet retained one very fine young woman when I was here last."

Kane understood she wished to clarify who was in the house to overhear any of their discussion.

"Only Nancy, *oui*," Bonnet assured her. "Her hearing has turned for the worse, poor girl. Come, do not worry over her. You know, I gather, that Madame St. Antoine is not here?"

"We hoped she might be here, but doubted," Gus said.

"I am delighted to see you, but not without my madame." Bonnet looked gutted. "I have not seen her... Not for weeks."

"So she *was* here?" she said in triumph.

"She came at the end of April. She knocked at the door of the servants' entrance to the kitchen late at night. Our kitchen maid was up and let her in. She awakened me, and I went to tend to her."

Bonnet sniffed, distraught at his tale. "*Madame* apologized for disturbing the household and said she came for only a few minutes to leave me funds to continue to run the house. She went up to her rooms to change her clothes. She left instructions that I was to burn what she left. I did that the hour after she departed."

"And her plans? Did she say?" Gus asked.

"She said only she had left Paris for good reason and would not return. She was very nervous—agitated, I would say. I dared to ask if she would tell me where she planned to go, but she said it best if I did not know. Vaillancourt was after her. She would not allow him to have her. 'He hated that I loved and married Monsieur St. Antoine, and he seeks to take his revenge. I will not allow it, Bonnet,' she said.

"*Madame* is no fool, Monsieur Whittington. Did you meet her before she left Paris?"

"No," Kane said. "I had not yet arrived in the city."

"You do not know her, then. But she is smart. What's more, *monsieur*, she loved my master. He loved her. He was just not young enough or healthy enough to protect her from this Vaillancourt."

Kane was distressed by all the butler had revealed. "Thank you, Bonnet. That's helpful."

"Bonnet," Gus said, her tone anguished, "we need to find her. Did she give you any indication of where she would go after she left here?"

"No, *mademoiselle*."

Gus worried her lower lip. "When she left that night, how did she go?"

"On foot, *mademoiselle*."

"Astonishing," Kane murmured, and sat forward. "Where in the city would she find help or a friend or…?"

"Pere Josef," Gus said, her eyes alight. "A priest who'd been canon years ago at the cathedral," she explained. "If he is still in the city. Do you know if he is, Bonnet?"

"I have not seen him in many weeks, *mademoiselle*. When one disappears for a long while, you begin to feel they have gone forever."

Gus inhaled, frustrated.

Bonnet looked at Kane. "You know, *monsieur*, that the archbishop fled the city after the royal family were seized in Varennes and taken to the temple. The archbishop has not returned. The cathedral is closed for services, but a pack of lawyers have moved in. Only one priest, this Josef, lives here in the city with us. But he is not out and about with us. He is afraid to be taken. Still, he does say the mass for a few in private homes. We never know where or when. It is a surprise, and word comes by mouth only within hours of the little priest's mass. The government, you know, still does not approve of the church."

But Kane knew this priest as their best hope here in town. "How might one find where the mass is said?"

"It is difficult, *monsieur*." Bonnet shook his head. "I know not where to find him. We speculate he lives with different families who hide him in their cellars. One must wait to hear the word of a day and time."

Kane accepted they were at an end with the priest.

Gus glanced to the hall and the stairs. "May I go upstairs, Monsieur Bonnet? You know Amber and I always left little gifts for each other. I dare to hope she did not forget."

"Of course you do, *mademoiselle*. Please." He swept a hand toward the stairs. "Do go and search."

Kane waited as she hurried away.

"*Monsieur*." Bonnet indicated Kane should make himself comfortable. "I will have the kitchen maid make your favorite chocolate, *monsieur*? A few small tarts as well?"

"*Oui, merci*." Kane held the man's gaze, and when he heard the last of Gus's footsteps fade, he began. "I am here as *mademoi-*

*selle*'s friend to help her find Madame St. Antoine. I am eager to remove her fear for her friend."

"I understand, *monsieur*. You have my discretion."

During the Terror, Bonnet had arranged many details for private meetings between Maurice, Kane, and their friends. All of them had been in the cellars here in town and at the main vineyard. "Thank you. Tell me, did Madame St. Antoine have any close friends here in Reims?"

The skinny fellow drifted near to Kane. He cleared his throat and spoke low. "Two. Both went off to Paris. To *la Force*, *monsieur*. Neither returned."

"I see." Kane exhaled. "I am sorry to hear that. Who of those in the city did not favor *madame*?"

"The local magistrate was particularly irritating to her. He is still here. A nuisance not only to *madame*, but to many. He has asked where she is."

"Did you tell him she came here?"

"Never, *monsieur*. She came in the night; she left in the night. My maid and I would die before we breathed a word that our lady was here."

HER SKIRTS IN one hand, Gus took the stairs at a clip. The delight at returning to the house had fled as soon as Bonnet told them Amber left weeks ago.

At the top of the stairs on the second floor, she stood absorbing the sunlight through the dome above. She remained still and listened. She heard not the pace of Amber's favorite maid, Nancy. The girl had a club foot, and she dragged it as she stepped. Even on carpet, her gait identified her.

Nancy did not come. Wherever she was, she had not yet learned that Gus was here. Once she did, she'd rush to see her. Such was their affection that a bellpull was not required to hurry

Nancy to her arms.

Gus hastened down the hall to the right and the large suites of the master and mistress of the house.

At Amber's quarters, Gus swung open the sitting room double doors. Save for the cloths draped over the unused furniture, all was as it had been the last time Gus and Amber had been here together. Last February it was, after a hellish snowstorm.

"If it clears quickly," Amber had told her, "it will be good for the grapes. I'd like a good harvest for the *vendanges*. The court favors our white."

Gus had pinned her with a look. "You mean Bonaparte prefers it."

So did Vaillancourt.

Amber had rolled a shoulder. "Good for business. Would that I have more than grapes to save me from him."

"Give up the network, Amber. It becomes too perilous."

"I can't. You know it. The system will not permit it. One above, one below. No one who knows any others. Besides, would you give up? Desert me?"

Gus shook her head. "Never. I hate them as much as you. They killed two of my friends whom they sent to their deaths in Carmes."

"Exactly." Amber turned her face toward the window overlooking the cathedral. "Do you suppose any of those kings crowned there imagined that one day they and their family would be swept aside like so much dust?"

"Never. Royals believe in their own right to rule. To them, God would not be so cruel as to destroy the very system he has created." Amber had snorted. Placing her hands upon the window ledge, she leaned forward to view those below in the streets. "I don't want kings, and I don't want those who imitate them." She shook off her reverie and spun. She caught up her bright copper red hair in her hand. "I think of cutting this off like you have."

Gus now strode to her friend's dressing table and sat upon the bench. She flung off the clean white cloth draped over the items there. Before her were her friend's combs and bushes, her hand cream and face cream, and her perfumes, all five of them. The bottles and jars were *mostly* in their exact usual spots. The comb, sleek. The brushes, spotless, without one bright autumn strand of hair.

Amber had been here. If she had not, the hand cream would be in the right-hand drawer, the face cream in the one below.

Amber never wished anyone to think she needed such emollients. Not even her maid Nancy.

Tonight, Gus cared naught for those.

No. In the third drawer was the treasure she sought. She pulled it open and saw its usual contents: ribbons. A jumble of them. Yellows and golds, greens, jades, teals, purples, creams, and pale blush pinks. And beneath, when one pressed on the bottom at the right back, the thick wood popped and one could lift the bottom out.

And beneath, Amber would hide notes.

There on two other occasions when Amber could not deliver a proper message to her second-in-command—after her husband Maurice died and after she had suffered her miscarriage—she had given Gus directives on whom to meet, what to take, whom to trust.

Now Gus held the mass of colorful ribbons in her left hand, and in her right, she held the bottom of the drawer.

Lying there at the bottom, however, was nothing.

SHE RUSHED DOWN the stairs and found Kane enjoying a small repast.

Bonnet had retired.

"We must go," she told him.

He studied her face. "What did you find?"

She closed the door behind her. "Nothing. Nothing useful. Yes, Amber has been here, but she left me no message. I am...mystified."

He put down his cup and saucer and glanced to the opposite chair. "Come tell me."

She wrung her hands and paraded to the window. Outside the world passed by in its daily routine, and inside here, she had no clue how to move forward. "Amber was here. I saw the evidence in her room. To describe how I know is...complicated. Take my word, it is so. But usually if she came here and expected me sometime later, she would leave me a message in a secret place." She whirled to face him.

But he was right behind her, his arms reaching for her.

She went to him, realizing in her sorrow and frustration that she was shaking—and that he was once more her succor.

He caressed her, the warm cocoon of his embrace a stabilizing influence.

She hugged him nearer, wanting more to fight the storm within her.

He cradled her close and nestled his lips in her curls at her crown. "Tell me why she would leave a message for you if she wished you to follow."

She pulled back, her gaze locking on his. It was time to share a few useful facts. "I think you know."

His steady appraisal of her told the tale. "Say it anyway, my darling. Let it be one clear, true thing between us."

"I work for her."

He cupped her cheek and lifted her face a little more. His lips blessed hers, sweetly, briefly. "And?"

She swallowed, hard and loud. Tears stung her lids. "I am a carrier of information for her. For her system. I have done this for over a year. She and I have worked together. Since she has been gone, I have only knowledge of how to send information down one path, but not up through her."

She let her tears fall and fell against his broad chest.

He spoke, his voice gruff with anguish. "Come sit with me." He scooped her up in his arms, strode to the settee, and sat with her spread across his lap. He dug a handkerchief from his frock coat pocket and dabbed at her cheeks. But he let her sit without discussion so that her tension drained away. "I expect now to see your feisty self."

She barked with laughter.

"Now, listen to me," he said as he stroked her shoulder. "You will taste this fine patisserie, a few sandwiches, and tea. Then you and I will take our carriage to the north road, to the St. Antoine vineyards. There we will talk with those you know. Hopefully there will be a few men remaining from years ago whom I remember, and we will see what we can learn about Amber's travels."

"You've been to the vineyards?"

"Once. I was young. Twenty."

"Why?"

He inhaled. "As you have given me your truth, now I give you some of mine. I was in France helping a friend of mine escape the Committee of Safety. We came north to Reims."

She thought on that a moment. "A perilous time. So Monsieur St. Antoine helped you, didn't he? How?"

"He hid us in his cellars."

She nodded and focused above on the heavy delicately painted crossbeams of the ceiling. "That is the place I expect Amber to be."

"Many a soldier has found a hiding place in the wine cellars of Northern France."

"And now Amber."

He pushed hair from her temple. The feathery touch of his fingertips sent little fires to every bit of her. She sank in his arms and nestled beneath his strong jaw.

"Have you ever heard that she has friends elsewhere in France?"

She frowned. "Friends? No. I know everyone she does. Except

for a few of her husband's friends. Why would you ask that?"

"A rumor she might have gone to visit someone."

"Or to hide?" She frowned but sat taller. "But who would say that, put it out in Society? You mean this was a Paris rumor?"

"Yes."

She faced him, her green eyes wide with the light of instinct. "The former wine taster."

He gazed away. "I can't recall his name."

"He blended the grapes from different vineyards. After Monsieur Maurice died, he took his pension and retired to live with his daughter and her family."

"Where?"

"Varennes."

## Chapter Sixteen

I N THE NORTHERN vineyard, Gus had talked with the servants, and no one had seen Madame St. Antoine for more than a year. Nor had Gus found any notes or indication that Amber had recently been to the vineyard or taken secret refuge in the cellars.

After they slept in the small vineyard cottage, the next morning Gus and he returned south to their hunting lodge outside Reims and prepared to leave for Varennes.

The following morning, they set out in their carriage from their lodge and took the northern post road east to Varennes. This time their hours held a different quality. They were optimistic about this venture. They had examined all the possibilities. Kane, in an attempt to say he had covered the remotest detail, even asked discreetly about Reims for any word about the priest who said mass. No one offered any clues. Kane had not held great hopes, but he could say he tried.

In the bumpy carriage, he gave up trying to read. The coach was suffering the hardships of too many miles and country roads too ugly for beast or man. He put his book away and told himself he was not going to sit here and obsess about what lay beneath his traveling companion's lovely, thin yellow cotton gown. The fabric was delicate. So was her skin. The bodice gapped. Her breasts rounded nicely above the line. His cock appreciated it all.

Meanwhile, she clacked away on her knitting.

Gus had two means of dealing with the challenges of life. Sketching and knitting.

Kane had seen her sketches of him, drawn as they rode in the carriage or by firelight in the evening as they sat in communion, waiting for the dictums of the next day. Her sketches were superb. He'd told her so, often. In fact, he was complimented by her renderings. His hard features softened beneath the stroke of her pencils. As days went on, he thought he saw in her rendering of him her fondness and desire for him.

He also recognized her art, her inimitable style—and he realized that the portrait Scarlett Hawthorne had shown him in her offices the day she assigned him to Paris was one Gus had drawn of her beloved friend Amber St. Antoine. How the paper had gotten into Scarlett's possession, he had no idea. But he liked to think the sketch had been an omen of how well he and Gus now worked together. How well—he crossed one leg over the other and suppressed his groan—they might combine as lovers.

*Ahh.* He winced and prayed for deliverance. And cursed her fumbling with the damn knitting needles.

The pair were of polished wood and of large circumference. The weave they made was by its nature large and would have, if in the hands of one more coordinated, made a handsome, bold garment.

What his darling Gus created with the clacking of those two long pins was, by the best definition he could muster, a mistake. If the item hanging from the conjunction of the two needles could be of use or beauty, he had no idea who in this world might welcome it.

He settled back and considered how the rise of her lower lip would taste sweet beneath his tongue. For her benefit, he'd tease the upturned corners of her mouth with little nips and entice her to open her mouth and let him all the way inside. Here in this carriage, that would be a fabulous way to pass the endless hours.

"You've been working that yarn on two needles for many

days now," he said when he could not talk down his cock any longer.

She paused and cocked her head, her gaze on him, her mind not yet present.

"What, pray tell," he said, and pointed to her creation, "is that supposed to be?"

"A shawl," she announced, as if he should be smart enough to see it.

"For?"

"You!" she barked, and chuckled. "One gets cold when one sleeps alone."

He sent her a quelling look. "You could invite me to join you."

"Ba! You would never come."

He'd been mad with nearly *coming* every day, every hour, since they'd left Paris together. It had taken all his control not to finish himself off day by day, night by night. "I have."

She blinked. "Come?"

He laughed at her, at him, at their hellacious conflict of wanting and not having. That was his fault, her fault, her aunt's too! *For God's sake.* "I like you, Gus. Too much. You test my mettle by your very presence."

"Do I?" she asked, sounding honored. "Don't you defy your own rule not to have me by even telling me that?"

"I do. You cannot imagine how I almost destroy my resolve every minute of every hour."

Her expression of surprise melted to one of naked desire.

"Put that down," he told her, his words low and desperate, as was his need to at least hold her in his arms.

"No." She went back to clickety-clacking.

"Gus."

"I can't, Kane. If I come over there, I may never leave."

"What fun," he ground out.

She dropped the needles to her lap. "This journey is too long, the road is too rough, and my...my shawl..." She held the silly purple thing up to the light from the window. "My shawl will never be beautiful. Besides, if I come over there, we can't do anything. Not in this carriage. It's too...lumpy. Bumpy. I'd be on the floor, and you..."

"Gus."

"Yes."

"Shut up." He crooked his finger.

OH, SHE WAS tempted. She kept up the business with the knitting not because she was lost in anxiety about Amber. Not lately. Not as much as before. She just knew this trip to Varennes would yield her friend. But this constant presence of Kane... The need. The urge to crawl into his lap and have his lips and his hands on her. She envisioned herself yanking off her clothes. If a woman could ever do that. Ripping them was more the expedient measure, yes?

"Gus, you think too much."

"I do. I think of having you all the time. Day. Night. In between." *Oh, hell!* She blushed like a pomegranate and put a hand over her face.

"Well, that is something I am so happy to hear."

She could not go on denying all that he was to her. "When I woke up last night, you were all over me." Not quite. But the sensation was one she adored. She hadn't moved a muscle, either. To be handled by him as she had been in the lodge, and in St. Antoine's house as he consoled her, was becoming her newest need. She thought of ways to have him touch her, or she him. He called her his darling or his dear, and she sank into the cheery aura of his delight in her. If she did the same for him with looks or words or deeds, she was now not certain. She only knew she wanted to be near him, with him, beneath his hand and his fine, bold body.

"Put down those things," he said, his gray eyes stark with an intent that made her drool. "I don't want to be stabbed."

She chuckled and tossed her head. "If I do," she told him while her insides gushed with need, "I'll never finish."

"Augustine." He beckoned again with his fingers. "Never finish."

Her mouth dropped open.

He reached across the carriage and pulled her into his lap. As he cupped her cheek and nestled his very erect, very large cock to her derriere, he growled. "I have watched you attempt that purple bit for days. Give over, my sweet. You cannot knit."

She inhaled the fragrance of him. This morning, he'd ordered baths for both of them in the little carriage inn where they'd stopped for the night. He used his signature cologne, and she loved the gentleness of it and of him. "It could be a blanket."

"For an owl with one wing?" he asked in such a mellow bass that she was lured closer to his lips.

She chortled, but stopped abruptly. "I want you, despite what I said in Paris."

He picked her up and shifted so that he put her down to the squabs, flat on her back. "All my defenses about not becoming entangled are drowning."

She caught her breath. "How?"

"I need to have you near me."

"Oh, good."

He rolled his eyes. "Good?"

She nodded. "Yes."

"Is that all it is, 'good'?"

"Well, what would be better?"

"If you kiss me, Gus. Kiss me like you did in the carriage outside the Louvre. Kiss me without thought. Hell, just kiss me any way you like."

She rolled her lips in. "And if I do it more than once, you won't laugh?"

"No."

"Or walk away."

"God, no."

"I can kiss you all I like?"

"All you want."

"And you'll allow me...this?" She arched against him.

He sank his head into the hollow of her shoulder and laughed. "Yes."

"Raise your head, then."

And when he did, she did what she'd wanted to do since the Malmaison road, in her days since she'd seen him in the Tuileries, and in all her hours since they'd come together with one fine goal. She put her mouth to his and enjoyed the welcome. The firm response of his lips on hers, the dart of his tongue, the play of hers with his, how he took her up and made her gasp and want and thrill. No kisses of any man, all three whom she kissed before, equaled his ecstasy.

"Gus," he murmured, and nibbled at her lower lip. "Gus," he called to her, and his legs tangled in her skirts. "*Gus,*" he praised her, and his hands were beneath her head and he was kissing her cheeks, her eyes, her throat, and her skin above her bodice. And oh my, she wanted to be free of all her layers and lie with him naked for the splendor of it all.

And then the coach bounced.

The horse neighed.

The coachman yelled and the groom echoed his cry.

Suddenly, she and Kane were sliding down toward one side of the cab.

"What's wrong?" she asked, bewildered, catching at him and the handle of the door, not a little angry that their tryst was at once ended by this lopsided business.

Kane struggled up, looked out, and asked their groom the problem. The man answered in a few words that made no sense to Gus. "That does it. We broke a wheel."

"A wheel."

His eyes held mirth and not a small amount of pain. "We're

stuck here."

She managed to sit up. Then she threw up her hands. Frustrated, hungry for all the kisses they'd discussed, she could tell Kane was about to laugh at it all.

She glanced at her gown—crooked, her hem above her knees. Him, his waistcoat askew, his cravat unwound. She traced a finger in the air at his condition. "Hmmm. Shall we hop out and help them repair the wheel?"

"We could, but I must wait a minute."

"I see." She did. He was in no condition to hop anywhere. She chuckled, crossed her arms, and waited until his erection had receded and the liquid, rushing need in her body stopped singing to her. "So shall we get out and let them have at it?"

They did. They were no sooner out and sitting beneath a canopy of trees than a bloody wild wind and rainstorm came along and doused them all in the space of two minutes. Soaked, Kane traipsed to the cab and opened the hamper, then retrieved a flask of whisky for him and Gus and another for their coachman and groom.

Tipsy and wet, happy and stupid with their condition, they enjoyed the sun as it reappeared.

The town of Varennes, which they should have reached that afternoon, appeared in their carriage window after midnight.

AFTER MUCH POUNDING on doors of three different inns, their coachman found one with the only vacant room available. The two-story inn looked well appointed and respectable, across the street as it was from the famous church where the Bourbon royal family had been discovered by a local *gendarme* in '93.

Their groom let down the steps for Kane. "*Monsieur,* the *propriétaire* of the last *auberge de calèche* said this is the most expensive in town. I hope this is satisfactory."

"It is, Albert. We are grateful. Go find your rest above the stables. We will not venture out early. Sleep well."

"OF COURSE," GUS groused once inside their room, "the only accommodations they have are meant for one person in this closet!"

She stood in profile to Kane and sucked in her stomach. He had his challenges ridding her of her stays. His fingers fumbled from lack of practice. Kane could not improve in the art of lady's maid, at least in doing the usual tasks. Many a fantasy Gus entertained, that Kane might abandon all thought of the stays and devote himself to touching her skin. Alas, he must be a Puritan, for his fingers did only their job. His diligence irritated her, and tonight, after so many like this one, she was testy.

She pointed to the bed that would hold only one. "It would be better if I were invisible. And that looks like even a five-year-old would cry over it."

Kane winced. "The linens look clean and the mattress firm. I'll sleep on the floor."

"On what? We have no quilts, no coverlets."

"We'll use my frock coat and your pelisse."

It sounded sensible, but less than an hour later, he was beside her. "Move this way." He put her to her side, moving her as easily as if she were a twig. Her derrière tucked against his hips. As usual.

She silently smiled into the black night. "This is no way to rest."

"What else would you like to do, hmmm?"

*So many things I have no experience to imagine!* But she elbowed him. "Close your eyes."

He nuzzled her nape and kissed her there. His lips were sweet and soft. "Mine *are* closed."

*And mine stay open to the possibility of what I miss here in this bed.*

But she could not ask. Would not lead him there. That way lay too much trouble. Regret. An end to their camaraderie. Awkwardness.

SUNLIGHT SEEPED INTO the only window in the room, and Kane gave up the quest for sleep with harsh blue invectives for the bed.

Gun ran her fingers through her wild hair and appreciated the sight of naked, masculine flesh before her. Oh, he had worn breeches to bed, and nothing else. But her breath hitched at the breadth of his bare shoulders and the lean agility of his hips in snug breeches. She tipped her head, licking her lips at the sight of him without layers and layers of clothes. She longed to draw her finger up the indentation of his bicep and trace the vein that curved from his elbow to his armpit. How was a man made so well that his torso rippled like the wind as he moved? And his melting gaze caught her admiring him.

She smacked her lips. "The innkeeper better have coffee and eggs."

"Bacon."

"And a hammer."

He stilled. "Why?"

"Unless they give us a larger room and bed tonight, I'm going to take that bed apart splinter by splinter."

He watched her get out of bed and pick up her robe to press to her chest, covered only by very thin muslin. "Hopefully our grooms had a better night in the stable loft."

She disappeared behind the paneled screen to find more clothes and ignore his interest in her night rail. "We should have gone with them!"

A YOUNG, LONG-LEGGED boy of fourteen named Olivier brought out their fried eggs, ham, a large boule of bread, and a crock of butter. The proprietor had disappeared after pouring their mugs of coffee.

"Do you know where the Verne family lives?" Kane asked, because Gus was not certain of the route. On previous visits, Amber's groom had driven the coach and Gus had paid no attention.

The youth thought a moment. "The road to Verdun. A brown cottage with a rusty plow in the yard."

Instead of disturbing their grooms and having them hitch up the carriage, Kane asked for two horses to be saddled. Gus donned her breeches for the ride. Once more Kane had the tormenting challenge of watching her round hips and long legs make the most of her sinuous garb.

He secured a strap to his horse. "I'm going to ask you to wear those breeches every day of your life."

She paused, at once serious. "Will you see me every day?"

He would be bold and honest. "I long to ask it of you."

"Would you not grow bored?"

*A challenge? A tease?* He snorted. "With you in those? Never!"

But she did not pursue the subject, and he pondered what his life would be if she were his each day. Each night. In Paris, he speculated there was much he did not know about her life that would unsettle his existence. Most of it would be his worry about what she did. And there was much yet he did not know...and much she knew not of him.

"Let's hurry." She worked at the reins. "I'm tired of this search. And if..." She rested her forehead to the neck of her mount. "Oh, Kane. What if Amber is not here? What will we do?"

He went to her and turned her to him. "We will not fret."

She scoffed. "How can we not?"

"Let us go, and quickly. Make no conjectures until we know what we face."

## Chapter Seventeen

T HEY ARRIVED WITHIN minutes at the small thatched-roof cottage with the old plow in the long grasses out front.

Gus quickly reestablished Madame Verne's memory of her years ago. The lady and she hugged and shed happy tears. "I hoped you would remember me!"

"I would, of course. You are so lovely, *mademoiselle*, and you have brought your beau to us? How kind of you!"

Gus had introduced Kane as her fiancé. To travel with a man of lesser relationship would raise numerous questions in the eyes of the lady who ran a simple country farm. To be in confined company with a man whom one would soon wed provided some rationale for the failure of propriety. Gus took a breath and asked if they had seen Amber.

The lady grew pensive. "No, Madame St. Antoine is not here. We enjoyed her whenever she came years ago with *monsieur*, her husband. To have her is so rare these days. She is too busy in Paris. And you, too, are gone to Society. Even when she came, she left so soon afterward."

"Madame Verne, did Madame St. Antoine come here recently for a visit?"

"She came in May. *Oui*, and she stayed with us briefly. She said she wanted to see the vines. But it was early spring and we had little. I wondered at her coming then and saying such. She knows too much about how vines grow to want to monitor their growth at that time of year."

"*Madame* stayed with you?"

"At first, *oui*, in the hayloft in our stables. She insisted on it. But that was only for a few days. Later, she took a room in a nearby auberge. Then she left and promised to return."

"Did she return?"

"One day, *oui*. With a man who had asked for her earlier."

"A man." Gus sent a glance toward Kane. He kept his tongue, but she could see he was eager to ask Madame Verne questions himself. "Did she introduce him?"

"No. He stayed down the lane, watching her. She said he was her friend and not to worry about him. She came to me to ask if anyone had recently asked after her." The woman wiped her hands on her apron. Her face drained of color. "Why do you ask me all this? Is *madame* hurt? Or…in trouble?"

"No. But my friend and I do not know where she is or where she went. We must find her. It is urgent."

→》》《《←

KANE STEPPED FORWARD. "Did anyone come and ask for her?"

"*Oui, monsieur,*" said Madame Verne. "Two men. The one who was with her when she came last to see me. The other, different, came yesterday."

"What did they look like?"

The lady got a look of distaste upon her pretty features. "The one yesterday was short and fat, with a long, sharp nose. He was a pockmarked, ugly man."

"He looks like a carrot," the little girl sitting upon the chair in the corner of her kitchen piped up. She was ten or eleven, old enough for Kane to credit her memory.

"Ho-ho!" Gus said to the child, lured by her funny remark.

She had greeted her when they arrived with a hug. "Why is he a carrot, Solange?"

"His nose, *mademoiselle*. It is a long carrot." Solange giggled.

Gus froze.

"Is his hair orange, too?" Kane noticed Gus's distress, but had to encourage the girl to give him more, give him anything.

"No. Like straw. Dirty, too. Mama would not allow that for anyone in the house. Bugs in the hair, you know."

"I do," Gus agreed. "Your mama is very wise."

"And the man who asked for Madame St. Antoine weeks ago?" Kane asked the girl and her mother. "Do you recall his looks?"

The lady smiled at Kane. "Oh, *oui*. Handsome. Hair like yours, *monsieur*, but with fire in it. Tall and fine. A gentleman."

*Ramsey. Let it be Ramsey!*

"Do you know what happened to that man?" Kane smiled at the lady, thrilled his friend might have found Amber.

Gus absorbed his smile with a question in her eyes.

Madame Verne shook her head. "He stayed at the *Petite Auberge* at the crossroads. He was particular about his bedding. Liked it very clean. The *propriétaire* told me days later that Madame St. Antoine was with him."

Triumph fired Kane's blood. He grinned at Gus in reassurance. Ramsey insisted on cleanliness, especially bedding. So he had been here—and Amber had been with him!

The girl said, "Madame St. Antoine went away with him."

"Solange!" her mother said. "How do you know?"

"I saw them together, Mama. And Olivier, who works at the *Petite Auberge*, told me they slept together in the same room and left together one morning before dawn!" The girl had a glint in her eye that told them all she had an inkling that when a man and woman slept together, more went on than resting. "Olivier says they laughed together. A lot." She raised her brows, happy with telling them her secret.

Madame Verne knitted her brows, confused at this news.

"We know the gentleman," Kane told her. "He was happy to have found her, I am certain. He would not hurt her."

Gus regarded Kane with hope in her eyes.

The woman and her daughter nodded, accepting his explanation.

Kane hastened to depart and took Gus's hand to lead her to the door.

With much affection and brief goodbyes, Kane and Gus bade the lady and her daughter *adieu*. Kane helped Gus mount, then climbed into his own saddle.

"Kane!" Gus held up a hand to stop him when they were out of sight of the cottage. "Who do *we* know who is *happy* to have found Amber?"

He could not help smiling, but under the circumstances had a feeling Gus was about to tear into him. "I'm certain you remember an English gentleman who arrived about the time I did in Paris? My friend Lord Ramsey."

"Ramsey, Ramsey." She mulled the name. "I see. And just *why* is Ramsey happy to have found her?"

"It is a longer story than can be told on the road, my dear."

"Do not give me 'my dear,'" she blurted, then shut her eyes and put up a hand. "Tell me, Kane. Why and how this Ramsey?"

He sidled his horse close to hers. "He is here in France to assist me."

She smothered a laugh. "He negotiates to buy products to send to Britain, does he?"

"No."

"Hmmm. I did not think so. He instead tracks ladies who are missing from court?"

"He does. He heard a rumor that Amber had come here to Varennes. I sent him onward to learn what he could. Clearly he found her and they got on well together. I am very pleased. You should be too. They were in company together, and he persuaded her to allow him to guard her, even at night. She is safe with Ram. And Ram will protect her with his life. And now, my darling, we will go back to our tiny accommodations, where I do hope the innkeeper has given us the larger room he promised, and—"

"And you will tell me why Ramsey reports to you."

"I head a group of British who are here to assist in projects for the Crown."

She gave him a sarcastic look. "But you are in charge of commercial purchases."

"I am."

"Along with other responsibilities." She did not ask. She stated.

"Yes."

"I see. And they include finding Amber?"

"They do." He did not wish to admit the next, but she was canny and would go on.

She frowned. "Was I your target?"

"You were. To lead me to her or for me to help you find her."

Her expression grew soft and sad. "Am I a fool here to think that—"

"I care for you, Augustine. I care very much about you. I said weeks ago what I showed you of my regard was no pretense. I meant it then. I mean it even more so now."

"I've not met any man I could trust." Her admission was sharp as a serrated knife to his heart. It tore him to shreds.

"But I am not any of them. I am who I say I am. What I say I am."

She stared at him, examining every feature of his face. "And you will tell me how this came about. All of it."

He wanted to reach out, take her in his embrace, and have this conversation all over again. But then it occurred to him that, separate as they were atop their horses, this was the best way to put it all before her. "I will. I promise."

"Then I will rage at you that you did not tell me before this that she might be here in Varennes. That, my dear, is a failure."

"An omission at the time. But yes, you deserve to learn everything."

She scoffed. "After *everything*, I will kiss you and then punch you in the jaw!" She wheeled her horse about, regal and very pissed, then trotted the mare down the country road.

He swallowed his grin and, quite pained, shook his head, then tried to catch up to her.

THEY WERE ALONG the road to town only a few minutes more when Kane examined a figure tracking parallel with their pace in the shadows of the forest. This figure was short. His own man who tracked them was tall and thin, and agile too. So this fellow was not Kane's—and he wondered who this was and where his own man was.

Gus followed his line of sight. "We have company."

"Let's make town quickly. I want you safe."

They entered town without incident. In the cover of the trees, their stalker kept stride with them.

Gus walked her horse close bedside Kane's. "If this is Carrot Nose...then I know him."

"I wondered at your reaction to Solange's description." He spied the squat, fat figure of so-called Carrot Nose and buried his good intentions in favor of the more immediate problem of ridding them of this nemesis.

He set his jaw. He did not see his own man about. So he had a diversion to effect.

The street narrowed, houses on either side, street *vendeurs* filling the cobbles with animals and wares for sale.

"I see him at the street over, toward the rear of the church." The Varennes church was the one in which the royal family had taken refuge in '93. A small stone building with one spire, it had gained notoriety as the place where the Bourbons had been discovered by a local *gendarme*, captured, then escorted back to

Paris—and prison.

Gus and he returned their horses to the stables and strode down the thoroughfare toward the inn. On the other side of the *vendeurs'* stalls, they saw the fleeting evidence of a fellow keeping pace with them.

"What a fool," she scoffed. "If he's trying to hide, he's a failure at it. He is one of Vaillancourt's men."

This vermin was sent by Vaillancourt! That filled Kane with a mindless rage. Vaillancourt had killed his friend Brussard, but, by God, he would not touch a hair on the head of this woman.

"How do you know he's the deputy's man?" Kane picked up his stride, and she did, too. He kept watch of their shadow.

"He tracked me on my errands to receive information."

Kane silently cursed. He'd suspected this and wished it were not so.

She gulped. "I saw him. He saw me. Take what you will of it. We saw each other on my recent visit to a bathhouse in St. Denis. I belong to a network of agents who send information to and from London."

Joy and horror raced through his bloodstream. There was nothing now he would not tell her. Who he was. What he was. What he did. He and she were a team, meant to work together. By all that was rational and all that was real and useful in life, they were meant to be together. He more than wanted her as his friend and his partner in work—he wanted her in his arms as his beloved.

He would have her, too. He'd end this madness that robbed him of sleep at night, robbed him of joy when awake. He would tell her all, his love and his hope and need. He'd ask her to be his own. And all of that, of course, had to come after he revealed all and she took him to task like a fishwife.

"My darling." He was beside himself, but he dared not stop walking. They had to reach the safety of the inn. He wove them in and out of passersby. "How long have you done this?"

"Years," she whispered, her fingers clutching the fabric of his frock coat. They walked quickly, and her riding outfit helped her keep pace with him. Many noticed, parted, and let them through. "I have never been followed. Never. But weeks ago, I cannot recall... I saw him with another man of Vaillancourt's, and soon after I came to you to ask you to help me find Amber."

He halted and gazed down at her. Awe and shock ran through him in poisonous alarm. This was the proof of all he had suspected. Now Gus would be his in the sight of man, and soon in sight of Bonaparte's court and God. For her protection first, yes. But also to salve his fear that Vaillancourt, others, would take her away from him.

He would begin now to make known to her who he was, what he did. They would have a union of like minds as well as purposes. That required honesty. He would state now the fact he had known and could not have declared to Gus before now. "Amber is involved in this network of agents too, then."

"She is my lead."

He wanted to rejoice. He wished to weep. He knew this of Amber. Now he must go on with all truth revealed between Gus and him. "Hurry. Let's cross the street. Avoid the church. He's gone, it seems." *But where?*

They ran forward, headed for the green of the church. At the side, Kane turned them for the clearing in back. If they reached it, they would make the front of the *auberge* in a few quick steps.

They rounded the corner of the church and came face to face with Carrot Nose. He had an evil smile, full of stained, broken teeth. He also had a pistol in his hands. "*Bonjour, madame et monsieur.* Or should I say Mademoiselle Bolton and *Monsieur le Comte?*"

Kane stepped in front of Gus, his palm up. "No need for that."

"I say there is. I think *mademoiselle* comes with me."

Kane sniffed. "You are so wrong."

"She's looking for that other *putain.*"

Kane took another step forward. "Go home, *monsieur.* Your mother wants to wash out your mouth."

"I'm after St. Antoine, and this bitch knows where she is. She'll come with me."

Kane barked with laughter. "Go away, *monsieur*..." He looked over the man's shoulder.

The fellow retreated a step, glanced over his shoulder, and...

Kane lunged forward.

But the pistol cracked.

A blast of fire burst through his upper arm. For a moment, he halted. His next step felt as if it were in midair, then he staggered.

Gus wailed like a banshee and ran around him.

Kane reached out...but she slipped through is fingers.

"Bastard!" she yelled at Carrot Nose in a French accent that could call the dead. Her arm up, she went for the fiend.

And he had her. Christ, he had her!

Kane's head whirled.

Around the waist, Carrot Nose pulled Gus to him.

But she fought.

Kane's knees buckled, but, mouth open, he watched her fight like Medusa. With fists and feet, she kept the poor sod busy.

Carrot Nose bellowed and cursed her.

But she broke free, faced Kane, her green eyes eerie with hate.

The bastard caught her back against him.

Kane blinked, his vision clear. He reached a hand to her...

Gus grinned at Kane in a triumphant, ugly sneer. Her left arm came up...and whipped down.

Carrot Nose howled like a wounded beast.

Gus walked from Carrot's sagging arms, free.

Kane gaped.

She came for him, smiling, all crisp matron. "Come now." With an arm under Kane's good one, she buttressed him and said, "He's down. The *auberge* for us, my love."

"But he...?" Kane found crumpled Carrot Nose on the ground, groaning, clutching his groin—from which a thin silver knife protruded and his blood ran dark and thick into the fertile earth of France.

# Chapter Eighteen

" A FLESH WOUND. Drink more whisky. You will live." Gus finished her ministrations of pouring half the damn bottle of spirits over his wound and winding clean cotton she had ripped from her chemise around his upper arm.

He could feel the floating effects of the whisky more than the sting of Carrot Nose's pistol. "You are very good with that knife." His words came out garbled from the whisky.

She grinned, pleased with herself. "I am."

"How did you learn that?"

"Aunt Cecily employed a master gardener at her home in Compiègne who had a talent with knives. He taught Amber and me how to use them."

"And where."

She looked into his eyes with only a small bit of remorse. "And when best to fell a man."

"He may die."

She busied herself with capping the bottle of whisky and rolling up the remains of her strip of chemise. "He will bleed to death, unless, of course, he can crawl to someone in the town who knows how to stanch a slice to an artery."

"You knew how to get him to hold you so that you could aim precisely," Kane said with not a little awe.

"Yes, he made the mistake of being too agreeable." She gave a smile that was more grimace.

"Your gardener taught you that?"

"He did."

"Your Aunt Cecily employs intriguing servants."

"She does." She came back to sit opposite him and take his hands. "I will go down and return with bread and whatever the fare is for supper." She rose.

But, catching her fingers, he coaxed her back to the bed beside him. "I can wait for that."

"I wish you wouldn't. You need food and rest. You have lost two thimblefuls of blood, but being shot is a shock, and I want you to live, Kane."

"Back there..." He cupped her cheek. "You called me your love."

"See? Not so wounded after all."

"Gus, sweetheart," he beseeched her. "Please, I will eat and sleep after you tell me what I need to know about your activities. I promise."

She placed her gaze on his. "I am a person who conveys information about arms, troops, rifles, other agents, anything at all—and sometimes silly bits that never amount to anything. I know the person beneath me whom I meet in the street of St. Denis near a bathhouse. I report to the person above me, who sends it on to her superior or sends important information down. That person above me is Amber."

He waited for the next revelation.

She gazed at the ceiling, then writhed a bit. Tormented, she clutched his hand and peered at him. "Listen to me. You need not know who that person below me is. Frankly, the less you know, the better for you. For me. For us all."

"And those who are 'all'?"

She set her teeth. "I do not know them. But they are diligent, efficient." Her mellow green gaze fell over him, and all at once, tears sprang to her eyes. "You need not know them. And you could have died today."

He pulled her close beside him on the bed. "So could you, my darling." He kissed her cheeks, her eyes, her nose, and fell back to the bed, taking her with him and blessing her lips with all the tenderness in his heart. "I died myself watching him catch you. I wanted to do more and yet stood there with my knees locked. You did him in, Augushtine Bolton."

She giggled.

"I shaid your name wrong, didn't I?"

"Augushtine is my name, and I rather like it from your lipsh."

He went to hug her but used the wrong damn arm. "Shiiit. Come here, Gush."

She kissed him then, and cupped his jaw. "I adore you, Kane. You are big and bold and such a brute. With you, I am..." She squinted at the walls around them. "I am safe. Protected. I knew somehow I had the power to hurt that man today. I knew it because you were there. Oh, yes, you had a wound to your shoulder, but I didn't know how bad it was. I panicked. I had to save you because, despite the fact that you had not told me about Ramsey—nor have you told me all yet about what you do here— I trust you. You have been a rock. My rock." Tears dribbled down her cheeks.

He brushed them away.

"And now, sir, before I become a gushing Augushtine, I am going downstairs, and you are going to sleep."

He kept her hand. "When you return, we will talk. I will tell you all."

As SHE SAT in the wing chair before the fire, she watched Kane sleep. She had donned her ripped chemise and her robe. She sipped a glass of whisky. She did not draw. She did not knit. She was at peace.

Curious, that. She'd not felt in control of her life for many months. Or perhaps, if she were honest, for many years. Not since she'd begun her work to filter news out of France to those who opposed the country's chaotic intrusion into other lands. Only working with Kane, living with him, laughing and striving, meant better days. That brought a smile to her lips.

She nodded. For, whatever the source of her tranquility, the logic made great sense to her. Kane performed a service for his country. She performed the same service. Perhaps she performed it for many other countries whose existence was now threatened by the first consul and his less-than-illustrious friends. Kane's work was for those same beneficiaries. He had as one of his duties finding Amber. She had searched for her dear friend not because Amber was her superior, but because she had been her dearest soul, save for Aunt Cecily, most of her life.

Now that Amber was at the moment found and in the company of Kane's friend, she was safe. Until and unless Kane had reason to find Amber himself—or Ramsey failed—he and she were without cause.

She stirred in her chair. Was Kane's and her work at an end?

She flinched. It hit her like a slice of her own knife. She put a hand to her temple and pressed the pain. If her purpose was gone, so was her need to be with Kane.

She shot from her chair and sought a strong portion of the remaining whisky in the bottle. If they were done, what was she to do with all her admiration for him? All her delight in his company? All her desire.

She refilled her glass...but stared down at it.

She sank to her chair.

She had never made a habit of brooding. But now the nothingness of what lay before her shocked her. Like the room that surrounded her, her days loomed in shades of gray and ashes of regret. The fire in the grate lured her. There was heat and substance, the reds of roses and cherries, wine...and love. One could live in black turmoil or find the passion of living.

Suddenly, to her surprise, she was sobbing into the torn hem of her chemise.

She gasped, covering her mouth and moving as far away from the bed as she could get to keep from waking him.

Kane stirred in his sleep, and she grew alarmed. Hurrying to him, she bent and put a hand to his forehead. He was cool. She ran her fingers through his hair, his thick black curls that always needed a good combing. She stroked his cheeks that always needed the perfection of his hand at his razor. His jaw that never needed more strength than it exhibited. His lips. His firm lips that she had only sampled. Never truly tasted. Never would again, if he and she were to part.

She held back a huge sob and shut her eyes to turn away.

But he seized her wrist. "My darling," he called to her, and pulled her down. "What's wrong?"

"I worry about you."

He slid his head to one side upon the pillow. In his long-lashed eyes stood a question.

*Perceptive devil.*

"Am I near death?"

She laughed through a fresh wealth of tears.

"Oh, sweetheart. You sob. Come here." He tugged her.

She relented and plunked down beside him.

"No missish stuff. Do lie down with me, Gus."

She could not help her smile. "You say my name correctly— and you must rest."

Both his long, dark brows rose in humorous delight. "Did you think we wouldn't?"

*I hoped!* She tugged to be free.

"Give over and come let me hold you. No tears tonight now, please."

She relented, because to deprive herself of his sweet company when she needn't seemed like a death knell. Curling close, she nestled into all the hollows and curves of his marvelous frame. She tangled her legs with his. Just to be entwined like errant vines was heaven. He was here and for now, hers. She would savor what she could.

He stroked her back and kissed her forehead. "This is better now. We are both warmer. Happier, too."

She burrowed into his shoulder. He wore a soft old shirt that she'd made him don when she got him to their room. He had on an old pair of breeches that he slept in always. But he was minus his boots and socks. The idea of his big body in little but his skin had her nigh unto swooning with want. Their bigger room, and their wider bed, was a godsend, not only to tend his wound but to lie here with him, spread out in comfort.

"Have you been awake while I slept?"

"I have."

He lifted her face to him, licked her lower lip, and tsked. "Drinking, too. Not like you. Tell me why."

She nuzzled her nose into his throat. Out of his sight, she swept her tongue along her lower lip and clutched at the grip of her desire to have him taste her, all of her. She fought for a reasonable response to him. "I celebrate that Amber is in good hands. And that you are not badly injured."

He continued to stroke her back. "Anything else?"

"No."

He cupped her cheek and stared down at her, then brushed tears from her cheeks. "Then what do you mourn?"

The sob that broke from her was not what she wanted, not what she needed if she was to part from him soon and never know him again. "You."

"I am not dead."

"To me, you will be soon." She rolled above him, a waterfall of tears destroying all her serenity. She was soon to lose him and never have him back. "I cannot see a future where you are not there."

He gripped her hair, his nails at her scalp, his eyes molten with urgency. "Then don't leave me."

That ripped her heart in two. "I don't want to, and yet...yet we are done."

He brought her lips to his. His whisper was a plea. "That is not certain. I trust Ramsey, but I do not trust Fouché or Vaillancourt. We should continue until we know all the details."

"I should not stay with you."

He combed her hair from her cheeks. "Why not?"

She dropped her forehead to his chest and cried bitterly. "I am ashamed."

He flinched—and she felt it reverberate through him. "Of me?"

"No. Never." Could she reveal how embarrassed she was to want him so dearly?

"But why?" He cradled her close, his lips to her ear. "Tell me."

"I told myself I was a thing unto myself. Alone. I did not want a lover," she blurted, letting slip in one raw word where her mind wandered. She lifted her face to tell him the awful truth. "I told myself that men were expendable. Changeable. Untrustworthy to boot."

His features melted to a yearning she had never before glimpsed. "Awful creatures."

She frowned down at him. "Don't laugh."

"I'm not. I want to make you laugh."

She let out her worst revelation. "I did not laugh when one man caught me by the skirts and forced me up against a wall and tried to ruin me."

He sucked in air between his teeth. "Who would dare?" he seethed.

"A deputy minister of justice, a friend of Vaillancourt's. Amber came upon him and beat him around the head. He fled, but, you see, I had lured him on, flirted with him. Innocent and stupid of me. But he took advantage, laughed at me, and spread rumors that I was his, until Amber had Aunt Cecily ask Josephine for his transfer to the south."

Kane kissed her cheeks and her lips. "When I meet Amber, I

will thank her for that service to you."

At his sentiment, she hugged him closer. She wanted more of his gentleness.

He swept a hand along her torso from rib to thigh. "Affection between a man and woman is not harsh or mean."

She blinked. He understood what she wanted from him.

"My darling, listen to me. What a man and woman enjoy is soft and sweet, wild and rapturous, but never cruel." He slid his hand to her mound and, through her thin chemise, pressed his fingertips between her folds. She heard the sound of her wet desire for him, and she startled. But he smiled and sank his fingers further between her lips. "I want to show you."

She caught handfuls of his shirt. "I want to have you!"

His face broke into the greatest joy. "This will be good. Just what you want and what I have wanted… Oh, God." He dropped his head against her chest. "What I have wanted of you from the first day on the Malmaison road." He caught her chin. "I will show you that you need me. And after this, you will tell me we are not finished, you and I." He rolled her to her back. "Tell me you will not leave me."

She arched up against him. "I cannot bear the thought!" She took his lips in a claim she had not dared to display. Full against him, she opened her thighs and let him sink between. This was what she'd yearned for, the heavy claim of him, as she'd had all too briefly back in Reims. The pleasure of his rippling muscles against her thighs and ribs and arms and the rapture of his kiss on her lips.

He urged her to one side. "You'll have to help me. Drop your robe. Take off your shift and help me remove my breeches and shirt."

She rolled away and stood to shrug and let the robe fall.

# Chapter Nineteen

H E GROANED, HIS eyes filled with the supple beauty of her curves. She was alabaster perfection. A throat, slender and sweet. Breasts, firm, sweet handfuls. Her nipples, pink chiffon, large and growing pointed as he watched.

That she had wanted him and he had not known honored him, but had him doubting how drastically he had controlled his desire for her that she would question herself. He had played disinterest too well. He now had largesse to show her otherwise—and he would not fail.

He pushed up in the bed and, feet to the floor, tested his ability to rise. His head did not swim, so he had the means to love her well. Tonight, he would also keep his brains and love her so well that she would forget the one man who had hurt her. And maybe, if he were truly admirable here, he would love her so well she would wish never to leave him.

She was suddenly shy. Her arms flew over her lovely breasts, then she tried in vain to cover the dark curls over the juncture of her trim thighs.

"Don't do that," he said, his gaze riveted to hers. Then he stood and stripped his shirt and unbuttoned the flies of his breeches.

"Oh!" She gazed upon his penis, her eyes wide and appreciative. "You are quite…"

He didn't have to look down to know he was hard as stone. "I am."

"Is that…" She twirled a finger at him. "Normal?"

"My reaction to you?"

She swallowed. "It gets bigger for different ladies?"

He snickered, hands on his hips. "I never measured."

"And…um…it seems to…" Her eyes widened with each word. "Grow."

"Indeed it does."

"So how does it…" She looked spellbound, as if making a scientific study. "Fit?"

"There are ways to ensure it does."

"Like what?"

He'd never seen her eyes so round, so with a grin, he stepped near and took her hands in his. "I'm going to show you."

"How it will fit?"

"All but that."

"Why?" She appeared to be a girl of fourteen, naïve and eager for instruction.

"Well, for one thing," he said as he put his hands beneath those lovely, warm breasts and stood against her luscious hips and long legs, "we want pleasure. All the pleasure we deserve for waiting so long to enjoy each other."

Her green eyes glowed with bright desire. "You've waited for this?"

"Every minute," he said as he stroked the lush gossamer of her nipples and she shivered. "Each one we've been together. I have wanted you next to me, hot and sweet."

"I've wanted you," she breathed against his lips, her hands to his back, his waist, and his buttocks. "You are so exquisite."

"That is a word for you."

"Use what you like. You are"—she tested the swell of his hip—"quite firm."

He gave a chuckle and stroked both his hands down to her

derriere. "As are you."

Her head fell back, her eyes closed. "I like your hands on me."

"And my lips?" he breathed as he let his mouth begin a tour of the cords of her slender throat.

"Yes, please."

"So do I." He licked the deep hollow between her breasts. Lifted them and sucked one nipple and then another into his mouth, letting each go with a pop.

At each loss, she made little sounds in the back of her throat that urged him onward.

"I like your navel," he told her, sinking to his knees. Nipping at her flesh around her belly button, he dipped his tongue inside and rejoiced as she squirmed. "I will lick your folds, too," he said, fingering the moist insides of her thighs.

She was humming.

He was swimming in madness to eat her up. He sent his careful fingers up the front of her thighs and, with his splayed fingers, urged her pussy open. The musky fragrance of her desire for him had him reeling. With his thumbs he parted two heavy folds and sent his tongue inside to sample her. She was swollen and succulent, his darling, his everything.

Her nails dug into his shoulders. "Again," she urged him.

"Then open," he commanded, "wider."

And she parted.

Then he had her. Licking and laving all she presented to him, he was gone, mindless in his need to take from her everything she offered. She tasted of rapture and offered utter surrender. He had to lick each delight from her to satisfy the hungry brute who wished to never let her go. Her lips were coated in her need of him. He moved his tongue over her plump flesh, frantic to make her his, only his.

She groaned. Then her knees gave way.

He rose like a shot to catch her. "Come to bed, sweetheart. We'll have all of each other."

She broke away and scrambled to the sheets. Naked, she lay

on her back, her eyes luminous with urgency, her arms out to him, her fingers beckoning.

He crawled above her, hovering, admiring, craving, stunned that he was so totally in love.

**❯❯❯❮❮❮**

HIS TOUCH WAS fire, his tongue the astonishing part of his lovemaking that thrilled her to her curling toes.

He paused above her, lost in some thought she could not fathom.

"Come," she urged him with hope and beseeching hands. When he just stared at her, she arched and rubbed her aching nipples against his chest. "Don't stop. I need you."

He put his palms to her inner thighs and spread her wide. "You are beautiful, pink, and wet."

She groaned.

He sank to her and put the tip of his tongue to a tiny part of her that sent her spinning in a whirlwind of want. Each lick was heaven, torture, a pulse of sparkling bliss. She throbbed, his touch so tender, too hard to bear, too soft to refuse. She moaned, deep in her throat. This ecstasy was nothing she thought possible.

"Kane," she cried, and he gave her even more. She thrashed upon the pillows, her legs pinned, not daring move lest he stop and leave her wanton and alone. But he rose over her, covering her body with his heavy one.

"Now," he growled, and she felt the tip of his cock at her entrance.

"Yes!" she urged him, coming up and off the bed in demand.

No sooner had she pleaded, he complied and drove slowly inside her. She moaned at his welcome invasion, his filling girth, and her mindless need for all of him. All of him. All of him.

And when he was seated and pulled her thighs wider, she opened her eyes to stare at him in surprise and abject want. And then…he was gone.

Gone!

She whipped the sheets. Lost.

But he was back, over her, his fingers stroking her, invading her, poor substitutes for the wonders he had given her with his full body and his hard cock.

"I'm here," he whispered, his fingers finding that same violently tender spot amid her folds. And there, he stroked and petted, patted and fondled. "Come for me," he crooned. "Come now and enjoy it."

In a few flicks, he had her climbing to that nirvana she'd briefly glimpsed. And in a moment, two, ten, she reached a stunning height where she shattered into a thousand brilliant stars. Then he left her to move to her side, and, face down, he moaned into the sheets.

It was glorious. It was unique.

It was done.

He wrapped her close into his embrace, molded her exhausted body to his hard, tender one, and told her how marvelous she was, how sweet and unforgettable.

GUS STIRRED, AWAKENING to the sound of rain pinging on the roof and in the trees outside their window.

She'd slept better than she had in many nights. Marking the languid rhythm of her breaths, she opened her eyes to the pale light of dawn shimmering through the leaves of the trees—and the sight of Kane. He watched her, propped up on one elbow. Smiling like a saint, he was. But, of course, what they had done last night was not the work of saints. They had even done it twice!

Memories of last night flooded her in waves of pleasure. At once, she was wide awake, blinking, feeling every caress of his hand, of his lips.

"Good morning," he offered, his hand up, a finger reaching to touch her nose.

She dashed it away. "Stop."

"Gus—"

She tugged the sheets up to her chin.

"Don't—"

"No. Don't touch me." She put a hand to her forehead. "I must think."

Sighing, he lay down. "Gus, what happened was—"

"What we'll forget."

"We won't."

"I will." She felt under the covers. She was naked. Had been all night. Had they made love more than once? Or was it all just one long, glorious episode of that shimmering tingling? No! She scrambled, clutching at the sheets. Where were her clothes? Had she no clothes? She pushed up on both elbows to examine the bed, the chair, the floor. *Ah.* The floor.

"Gus, listen to me."

She shook her head.

He had her cheek in his hand, turning her face toward him. "Please look at me."

She seared him with her despair and her anger at herself.

"All right. I won't touch you." He backed off. "We must talk."

"We've said enough."

"Evidently, we have said nothing."

There was no recourse. She'd have to arise from this bed naked to retrieve her shift.

"Gus!" He caught her arm just as she would have stood, but he pulled her back to him and cuddled her against him. One leg over her hip, he held her to him.

She shut her eyes. She could not block him out. The sinuous power of him was as erotic to her as his kisses to her ear and her shoulder. "Please don't do that."

"Listen to me. What happened last night was inevitable. All our days and nights together brought us here."

*Foolish to believe it so.* "I did not care for you on the road to Malmaison."

"No. But in Paris, from the start. You knew who I was then. What I was about."

"Not all, I'm afraid. You did not tell me you were here to find Amber."

"How could I? I hoped you would confide in me about anything you knew of her whereabouts. But I could not reveal all I wanted and chance what your contacts were. I had to learn who you were, truly. Just as you had to learn who I am. Trust began the journey. Friendship brought us together. Desire sealed the pact."

She could not argue with that.

"Yesterday, you even forgave me my omissions." He pressed his lips to her nape.

She shivered. "I still have to punch you in the nose."

He snorted. "You do."

"But now we return to Paris. And this," she said, and curled her shoulders, "this is done."

"I don't want it done."

She shook her head.

He cupped her shoulder and rolled her to her back. "You were right last night when you said Amber is safe with Ramsey for now. But we know not what they plan to do."

"She will not abandon her role." *It is too dear to her.*

"We don't know. But whatever she does, she does it with the full knowledge of Ramsey. And one thing I do know is that my friend will not let her from his sight until he believes she is safe from Vaillancourt and anyone else who might wish her ill."

Gus could trust in that, but then Kane might question her decision about her future. "I will not abandon my role either, Kane."

"I would never ask it of you. But realize: you have been followed from St. Denis to Montmartre, discovered in Varennes, and attacked one of Vaillancourt's men."

"I killed him, let us not forget." How she hated to admit that.

"Perhaps. We do not yet know if he lives. One fact is certain: if the man does not report for duty, Vaillancourt will seek the reason. We don't know if anyone witnessed that scene yesterday. Plus, if he *is* dead, there is a body to be identified and buried. If and when Vaillancourt comes for you, I will not let him hurt you." Kane sighed. "And he will come. You know it as well as I."

She looked away.

"Gus, you and I have much to do. We must return to Paris. I know not where to find Ramsey, so he will look for me at home. I must return. You will come with me because, first of all, you go nowhere without me, and secondly, we are having an affair."

"It is over."

His brows knitted. Thunder rolled, and she thought it intriguing that even the weather conspired with him in his anger. "We are just beginning."

"No. I want no more to do with you."

"You do, my darling. And God knows, I am willing to give more."

She made to leave.

But he pulled her back and rolled over her. His weight was a blessing and a curse. "We return to Paris. And the day after we arrive, you and I will marry."

"I'm marrying no one." *Caring for no one.*

"I have a house, four men who guard it, countless others who are my guards and agents. All will die to protect me and mine. You will be mine legally and in sight of God. Then Vaillancourt cannot touch you. You and I will marry four days hence. Do not argue. You are mine." He kissed her quickly and with determination. "And I am yours."

"Whether I want you or not."

"You want me." He smiled and cocked an assured brow. "I vow to make you want me more."

"It's dangerous to delude yourself."

"It's more dangerous to ignore the truth."

## Chapter Twenty

IN THE PUBLIC room of the *auberge*, Gus ordered a tray of bread and eggs from Olivier the waiter to take to Kane. It was early, and many villagers came in for a coffee. They huddled together, drinking and giving Gus the evil eye.

Olivier brought her a steaming mug of coffee as she sat on a stool at the bar. She inquired what the others discussed.

"A man was knifed behind the church yesterday."

"That's terrible." Her pulse jumped. But she had to commiserate, didn't she? "How did it happen?"

"No one knows." The boy shrugged, unconcerned.

"Do they know who did it?"

"No."

"Is he alive? This man?"

"Died this morning, so says the *boulanger*, Monsieur Carville."

"A pity," she offered as Olivier returned to his work, unconcerned with a mysterious death in his midst.

SHE HURRIED UPSTAIRS with her tray and coffees. Laying out their breakfast, she tried to ignore Kane's state of undress. A maid had arrived earlier, bringing fresh water to wash with, and Gus had quickly availed herself of the pleasures before she went down-stairs.

"Smells wonderful," he said as he closed the door behind her, then toweled off the excess soap from his jaw. Shaven and bright-eyed, he looked recovered from his ordeal. But he was also naked to the waist, and the sight of his rippling good health was what Gus wished to keep out of her sight. That was exceedingly difficult. The room may have been the largest in the *auberge*, but it was still too small to keep such a secret.

She looked away. "Our man with the long nose died this morning."

Kane hung the wet towel over the linen rack and sighed. "So we have some time. A week or ten days at least before anyone from Vaillancourt's staff can come to investigate, then return to Paris with news."

She'd be in the Loire by then. A friend of hers and Amber's lived in Blois along the river. She was married to a gentleman who had been a close friend of Amber's husband, Maurice St. Antoine. Giselle would happily have her for a few weeks. Gus would create some story to cover her need to stay out of Paris.

Kane sipped his coffee from a chair by the fire. "You are quiet. No need to be concerned. By the time we are back in Paris and married, no one will be able to touch you."

Anger and a tinge of fear for their future had her whirling on him. She had more reasons to point out. "You do not listen. You need not marry me."

"Need? Yes, I do need you. But I want you more as my wife and my lover, Gus."

"No, no. Kane, please. Be reasonable. Last night, you did not give your seed." She blushed to say it.

He locked his gaze on hers. "That which I did was no guaran-tee you are not with child. And I will have no bastards."

"There is no point of honor you must perform here, Kane. You did not deflower me."

He rose to his feet, a nerve in his jaw jumping as he strode over to their bed and threw back the quilts. He pointed to the spot of red on the sheets. "On the contrary, Gus, there was blood. That deputy minister of justice did less than you imagined."

That had her flexing her fingers. "No marriage can be legal. We are not in England. We have no vicar to do the service or bless the marriage. No church register to record the union."

"I will see that it is legal. We'll have the temporary man, Minister Anthony Merry, do the ceremony. Later, I'll find a vicar or a man of some cloth to do the service."

She shook her head, weary of this argument. "Why marry me, Kane? I do not want a husband."

"I did not want a wife, either. Then I found you." He strolled back to his chair and their breakfast. "Come eat. I'll go talk to our coachman and groom."

"Yes. Get them to hurry." She did not want to sit with him in a confined carriage again for three or more days. The lure of his person, the mellifluous sound of his voice, the way his fabulous lips formed words, the power of his hands that she wanted on her again as they had been last night—all too much to contemplate. Alone and ever so near, he was her tormenting temptation. "As soon as they're ready, let's leave for Paris."

KANE STEPPED OUT of their carriage at the broad steps of Countess Nugent's mansion on Île Saint-Louis. Dusk shaded the grand ivory stone mansions of the Paris island in shades of blues. Offering up his hand to Gus, he wondered if she'd take it.

"I'll call tomorrow at four o'clock to confirm the time for the ceremony. We arrive so late this evening, I will not be able to call upon Merry until tomorrow." The British envoy would be the one to marry them.

Gathering up her skirts, she lifted her chin in defiance. "Send a note to me."

The two of them had already fought over the issue of Kane going to her aunt to divulge their plans. That Gus had decided that she would marry him after all was the bigger victory. Kane was not about to question that or belabor the point he'd already won.

She climbed the steps to the front door, and the countess's *majordom* was at the ready, standing aside the open portal for Gus to enter.

Kane knew there was many a slip that could occur before he had Gus before Merry. She could leave Paris, escape to anywhere, and he would not be able to find her easily or quickly. But at least for now, she seemed to have concluded that marrying him was the best choice she had. Going into the world alone was the other, and that did not appeal.

He left her at the door. "Tomorrow, then. A note."

He was down the steps, telling himself he trusted Gus to keep to her promise to marry him. They had progressed far in two weeks. From sparring partners, to friends, to lovers.

GUS RACED UP the stairs with a word to the *majordom* that she would see her aunt at once if she was free. She'd lose not a minute in informing Aunt Cecily about Kane's and her trip north. The lady would want immediate news, despite Gus's need for a bath and clean clothes after so many days in a carriage.

Her aunt sat in her library writing her social correspondence. At the sight of Gus, she rose and strode to her, arms out in greeting. "Tell me the news quickly before I faint from lack, *ma cherie.*"

"I will wed Ashley day after tomorrow in front of Anthony Merry." The more she'd thought of the prospect, the more she coveted him as hers. Hers alone. She'd never wanted another man. This one was too unique to let go. She would have him—

and she would still be herself, unchanged, belonging to herself as she had always been. "We ask you to attend as our witness."

"You will not be sorry. Perhaps even very happy with such a virile husband in your bed." Her aunt cocked her head. "I do not fully approve, and you know it. But I will not argue. Tell me your other news."

Summarizing Amber's association with Lord Ramsey and a description of Kane's and her travels, Gus watched her aunt imbibe it all with composure.

Gus stared at her aunt's stoic expression. As often before when her aunt had lost a friend to illness or death, the lady showed no public display of grief or despair. Once more, Gus marveled at her dispassion. For decades in the midst of chaos, her aunt had endured so much. The loss of her first lover, the Prince of Wales, to convention. The loss of her second lover, the Duc d'Orleans, to the guillotine. The near loss of her own life, imprisonment during the Terror. Now this loss of one of her two "beloved girls"—and the continuing lack of Amber's return to normal existence.

"But you know not precisely where they are?" her aunt asked, hands clasped before her as she faced the fireplace unmoving.

"No, ma'am."

"Ashley does not worry about this lack?" she bit off.

"No. He trusts his friend."

Her aunt sniffed. "Vaillancourt has not been a happy man since you disappeared."

"How so?" Gus asked, but marveled that her own fear of the man was not what it had been. Was that because Kane's continued presence in her life—and now his proposal of mar-riage—offered her safety?

Her aunt turned around. "Word is Vaillancourt sent out men to find you both."

Gus did not tell her aunt about the appearance or fate of Carrot Nose. Kane and she had discussed the matter on their way home and had decided, for Gus's sake, that neither would tell anyone about the man's sojourn in Varennes. "Clearly, they failed."

"Vaillancourt will be angry about that too. But once he hears you are to wed Ashley, he will announce his displeasure for all to mourn with him. It will not be pretty."

Gus arched a brow. "Such a pity for him."

Her green eyes pinned Gus in place. "Tomorrow night Madame Lery gives a ball and dinner. We will announce your wedding there. The ceremony must not occur in secret. That would make many matters worse."

"Announce it yourself, Aunt. Let the court buzz about it. I care not. I doubt Kane would crave an announcement."

"If your marriage is made public, Vaillancourt will not seek to trouble you more. He is so angry that Amber disappeared, but he has always thought he could threaten you to bring her forth."

"Now he has failed." Gus credited Kane with the foresight of that.

Not for desire alone had Kane offered to marry her. Not for lust alone did she want him as her husband.

Gus left with haste. She was done discussing Vaillancourt and his ambitions.

In her bath, she focused her mind on more seductive thoughts. A tub. Hot water. Bubbles. Soap. Shampoo and Kane. She sank to the warm water and submerged herself entirely, hair, face, nose. But he filled her thoughts.

For three days in that blasted carriage, she had tried to avoid conversation with Kane by knitting.

He had mentioned her poor skills again.

"Have you ever tried to knit?" She'd flung her ugly, misshapen project to the squabs.

"Perhaps you could teach me."

She closed one eye to threaten him with extinction.

"Or I could tell you tales of my childhood?"

"Do," she urged. "Why will you have no bastards? Men do. You are an earl. Is it not a mark of pride to sprinkle yourself everywhere?"

"I do not sprinkle. Well you know it."

She'd blushed with a violent heat as he told her his aversion to having illegitimate children was due to his father's penchant for not caring where he spread his personal benefits. His older brother had sired two illegitimate children whom Kane now supported from estate income.

Again he affirmed his dedication to legitimacy. "I will support children who have my name."

"And no mistresses?"

"None." His gaze had absorbed her like sunshine after rain. "Ever."

She had picked up her poor knitting, satisfied in one regard. She did not need any further clarifications of his reasons for failure to finish during intercourse.

More was the pity for her continuing appraisal of his marvelous person. That she could not stop. That he often caught her at, too. Damn her delight in his masculine appeal.

The woman who rose from the water of her bath minutes later admitted two truths. She felt better physically, clean and alert after far too many days bumping along frightful roads in a conveyance.

Secondly, she felt the lack of her traveling companion, soon to be her lover and husband. She was at odds and ends without Kane. None of his smiles. Or jibes. No demands. No scintillating gazes from those gray eyes that melted her bones and stirred her insides to raw appetites.

Her future would be filled with no need to fend off his kisses and caresses. Within hours, she could freely embrace all her hot, wet yearning to have them. All he had to give.

## Chapter Twenty-One

K ANE STOOD BACK from his floor-length mirror and lifted his chin as his valet tied his cravat. "Make it simple, Clement."

"But, *monsieur*, to be wed requires a dashing appearance.

Kane was already dashing to his bride. Wasn't he? "Only my fiancée's aunt will attend, Clement." That was the best part—and the worst of this morning.

Yesterday afternoon, Countess Nugent had sent him a note filled with her displeasure at his impending marriage to Gus. She declared she would go as witness to their union, but for appearances only. He perceived in her reluctance a disapproval he wished did not exist. However, he would not address it. If he attempted, the lady could argue with him. He would not have it.

He would have Gus to wife. Her aunt and British marriage laws aside, Gus had agreed, and if that was to taste bliss with him again or if it was to secure his protection from those in power, Kane cared not. He wanted her in all the ways he could have her.

Even though he witnessed hesitancy from his bride, he vowed he would wipe it away with kindness and sex. Even love, if he could show it to her before he dared express it in words.

"Finish this, Clement. I will not be late."

Anthony Merry, the British envoy, had a few foibles. One was that he was always punctual. It helped compensate for the fact that he had never learned the art of diplomacy.

"Ass," Kane muttered, and his young valet paused.

"*Monsieur le Comte?*" His servant's hands fell to his side, Kane's cravat in his hands.

"Not you, Clement. I wonder at the finesse of a member of our delegation." Kane had heard that Bonaparte sarcastically called Merry "*Toujours mai.*"

Kane snorted. "Ever Happy," *my foot*. The man had received Kane weeks ago as if Kane were his puppet. Keeping him waiting for two hours yesterday, Merry had relented and agreed, after much ado, to eleven o'clock this morning for the wedding.

Kane would have had it at eight. But Merry was not congenial until after eleven. Or so the man said with frustration at Kane's insistence.

*All I want is this marriage done, legally.*

Kane had certainly had enough of waiting for his right to have Gus. Sitting in a carriage, biding his time, especially the last three days on their way back to Paris from Varennes, had been a trial. He'd been hard every day, every hour, for more than two weeks in Gus's presence. The temptation to kiss her senseless and seduce her had been grueling.

He shifted his stance now as Clement reached for his frock coat. The mere thought of Gus as his own in only an hour had him hard as the floorboards beneath his feet.

"Remember what I said about after the ceremony, Clement?"

"*Oui, monsieur.*" The young man bit his lower lip, attempting to hide his grin.

Kane reached out and ruffled his hair. "I suppose it is no secret?"

"No, *monsieur*. the whole house knows. Else how—"

"Exactly."

"YOU MARRY IN fashionable June," Aunt Cecily said with a

satisfaction Gus had not seen since her return and engagement announcement. The lady fidgeted, her hands restless, unusual for one so tranquil. Gus had no time or presence of mind to ask why that was.

Their carriage neared Anthony Merry's rented house, and Gus's excitement sent thrills through her blood. She told herself to ignore her aunt's behavior. Instead, she examined those in the streets on their way to the shops along the Champs-Élysées. "To whom does it matter?"

"Those in London. It's the season for weddings there."

"I care not." In her haze of desire for him, she had put aside temporarily her need to complete her work for Amber and whatever part her network remained in operation. She was not proud of that, but she itched to have this man. Have his hands on her and his body inside her. The only thing of importance to her this morning was that she would be with Kane within minutes. *And forevermore.*

Or at least as long as she appealed to him physically.

She recoiled at that nagging possibility. It had picked at her all through the night. Each time she awakened, the possibility loomed like a ghoul. The only fact that had lulled her back to sleep was his statement that he would not take mistresses. And if Gus were his only source of pleasure, then he'd come to her. *Will he? Always?* Her pride would die a thousand deaths if he shamed her thus.

She had no way to know. But she could do things to ensure he always came to her, couldn't she?

And so she had committed to that this morning when she left her bed at dawn. Even her resolution to welcome all his advances and make many of her own had not improved her looks. One glance in their mirror gave raw evidence that her nightlong questions had certainly made her look like hell. Warm compresses to her cheeks and cool to her eyes had improved her appearance. At least partially.

Her aunt stirred in the carriage. She even smiled. "It is a good marriage, Augustine. I have been less than agreeable about this. But it has merits. Ashley is an earl. Though he may not come from a family that comports itself with credit, Society cares not, if the man has land and prestige. I understand he has little money, however. Your forty thousand is in British banks in London. Use it as you will to make yourself happy. If that means using it on him and your children, then so be it. But it will be imperative that you—"

"Aunt? Please. No more." Gus could not look at the lady. She would see how Gus wanted him. At the moment, Gus could not hide it. Nor did she wish to.

*All I want is to be done with this ceremony and away from Paris again. With Kane. And in his arms in a comfortable bed where I might lose myself in nothing and no one but him.*

THE CEREMONY WAS quick. Merry, not merry. Cecily, wary. Kane, his eyes dancing, irresistible in morning attire of gray satin waistcoat and cerulean-blue frock coat, breeches that fit his thighs like his skin, and a regard of Gus that set her heart aflutter.

One day long ago before Amber wed Maurice St. Antoine, Gus had marveled at her friend's giddy anticipation of her wedding. Amber, never one to gush over any man's lashes or jaw, had remarked that the only thing she wanted to do at that moment was press her lips to Maurice's belly button.

Gus had chuckled. Amber had loved the man with a passion almost at first sight, never thinking twice he was thirty years her senior. She loved him for himself. "You have seen his belly already and like it, do you?" Gus had asked.

"I adore all of him. But that, yes. I want him beneath my lips. All of him. One day you will want a man desperately, and you will need to taste his skin…everywhere."

Gus had waved a hand, disregarding the probability she would ever want a man that badly.

But now, as she vowed to love and treasure Kane Russell Whittington for the rest of her days, she understood. Her need to see Kane, touch him, discover all he was, did not scare or repel her. The stirring deep in her womb was unbearable this morning. Her eagerness to leave unhappy Merry and critical Aunt Cecily grew like hot lava in her loins. She'd erupt if she and Kane could not be alone soon.

At last, Merry offered Kane and her a dipped pen. "Sign here." He pointed to boxes that marched across his open diplomatic journal. She wrote her maiden name and birthdate, her parish where her birth had been recorded, and her age. Kane put in his own. Aunt Cecily autographed as witness to their marriage.

"When you return to Britain, you should go to Doctors' Commons, Lord Ashley, and notify them of any need to reaffirm your vows. Because France observes no religion, not even of the Catholic faith, and because I am only minister ad hoc, you may wish to wed again before Anglican clergy. For now, you are both married legally. Congratulations and good day."

Merry left as if he had a fire in his shoes.

"I thought he'd never stop talking," Aunt Cecily complained as Kane and Gus walked her to her carriage.

"So poorly named, isn't he?" Gus asked Kane when they were settled into his coach.

Kane sat across from her, his grimace nothing feigned. "He is a marvel. Why the dour fellow was appointed temporary minister is a mystery. Bonaparte finds him tedious."

"Smart man!" She patted the seat beside her. "Are we not so well attuned by now that you can sit near me and we won't cause a scandal?"

"If I sit next to you, I may squash you."

She batted her lashes. "Come squash me, then."

His hot gaze dropped to her lips. "You don't know what you invite."

"I'd like to."

"I've spent weeks wanting you as mine, Augustine Whittington."

She beamed at her new name. "That means you must have ideas about what you and I can do legally."

He scoffed. "In this carriage?"

She considered how his sculpted thighs had to flex in the confines of the coach, how his knees bracketed hers, and how beneath the points of his frock coat and waistcoat, his cock rose even as they spoke. "Here, yes," she said, and rose to sit on his lap.

Even at that, the air was close, the appointments of the squabs and walls very near. She lay in his arms, wiggling to find a comfortable spot on his lap, and he yelped, fighting beneath her derriere to rearrange his accoutrement in comfort.

She giggled.

He glared, his outrage pure fluff as he yanked away her little ribboned hat and fisted the wealth of her hair. "You are a tease."

She brushed her lips on his. "You like me, though."

He lifted his hips and her, then put her down on him in a manner that told her he was more at ease and more erect than a moment before. With a nip to her lower lip, he whispered, "I like you, though."

"How much?" She circled an arm around his massive shoulders.

"More than you know, wife." His stare could melt her down here and now, as if she were his golden trophy.

"Show me," she mouthed.

He had kissed her before. In desire and in the dark, he had taken her mouth and taught her that the beginning of want continued with the satisfaction of mindless tastes of lips and tongues and endless enchantments. But here, she now his to do with as he wanted, and he hers to do with as she had only imagined, the way he kissed her was as if she were his prize. His infinitely priceless treasure.

She broke away. "We're going home, I hope."

"We are," he said, and crushed her up against him. "Home to

bed."

"Oh, thank heaven." She closed her eyes, feeling the press of his lips to the line of her bodice, his hot palms searing one breast, her nipples rising to the occasion of her own ravishment. "I thought you'd never ask."

He chuckled against the hollow between her breasts. "Should I ask for permission in the future?"

"Never."

"Such a good wife you are, my darling," he said, and took her lips once more.

The coach rumbled to a stop.

"Nooo," she objected to the interruption, and burrowed her face in his shoulder.

"We're home. Come now, wife. Smile to the servants."

She swallowed hard and sat up. "I want you here."

He put her to her bench. "Trust me. You'll like better what I have for you."

Her eyes flicked down to the juncture of his impressive assets. "I already do."

"If you do not move quickly when this door opens, you will have me coming before you can enjoy me. Then you will have to wait."

She thrust up a hand as the footman opened the door. "I'm leaving already."

## Chapter Twenty-Two

S HE TOOK THE stairs like a queen leaving her audience, and Kane followed, his eyes blind to all but her.

Corsini had pulled open the front doors the moment Gus set foot on the stones. The footman, one of Corsini's best, had stared only at the drive. Kane had knitted his brows in mirth. He'd ordered the staff's discretion for their return to his house, but this display was exceptional. He'd praise Corsini later. The other servants, as per his strict orders, had disappeared like ghosts.

At the landing to the third floor, Kane circled Gus and took the lead. Grasping her hand, he tipped his head. "This way."

In a trice, he had the door to his suite open, her inside, the door closed, and she against the wood.

"I'm impressed," she managed to get out before he kissed her again, lavishly this time.

"I hope not half as much as you are about to be." He ran his hands up her hips to her ribs and her luscious breasts.

"I'm interested in all your proofs," she said as her fingers grazed the buttons of his flies.

He took her hands away and wrapped her arms around his waist. With two swipes, he lifted her skirts. "I doubt I told you how I love your wedding gown, madam."

"But you don't love it enough," she said with a laugh.

"To leave it on you?" He rucked up more of her skirts and found the bare skin of her inner thighs. "No."

He wedged one hand over her mound and played among her folds. He heard how liquid she was. Her eyes watered with the sound. And he sank his fingers inside her.

"Not fair," she told him, her arms around his shoulders in a fast embrace. "I have nothing to caress."

He picked her up in his arms and strode with her to the next room and a bed, already turned down.

She grinned at him from the center of the bed as he fumbled with his clothes. Coat, cravat, waistcoat, shirt, boots, breeches. "Mine," she said, and with open arms welcomed him, naked and painfully erect. "You are mine."

He tugged to get her to sit up. "You must be free too."

"No, later." She ran one hand over his jutting cock. "Now I want you." And she scooted backward, leading him with her hand and opening her thighs to have him.

He looked bewildered by her offering, reverent and oh so eager. Open-mouthed, he scooted close on his knees and pulled her thighs wider. "You are beautiful everywhere, my darling wife."

WHY SHE WAS not shy but brazen in her display, she could not reason. Her mind was gone to him, and this, and all the pleasure he had given her once before and would do again.

He sank down, and found that one delicate point in her universe that set her keening at the dip of his tongue.

She lifted her head, watching him, his concentration, his delicacy to approach her to lick her hard and set her aflame and send her down to a growling appreciation. Once more, he touched the tip of his tongue to her, and she throbbed, head to toe in the brilliant pulse that only he could provoke in her.

He was at once one with her, groaning, his head to her shoulder. Inside her where he was meant to be. She arched up into him as he ground out and came inside her.

In minutes, he had her against him, both to their sides. Still inside her, he cradled her to him.

For minutes, she knew not how long, she inhaled the special flavor of his scent and drifted in a euphoria that his care had brought her.

Then he was up, urging her to stand and remove the clothes neither of them had taken time for. Turning her around, he worked at the buttons of her gown. She smiled, besotted, chuckling at the memory of her fear this morning that those tiny things would be too small for his fingers. He made short work of them, and the gown was gone.

"You were beautiful in this," he said as he held her against him and dropped the Lyon peach silk to a chair. "You'll wear it again for others. For me now, only your skin is what I wish to savor."

And so he did, nibbling at her shoulder, kissing the hollow of her breasts, and laving her nipples, hard and aching as they were for his attention. Then, devoid of every bit of cloth, he swept her into his arms and marched with her to his small, warm boudoir, where a steamy tub of water awaited her. He set her in, over her objections, and, picking up a small towel, washed her intimately everywhere.

He led her up and out, wrapping her in a huge piece of soft toweling. Then he led her back to bed.

"I want you again," he told her, his hands framing her face. "But I don't want to hurt you."

"Come make love to me, Kane. I want no respite from the delight you bring me. Dare I hope you want none from mine?"

He kissed her, a ravishing claim. "You are sweet."

She laughed. "Never did you think so."

"Not on that blasted road, no. But then, neither was I."

She ran her hands over his dark stubble, already growing at

this hour so soon past noon. Up in his thick, curling hair, she drove her fingers to his scalp. "I want you again. Now. We need to make proper babies for your earldom."

"And to ensure you are truly mine."

"I wish to be no other's. I never did."

The fire in his eyes matched that in her words, and she smiled.

"Know this, my darling wife. I take you to me not to make progeny, but to make you my only love."

"Might I be that?" she asked, breathless with the possibility.

"You are, my darling. You are."

If his love was so evident a thing, in deed and in some words, he did not declare it directly. But for now, she'd take the other words and call them her endearing prize.

NOT UNTIL THE sun sank low into the earth did they leave their marriage bed.

They made love. They slept, only to entwine once more and join, countless times.

A heavy knock upon the outer sitting room door had Kane reaching for his breeches and banyan and leaving her.

She heard conversation between Kane and the butler, she assumed. Then the servant was gone and Kane appeared at her side, a gown dangling from his fingers. That had her sitting upright.

"That is quite lovely." She reached out for the transparent while muslin, embroidered with roses and chrysanthemums in the lightest of stitches.

"Yours. I had a few made for you."

"Quickly, too." She sat up, grinning. "I do like presents."

"I will note that." He held up the gown and dropped it over her when she stood next to him.

"This, my dear man, is so sheer it covers nothing."

He swept an arm around her waist and held her to him, chest to knee. "It is not meant to."

"Do I get to view you in such a garment like this?"

"If you wish."

"I'll have one made." She waggled a finger at his wine-red banyan. "No more heavy satin for you, sir."

"We both will catch our deaths of cold."

"Never get ill." She clutched the thick fabric of his robe. "You may not leave me for eight or nine decades."

"May it be so." He kissed her quickly. "And now, come see what else we have."

⇥⟫⟫⟩⟨⟨⟨⇤

HE LED HER through to his sitting room, where Corsini had done as Kane asked and wheeled in a cart dressed in white linens, with dinner offered. Kane's Parisian chef had outdone himself with a filet of sole in lemon sauce and a sliced beef *au jus*. He'd added *dauphinoise* potatoes and a green salad with olives from the south. Dessert was a *gateau* of chocolate with candied berries.

Uncovering each new dish was a moment for his wife to exclaim over their beauty and close her eyes at first bite.

"How good of you to know we would be hungry," she declared with dancing eyes.

"I dared to hope." He winked at her as he dipped his finger into the rich *gateau* and offered it to her to lick clean.

The silly little moment turned into a torrid affair as she came to sit in his lap and kiss the sugary stuff from his finger and then his lips.

He dipped to push aside the muslin from one breast, his heart pounding that she could display her desire for him so openly.

Then she told him, "I hope you have many more surprises for me, sir. I am now so trained to respond to your generosity."

His cock, randy fellow, was ready to have her again. "Shall I kiss your other breast or show you more surprises?"

She hung in his arms, beautifully sated, as she feigned a frown and considered her options.

He did not wait, but set her to her feet. "I'll show you."

He tugged her along back into his bedroom and opened a door in the far wall. "Here. Your rooms."

Her face fell at the sight of the bedroom. As large as his, this belonged to the mistress of the house.

It was done in creams and pale golds, and the touch of pale peach to the appointments gave the bland room life.

"Mine," she said with no enthusiasm.

"Yours," he told her, and then, understanding her displeasure, strolled in front of her. "Look at me."

Her gorgeous green eyes held no life.

"This is where your clothes will hang in the far dressing room. And there," he said, and pointed to another area, "is your bathing room. And that"—he pointed again—"is your sitting room." He held her delicious body close. "But it is only for those purposes. Never will you sleep here. Never will you wish to, I dare to hope, and I hope to dare to keep you with me."

The tension in her body seeped away, and she melted against him. "Oh, Kane."

"You want me still," he murmured. "How could I be so fortunate? I've never had anyone wish for my company so fervently." He lifted her chin. "How could I bear to part with you even this far? I cannot."

She pulled away and would have tugged him back to his bedroom.

"One more thing before we make love again."

"What?" She was all business, eager only for one thing...and he smiled.

"I had one item brought up so that you wouldn't get bored with me."

She let out a snort. "Let's see it."

He took her into her sitting room. Except now there was little room to actually sit.

"The piano?"

He nodded.

"From your music room?"

He smiled.

"Kane, darling, why is that here?"

"I thought my desire for you might take many days or weeks or more to quiet."

"So you plan on leaving me after a few weeks?"

"Never."

"That is good to know. But the piano?"

"Is for you and me."

A smile broke over her face. One fine black brow arched. "For us to...play?"

"Together."

"Do we need a piano to do that?"

He laughed at the ceiling. "I doubt it!"

"So do I. But I appreciate the gesture." She glanced around. "Did you bring my knitting up here?"

"Hell no. You do that when you're nervous. You won't be here."

"I agree on that."

"I did have the maids set out your drawing pens and pads."

"You think I might like to draw in between...?" Her eyes went round.

"Perhaps. I have a few tasks I must complete now that we're in Paris, and so I thought you might appreciate your items."

She went to him then. "As long as you promise to come back to me."

"My darling, I'm never going far from you ever again."

THEIR HONEYMOON WAS an idyll—and neither spoke of an ending. They took their meals in the master suite, conversed, and laughed. They played chess and, with the loss of each piece, lost an article of clothing. Not that either had much to lose from the beginning. But the bet produced as much delight as the win...or the exciting loss.

Servants came to bring their meals at appointed hours. They also changed the linens for bed and baths daily. None of them ever saw their mistress. Occasionally, Kane used the bellpull to summon Corsini. Once a day, he left their rooms and descended to his library or study to work. The first day he had to leave the house, he planned to meet with a *vendeur* of corn. Excess supplies lay in French ports, so said one Paris newspaper. Kane sought to buy it and ship it to England. The next day, he changed from his own carriage to a hired fiacre so that he might meet discreetly with two whom he wished to recruit to work for his network. That same afternoon, he met with a new man whom Scarlett Hawthorne had recently sent to Paris.

Later that day, Corsini knocked and told him he must come to the salon to meet with one of the staff. The man who appeared was the one who had followed them to Reims and Varennes. He apologized for his failure to protect them. He had fallen ill from what he suspected was spoiled food.

"I know not, *Monsieur le Comte*, but I suspect that I was discovered by one of Vaillancourt's men and fed bad food. I was so ill I could not travel until a few days ago. Forgive me."

Kane quickly absolved him of any wrongdoing. "I am glad you have recovered and returned to explain to me what happened. I worried about you."

He returned upstairs to Gus, and much like other times, he found her playing the pianoforte in the mistress's sitting room. He sat down beside her, and they played together. One day, he played a piece by Bach. Gus frowned but complimented him on his expertise. She claimed she played that man's works only when she was upset and needed to bang at the keys. Mozart was her favorite. Kane sought to learn the pieces she adored and tried to provide accompaniment. But often he simply sat, marveling at her skill, his hands in his lap until he could bear them empty no longer. He would draw her against him, lost in her generous affections.

A few days after their marriage, Gus told him that the next day she had to go to the bathhouse in St. Denis. Her contact would be there, and she would not fail him. At first, Kane objected. She told him point-blank she had her duty. She would do her work, even though she had no means to convey to Amber any information her contact would give her.

Kane knew he had to divulge a secret to her. There was nothing for it—and she might recoil at what he had to say. "I must tell you, Gus, I know the man you intend to meet."

She was aghast. "No. How...how can you?"

"I know Luc Bechard. He is a friend. A lifelong friend."

"But... You did not tell me when I mentioned his name." She rose. On her face, disappointment mixed with anger. "How could you not?"

He took her hands. Fearful this would destroy their new-found pleasure, he blurted a response. "Our friendship was young. I wanted you to learn to trust me."

"I did! Still you did not tell me." She broke away to walk the floor. "How could you do that?"

"In honesty, my darling, I forgot. We had other issues that occupied us...and now, we are married and—"

"And fully engaged in that, aren't we?" She had one hand on her hip.

"Gus, please. I did not mean to hurt you or your work. I would never tell anyone and betray you."

She frowned at him, wary. "Not even the person to whom you report in London?"

"No. My actions are my own. I send no written descriptions."

"Why not?"

"Letters can be stolen. Destroyed."

"How does your supervisor know you do as you were instructed?"

"I send word back to her with those whom we both trust."

"Her?"

"Her."

"And if those persons disappear or are arrested?"

"Then word never reaches her. She waits."

Gus scoffed. "Not very efficient, is she?"

He would not answer that. "Gus, you and I, we do the same work."

"So we do," she said with no delight.

Then she walked away, her hands fisted. She stayed away in her suite that afternoon. For hours, he heard her attacking the pianoforte with hard notes by Bach. She was still upset with him that night when Corsini arrived with their dinner.

"Tomorrow," she said without a drop of good cheer, "you and I will dress like fisherfolk from Calais. Corsini will bring us the change of clothes. We will go to St. Denis in a public fiacre and change at least once. I mean to keep my appointment with Luc. You stay in the carriage."

Kane nodded. He would be with her. He would also have Corsini post all but two of his footmen as disguised passersby.

The next day, his wife left their carriage in St. Denis to scan the street in front of the bathhouse for Bechard. Luc did not appear.

Gus returned to their hired carriage.

That night, she was all fire in his embrace. His wife—he was relieved to learn—could forgive. For that, he counted himself a fortunate man. They were once more enthusiastic lovers, finding solace in each other and their new relationship.

Gus found in the grand library of Kane's house the usual staples of French literature. Charles Perrault, who wrote fairy tales. La Fontaine, who wrote allegories and used animals to illustrate human truths. Rousseau. Voltaire's *Candide*. But after Corsini knocked one day offering books he had discovered behind a secret door in the library downstairs, Gus read English novels by Jonathan Swift and Daniel Defoe. Her favorite was Richardson's risqué *Pamela*. Her least favorite was Defoe's *Robinson Crusoe*.

For Kane, their days and nights formed a unique respite from what his life had always been. His childhood had been spent with his father's villagers, learning farming and husbandry, reading at night. His youth, filled with applying himself to learn the wayward pastimes of his brothers, had been misspent. By nineteen he knew he was unfulfilled, and he drifted toward a renegade's existence when a friend of his persuaded him to spy against France during the Terror. For years, Kane had been living on the run, by his wits, stealing information from politicians, military couriers, and ladies of ill repute. His latest assignment by Scarlett appealed to him more. Using what he knew of France, its people, and its products, he garnered information valuable to Britain in what he was certain would be a growing conflict with the new French government. So in these days alone with his new wife, he learned that he preferred this quieter existence. He used all his knowledge and his skills, and could become more the diplomat than saboteur.

"You do possess finesse," his wife told him one evening after their supper as she sat in his lap running her fingers through his hair. "More than Anthony Merry, my darling."

"He has more credentials than I. Plus the newly appointed ambassador is much more experienced."

"But the future approaches."

He smiled at his trusting spouse. "You assume I will grow into that role."

"If you want it. Think on it." She brushed her lips on his. "Is diplomacy not the ultimate reward for spies who have seen the truth firsthand?"

He wrinkled his brow. "I am not certain you have a very fine opinion of what you and I have been doing these past few years."

She stroked his jaw. "Ambassadors weave tales made of objectives and fantasy. They are spies who tell tales that are more polite than others."

Kane had promised to think on that when a knock came at their sitting room door.

"One moment," he said, as Gus left his lap and strode into their bedroom for a heavy robe.

Corsini appeared at Kane's summons, and his face was ashen. "*Conte*, you have a visitor."

Most in Paris had allowed them their honeymoon, uninterrupted. Kane was not pleased with the disturbance. "Who is it?"

"Your friend, Lord Ramsey."

Gus appeared in the doorway, anticipation ripe on her face.

Kane stood. "Where is he?"

"In the small parlor. Do you wish…?"

"Brandy. Wine. Crudities. Whatever Chef has." Kane turned to her. "Come meet him?"

"Yes, I will dress and be down as soon as possible. Corsini, send me my maid."

## Chapter Twenty-Three

R AMSEY STOOD BY the fire, his hands behind his back. Kane noted the characteristic set of his friend's shoulders and wide stance, which implied the man's ease. Kane had to stop on the threshold and shake himself at the surprise of it.

Ram heard the hall door open and spun. A smile greeted Kane.

"Good God, am I happy to see you!" Kane strode, arms out to embrace the man whose fate he had worried over for weeks.

They patted each other on the back, then broke apart.

"Come sit down."

Ramsey was usually sartorially well turned out. Tonight he wore a finely tailored frock and waistcoat, a simply tied cravat, and fawn breeches and boots. All of it was dark and modest, as that of a bourgeois merchant. Ram was clean-shaven and had added a splash of woodsy cologne. All of that told that he had prepared for a secret trip here and that, in doing so, he was at comfort.

"I came in the back door through the gardener's shed and up into your orangery." Ram arched a burnished brow in humor as he crossed one leg over the other. "We are newly arrived in Paris. I wished you to be the first to know."

"Madame St. Antoine is with you?"

"She is. And has been in my company for many weeks now. She is healthy, whole, a challenge—and at times a real hellcat."

Kane burst into a short laugh. "Whatever the circumstances, I am overjoyed, Ram, that you found her and that both of you are well. I feared. But then, I am sure you know what misery that was. I am thrilled you are here and well. You look, dare I say, happy?"

"Please!" Ramsey grimaced as he fastened his pale blue eyes on Kane. "Grace me with no flowers, Whit. The duty to find the lady was nothing to the challenge of persuading her to allow me the honor of protecting her."

Despite his words, Ram looked nothing other than sated. How could that be? Kane was used to looking at his friend and seeing in his demeanor an irritable lack of contentment. A restless need to do, to acquire, to seize, to enjoy. But as Ram fixed him with a generous smile, Kane saw that something in the past weeks had changed his friend.

"Amber and I arrived in Paris day before yesterday. We read in a scandal sheet you recently married Augustine Bolton. I bring you congratulations from Amber and from me, my friend."

"Thank you. We are, I am pleased to say, very happy."

"I am thrilled for you. It is what you needed."

Kane was shocked at Ram's concession to the power of love. Kane grinned at his use of the term, even if it was only in his mind and not on his lips. But that was what his life was now. He was a man in love with his wife. That Ram, who had always scoffed at sentimentality, would offer this spoke of Ram's own change of disposition, if not, indeed, his change of heart.

"I did. But no man voices it, does he?" Kane said with a sharp laugh.

"Never good for one's image." Ram ran a hand down his thigh. "Let me get to this. I come for a few reasons. I want them said quickly, and then I return to Amber. I do not want her without me for long. I have hired men as guards, but you know how that goes. You have five, your opponent has ten. It's never safe for long."

"Do you fear Vaillancourt knows where you are?"

"I gather your wife has told you how he hounds Amber."

Amber had obviously shared much with Ram about her own life and Vaillancourt's pursuit of her. "She has. We encountered one of Vaillancourt's men in Varennes."

Ram sat forward, frowning. "You were there?"

"After the two of you left. We talked with Madame Verne and her daughter, Solange. They were helpful. But we met one of Vaillancourt's men in the town, and he is dead now."

"How?" Ram went stiff with shock.

"My wife has a skill with knives. He attacked us, but she got the better of him."

Ram blew out a breath. "Good that these women have talents. Amber can handle a knife and pistol."

"To your advantage."

The hall door opened, and Gus stepped in.

Kane and Ram rose.

Kane stepped forward. "My darling, you may remember my friend, Lord Ramsey."

She stepped toward Ram and thrust out her hand. "I do. We are so very happy to see you here, sir. Thank you for coming."

They shook hands. Gus indicated they should sit down again, Gus to the settee, the men to chairs. "You are very welcome. I come with loving regards from Amber."

Gus breathed deeply. "She is well?"

"She is. So has she always been these past weeks. I like to think it is I who have kept her well, though she would not tell you that."

"I'm certain," Gus said with a sympathetic smile. "I hope you will tell me all. We have been very worried about you both. So is Aunt Cecily. Have you been to see her? Will you? Will Amber?"

"That, I doubt."

Gus shook her head. "But... May we tell her?"

"Do not. Amber has her reasons. Not all of them does she

share with me."

Gus sighed. "I know. That is her way. But then, she must have approved of your coming here."

"She did not want you to worry any longer. She was certain you had. Especially when we heard rumors that the two of you had gone away on a lovers' escapade. Amber saw through the ruse. She knew you would not go away with any man without excellent reason."

Gus scoffed. "How good of her."

"She is a very fine woman."

Kane could have fallen off his chair. Ram, his surly friend who admired few people, had just praised Amber St. Antoine.

"She is indeed, Lord Ramsey," Gus said. "Now, tell us why are you here tonight."

"I was just informing Whit that we arrived in Paris only day before yesterday. We are getting settled."

"In her house in Rue Dauphine?" Gus asked.

"No. We are in a small house on the left bank in Saint-Germain-des-Prés."

Gus shook her head. "Why? Do you not wish to announce you are in the city?"

"Exactly."

"Wise. But then why return here at all?"

"Amber insisted we return because she had lost the threads of her work."

"She has been away from Paris since mid-March," Gus said. "Of course she has not worked."

"When we heard that you both were looking for us in Reims, Amber considered returning. But would do so only if she were still invisible to Vaillancourt."

Kane looked at Gus. "The man is relentless in his pursuit."

Ram nodded. "And Amber is determined he will not stop her."

"And you agreed?" Kane asked.

"Only if I were her companion. Yes, we live together. We

CERISE DELAND

have developed a trusting relationship." Ram glanced at Gus. "I hope I do not offend you when I admit that your friend and I are intimate?"

Gus smacked her lips. "No. Amber would not do anything unless she believed it to be right. Will she remain incognito? Indefinitely?"

"She says she will. I encourage it. Three of the deputy police chief's men found us at various points along the roads. They are ruthless creatures. I do not want Amber in public. They would take advantage at their chief's command. I think him capable of anything." He looked at Kane. "I will keep her by my side for as long as is necessary. No one will hurt her."

Gus let out a shaking breath. "So I conclude, then, that I will not see her."

"I came alone. I will go out with her on her journeys, and I will not come here again. She tells me she will be too busy. She congratulates you on your marriage and hopes you are very happy." He glanced at Kane. "I bring you my own fond regards for a happy life together."

Kane noted the hint of sorrow in his friend's soft blue eyes. What that denoted, he could not define, because Kane had never seen such tenderness in his friend's countenance.

Kane had to share with him what he knew. He took his wife's hand in his. "Ramsey, we fear Vaillancourt's orders to do anything to find you both and take Amber from you."

"That is not news. Amber has told me the same for weeks."

Gus whispered, "He wants her to reveal her network. Perhaps he wants more than that."

"He does," Ram replied. "But he will have her over my dead body."

Gus stared at Ramsey, absorbing the full meaning of that statement.

A knock at the door came, and Kane called to Corsini to enter. The man had a tray.

"Would you like any refreshment?" Kane offered.

228

"None for me, thank you," Ram replied.

Corsini took his cue and drifted away, closing the door behind him.

Ram got to his feet. "And so, if you will forgive me the brevity of my visit, I return home to Amber."

"You will let us know how and where you are, I hope?" Gus pressed him.

"I would like to say yes, my lady, but I cannot. To come here taunts the devil. It took me hours to change course and defy anyone who might have discovered me. I shall return now by different routes." He took Gus's offered hand and bent to kiss it. "No news will be good news."

Kane said, "I will walk to the orangery with you. Pardon me, my darling. I will have a few words with Ramsey."

⇶✳⇷

"LISTEN TO ME, please, Ram," Kane said when they stood amid the fragrant orange trees in the warm room at the back of the house. "I have men here to help you. If you need assistance, I can send them to you now. Also, if you need money, I have that too. Scarlett was more than generous. So whatever you may want—"

"I have men enough, Whit. Money is a challenge. If you can deposit an amount with my *majordom* in my house off Rue d'Orleans, that would help."

"I gather you are not pleased to return to Paris."

"God help me, no. But Amber would not listen to reason. She is beside herself and thinks that Bonaparte makes way for himself to destroy the consulate. Dirk Fournier thinks the same."

Kane was shocked. "You've seen Dirk?"

"No. Not since he and I parted weeks ago in Verdun. But while Amber and I were in Verdun, we learned that the citadel there receives a huge supply of muskets as well as new cannon. Rumors there are bad that Bonaparte wants the territory along the border with German Baden. Napoleon offers land and money to the margrave. That man wants to be a grand duke."

"Dirk's grandmother's territory."

"Exactly. When I left Dirk in Verdun in late May, he was in a hurry to get to Karlsruhe. Unless you have heard from him, I assume he is still there."

"I have had no communication from him. So he must be still in Karlsruhe."

They embraced.

"Despite the pressure of protecting an independent woman, you look happy, Ram."

The man hid his emotion with a chuckle. "Let me say the same for you."

"*A bientôt*, Ram."

"*A bientôt*, my friend."

⇥⟫⟪⇤

GUS WAITED FOR Kane in her sitting room, having a bad time recuperating from the interview. She played Bach.

Kane came to kiss her shoulder.

She paused a moment to enjoy his lips on her skin. "I'm pleased they are back and healthy. But Amber returns to work. That presents so many problems."

Kane said nothing. This was exactly what he had told Gus long before they left to seek out Luc Bechard in the bathhouse in St. Denis.

"We must learn what Vaillancourt truly intends for Amber."

Kane let his eyes close. A debate with his wife was nothing he could win.

"I think you and I must return to Society."

He sat down next to her. For a few bars, he accompanied her.

"I know you don't want to return, Kane. But on the other hand, we must leave our rooms here sometime. Now is as good

230

as any. We can put our ears to the court rumors and send messages to Amber."

That was when he stopped playing.

He rose and paced.

Gus stopped attacking the piano too. "Kane, you know if you do not agree to go into Society, I will go by myself."

"I do agree with your premise. I do not agree that it is wise for your safety."

"Or yours."

He said nothing to that.

She came to him, opened the panels of his banyan, and enfolded herself in them. Curling her arms around his waist, she laid her head on his chest.

He held her to him, angry at the world that threatened her very life, torn that he had his own mission to accomplish, and that if they left this cocoon of pleasure, the departure could mark the end of their separate work—and end their lives.

But there was nothing for it. They had to leave. They had to begin. They had to work.

# Chapter Twenty-Four

"THE EARL OF Castleton arrived in Paris while we were gone," Gus told Kane as they entered the rented Parisian manse of the British gentleman a week later. Kane and she had accepted Castleton's invitation to attend his ball because it would be so well attended. Even Josephine hinted she would come. Like Kane's house, Castleton's was a huge, old mansion once owned by French aristocrats gone abroad or to their maker.

Cecily led the way into the ballroom, ceasing her complaints about the torrent of rain outside. The lady put a smile on her face as they were announced by the earl's hired French *majordom*.

Gus and Kane had called upon her aunt three days ago with their announcement that they were emerging from their honeymoon and returning to Society. Aunt Cecily was overjoyed.

"Many wish to know if the euphoria lasts. I see you both look healthy. I am pleased." The way she'd regarded both Kane and her told Gus that indeed her aunt was very happy that they were content with each other.

"Do you know this fellow?" Gus asked Kane as they wove their way through the crowd in the ballroom, renewing old acquaintances and gaining new ones. Gus was impressed how so many British spent so much money to come to Paris and pretend they had always loved those in it. "He's done well for himself to invite so many."

Kane grimaced. "I only know of him. He has quite a reputation as a gadabout. And clearly, he loves a party."

Cecily turned to them. "He even sailed here from Brighton on a schooner with fifty-six of his so-called dearest friends. I'd say he has three hundred more here tonight."

"It is a crush," Gus admitted.

Cecily worked her fan furiously. She disliked pretentious men—except the two who had been her lovers. She leaned close to confide, "This one always likes a crowd. He's got more mistresses and children than God allows."

"He was a friend of my father's," Kane said with a look of tolerance. "'Never Alone' is his moniker."

Gus knew how Kane had rued his father's coarse behaviors. "Birds of a feather, were they?"

"Indeed. Well, here he comes."

The earl was a pretentious twit who used a monocle to acknowledge Cecily and turn much too quickly to examine everything about Gus. "I say, lovely woman, young Ashley. Your father would've liked her. Indeed. Word has it, Lady Ashley, that you are a favorite of the first consul and his wife."

Gus nodded. "We are friends, yes."

"Lord Castleton!" Kane said through gritted teeth. "I hear you sailed the Channel to get here. Rough weather?"

"Course! Course. What can you expect, eh? But we had to come and taste the pleasures. I say, Lady Ashley, will you honor me to dine with me at the midnight buffet?"

"I beg your pardon, sir. My husband and I will leave before the buffet. Another time, perhaps."

"I do hold you to it, my lady. Going home early is a fine custom, Ashley. Were she mine and new to me, I'd rush her home myself." He elbowed Kane, who already had his fists curled.

"Sir?" Cecily tapped the odious man on the arm. "Control yourself. This is Paris. Not your home. Civility is required."

"I will, indeed." He grinned down at the lady who was not

amused. "Ye're lovely, madam. Understand how Prinny and your old Orleans could give you a good go."

"Sir! Do shut up," Cecily reprimanded him.

"I think we must go." Kane grew near purple with rage.

"Now, now. Don't be testy," the blubbering idiot told them. "We'll open the dancing as soon as Madame de Lucay arrives. She takes names for Josephine to remember us all. She's like a forgetful schoolgirl, I am told. After that, we can dance. Silly. But this is Paris."

"It is ritual, sir." Cecily was not about to let the man criticize the procedure. "Madame Bonaparte will arrive and receive."

"Good. I will rush to greet her," Gus put in.

Cecily all but rolled her eyes in Gus's direction. Then she took the man's arm and led him aside. "Allow me to educate you, Castleton. If you wish to be accepted by the first consul and his wife, observe the rules. She will greet you, host that you are, only after she has risen for her husband's family and all ambassadors and their wives. She will only bow her head to you, sir."

"But I buy the wine tonight."

"And grateful we all are, sir." Cecily forced a smile. "Come, Castleton. All of us will now find our friends."

Kane regarded her departure with aplomb. "She gives us leave to have fun."

Gus wound her arm through his. "She does. Let's." She surveyed the room and found a group of her friends in one corner. "Come with me. I have more pleasant people for you to meet."

She introduced him to two friends of hers and Amber's, both of whom stood with their brothers. After Josephine arrived and greeted all, then took her chair to greet Castleton, the orchestra began the first set.

Castleton took out Madame Tallien, who had arrived with Josephine, and a few took the floor later.

Gus leaned close to Kane. "In Paris, one allows the host and hostess to perform most of the first set alone, with only a few close friends joining in."

"I'd like to dance with you."

That warmed her. "Do you like to dance?"

"I see by the smile on your face the idea pleases you. And my answer is yes, I do like it."

Gus said, "But I understood that in London it is not done for married couples to dance together."

He looked out at the few gliding upon the chalked floor. "You and I will be the exception."

On the next set, Kane took her to the floor, and they laughed together as they danced. Afterward, as was customary, Kane asked Gus's two friends to take the floor, and the young ladies' two brothers danced with Gus.

Suddenly before them all stood Rene Vaillancourt. With his hand out to Gus, he formed the perfect picture of a man who simply wished to dance.

Refuse him and Gus would create a scandal.

The minuet was not only long, but a form she did not care for.

"You have been away from town, *Madame la Comtesse.*" Vaillancourt presented a dazzling figure. Tall, lean, and dapper, he had a smoothly sculpted face of even features. To many women who knew him not, he was desired. To Gus, who knew his relationships with Danton and Robespierre, and now with Fouché, he was a handsomely presented human, corrupt to his core. Odd that a man so perverse would be so handsome, but then, God created oddities so mortals debated their value.

Over Vaillancourt's shoulder, Gus detected the tense features of her beloved husband. They were so very unlike each other, the two men.

Her husband, containing his displeasure with a face void of any emotion, save stark observation. The man before her, smiling like a cavalier, untrustworthy from his even white teeth down to his highly polished dancing shoes. Her husband, six inches or more taller than the fellow in front of her. Kane blinked, his eyes on hers as she took the devil's hand and went with him to the center of the floor.

"Forgive me, sir, if I do not recall the minuet well." She wore no smile, only blank civility. "I do not wish to embarrass you."

"*Madame la Comtesse*, to appear with you on the floor in front of Madame Bonaparte is an honor. I am certain you will execute yourself very well."

The word "execute" jarred Gus. But she had to play the *bonne vivante* here. "*Merci beaucoup, monsieur.*"

"I am delighted you and your husband have returned to Paris."

She smiled.

"Where did you go on your travels?" He asked it so innocently, she might have thought him an actor in the *Comédie-Française.* "Anywhere exciting?"

"To bed, *monsieur.*"

His shock led right into a robust chuckle. The man had a sense of humor, even if he was a scourge. "And you enjoyed it so much, you decided to marry the fellow."

To which she did not reply.

"He must be talented."

*He is.*

"And love you dearly."

*I think so.*

"I envy him."

She arched a brow. "You like Englishmen?"

"Never. Especially not men who take what I want."

"If you wish Madame Bonaparte to censure you, sir, you will say nothing more to me."

"No? What can you do to me?"

"Leave you where you stand, *petit crapaud.*"

Calling him a little toad brought forth red splotches on his cheeks. "You dare—"

"I have been in many situations, sir, where I dare. *Oui.*"

"I know what you did to my man in Varennes."

She glared at him. "You dream, sir." And then, picking up her skirts to visibly and sharply flick them away from the slightest touch to his trousers, she left him where he stood.

The gasps that rose from the French were a pleasure to Gus's ears.

Castleton watched, open-mouthed.

Two steps off the dance floor and Gus had the arm of her husband.

They gave their excuses, their thanks to their host, a gentle bow to Madame Bonaparte, and left the ball.

KANE COULD NOT take Gus away quickly enough. They took the stairs down to the main entrance, where Castleton's *majordom* awaited.

"Our carriage, *monsieur.*" He handed the man his card with his grooms' names. The servants would fetch them both from the kitchens, where all the guests' grooms waited for their masters and mistresses to leave for home.

The *majordom* summoned a footman standing behind him and handed him the card.

Kane seethed, his arms around his wife's waist. Vaillancourt had more gall than ten men. But then, hadn't Kane seen the worst of what the man could do?

Vaillancourt had tortured his friend Brussard. From one of the men who had observed the *gendarmes* that horrid day on the Malmaison road, Kane knew it had been Vaillancourt who did the deed personally. Ripping a man to shreds took more than nerve. It required grit mixed with an insane measure of cruelty. Vaillancourt had learned the art of it—and the taste for it—under Robespierre. That man was gone, but his cruelty lingered on.

Gus curled against Kane as they stood in the foyer waiting for their carriage. "We will be criticized for leaving before Josephine."

"We can send our apologies tomorrow."

Gus kissed his jaw. "We will be forgiven. He was at fault."

Whoever saw their affection be damned. Kane brought her nearer. Her vibrant warmth was reassurance that the man had not hurt her. "I saw his rudeness, and I was not the only one. But never fear—he will pay for this tonight."

She tipped up her face. "What is it? I hear danger in your voice."

"You do. Perceptive, my darling. But never fear, I have this in hand."

"How?"

Kane glanced about the foyer. Grand as it was, alcoves abounded, niches in the walls, a butler's coat closet with door was within two paces.

"Not here." He sensed prying eyes and ears.

The footman reappeared and spoke into the ear of Castleton's *majordom*.

The man took four steps toward Kane. "*Monsieur le Comte*, your men are on their way to bring your coach around."

Kane offered his regards.

Gus peered out the tall, dark window into the night. She shivered against him. "It's raining harder."

"The storm is a deluge. But we need the rain for the crops."

Long minutes passed, and Kane frowned at his servants' tardiness.

"Don't be upset," Gus told him with sweet tolerance for the delay. "It's difficult to park all these carriages nearby. And we have all these people here."

But still their men did not come with the carriage.

Kane turned to the *majordom*, who was also, by this time, frowning at the failure of Kane's carriage to arrive. "Might you know in what street our men went to retrieve our conveyance?"

The man opened his mouth to speak and noticed Kane's carriage pulling to the circular drive.

With thanks, Kane and Gus darted out into the rain.

Kane's footman bent over, his cap tightly drawn over his head, as he opened the carriage door. The rain was a torrent.

Kane handed Gus inside. Both of them were soaked to the skin.

The door slammed shut, and Kane attributed the abruptness to his footman's need it get out of the rain.

The coach jerked forward.

In her seat opposite, Gus shivered once more, pulling at her silken gown. "No need to wet down this dress to appear fashionable, eh?"

He removed his formal frock coat. "I think this has shrunk. Let me give you my waistcoat." He remembered how sensitive Gus was to colder temperatures.

"I don't need it. Honestly, Kane."

"Take it." He swung it around her shoulders, then moved beside her. "Come here. Let me warm you."

She snuggled next to him. "Better than your waistcoat. Hmmm. The coachman is driving very fast through these narrow streets, don't you think?"

"He probably wants to get home out of the rain," Kane told her, but he was worried at his man's reckless behavior. Speed was not like him.

Suddenly, the carriage lurched forward. Kane parted the lace curtain and saw that his man was taking the riverbank road. In the black night, only a few candles glimmered on barges in the Seine. Across the river on the left bank, a few more candles lit the tall houses of merchants. The carriage was also traveling west, not east toward Rue Gabriel and home.

"You are scowling," Gus murmured. "What's wrong?"

As if in answer, the coachman yelled to the groom, the carriage careened to one side, and shouts pierced the night.

Kane reached under the seat and brought out his pistol.

Gus opened a compartment in her armrest and extracted her gleaming stiletto.

Kane held her close. "I will kill whoever opens that door."

She gripped her knife. "I am for the second one."

Men yelled, a raucous din. The carriage door flew open. An ugly creature with a scarf over his mouth snarled.

Kane fired.

The creature was dead before he took another breath.

A churl behind him reached in, and another beside him tore Kane from his seat.

As the two beat him about the head and dragged him along the cobbles, he heard his wife behind him.

Screeching at them to let him go, Gus struggled with her attackers.

Kane heard her curses and, in his soul, felt her struggles. He heard the cry of one man and the shout of another.

Both cursed.

Gus had cut them.

But then, Kane went deaf. His ribs and stomach exploded in flames. His guts churned. He heaved up bile.

At once, he was free. Seeking his wife, he ran to her and seized her attacker by the scruff of his ragged coat.

Behind that man came one of Kane's, a huge fellow that Corsini claimed could stop a bull—and he did.

Kane clamped his arms around his wife, drawing her back and away from the villain who had attacked her and who was now under siege from one of Kane's men. Gus, angry as a wet cat, still slashed at the fellow, her hand poised to cut her assailant to bits.

All masked attackers swirled into the fists and raging pistol fire of Kane's guards. Four were down, their fight gone with their breaths.

Kane counted six more, hands up, surrendering and panting on the soaked cobbles.

"Let's tie these vermin," he said to his men. "We will visit their master."

His guards grunted their approval.

Kane would praise Corsini for his bloodthirsty taste in servants.

## Chapter Twenty-Five

RENE VAILLANCOURT, THE debonair deputy of police, was known to remain late at the few social events he attended. Even afterward, he remained inspired, vigorous in his appetites for more. He would journey on to other, more private parties with personally chosen participants who yielded to his special tastes.

A few minutes after five the morning after Castleton's ball, he arrived at his home in Rue St. Martin.

He wore a self-satisfied smile as he flung open the two doors of his salon and took two long strides into the dark room. Then he halted. His smile disintegrated.

Gazing upon his uninvited guests, he grunted. "I see I must dismiss my *majordom* for allowing in street scum."

Kane lowered his arm from the man's marble mantel, then clicked shut his pocket watch. "Don't be harsh with him. If he disobeyed me and gave you any indication we were here, he would have died on the spot."

Vaillancourt spied the six muzzled men who were seated, tied, hands and feet, in the middle of his fine Aubusson. He gave his evil smile. "I gather you have subdued all my household?"

"We have." Kane strode toward him, his hands out to denote the six who glowered at him.

Vaillancourt's blue eyes slid to Gus. "I would never hurt you."

She chuckled softly. "I'm certain that's what you tell all the women you seize in the streets."

"I take only those who deserve it."

Contempt rolled out of her like lava. "I deserve your attention because I am Madame St. Antoine's friend."

Vaillancourt indicated one Louis Quatorze chair. "I hope you don't mind if I sit."

Kane gave a royal flourish with one hand. "Please."

Vaillancourt licked his lips. "Of course you are St. Antoine's friend. But I do believe you are much more than that."

Gus cocked her head. "*Madame la Comtesse* Nugent's niece."

Vaillancourt huffed. "Immaterial."

Kane scoffed. "Whatever your motive to attack my wife, *that* is immaterial to what is about to happen."

Vaillancourt tipped his head to and fro. "Get on with it, Ashley. It is late."

"Later than you think," Kane responded with glee. "This morning, in a few hours, in fact, the balladeers on the Pont Neuf and the printers of *libelles* and *chroniques scandaleuses* in the Quai de Augustine will have news of your actions earlier this evening."

"Ba! That your wife insulted me in front of the premier of Society?"

Kane smacked his lips. "That you have a curious relationship with a certain gentleman in your household."

"*Merde.* Is that all you can think of?"

"That you persuade men in the first consul's household to join you and a favorite of yours is a subject many will enjoy hearing and reading."

"I am pure. You have no proof."

Kane shook his head. "What proof did the authors of *libelles* have against the Bourbons? What proof was necessary for the fiddlers to chant about Madame Pompadour or Marie Antoinette?"

Vaillancourt crossed one leg over another. "Just as those misfits were sent to *la Force* and the Bastille, I will catch them."

"Perhaps. But not soon enough to douse the displeasure of the first consul and his dear wife."

"I have my ways."

"You'll hire more like these poor souls?" Kane swept out a hand toward the six thugs. "Bonaparte has learned the lessons that fired the revolutionaries who took control of Paris in the early nineties. The first consul won't allow his family to wed certain unmentionables. Soon it will be all in his regime. Come now, Vaillancourt—you know as well as I that Bonaparte is as dedicated to public morality as a poor English vicar. He has no tolerance for—shall we call it—divergent behavior?"

"You will not win."

"I only need to plant a seed, Rene." Kane inhaled. "Now, on to this business here. As for these six little bunnies, they failed. Not their fault. Really, it isn't. I merely anticipated your actions. I had more men than they. Plus, mine are trained. These are street dregs. Nonetheless, they should not go in want for your failures. You must honor your commitments to them. How much did you promise them for their work this night?"

One of the men huddled on the floor muttered beneath his gag.

Vaillancourt glowered at him.

"How much? One *sou*? Two?" Kane offered. "I will see you pay them now. Pull your bell for your *majordom*."

"You are mad."

"Very."

Vaillancourt stood and went to his pull, called his man, then resumed his chair.

"Good. Now, as we await him, let me tell you what will happen tomorrow. You will go to Fouché, express your regret for your poor actions at Castleton's ball. Your superior is such a good family man. He detests those who disparage women. You will, if Fouché requires it, go to the first consul and apologize. The first consul will have in his morning correspondence a few little *libelles* from the streets. No excuse for the scarcity. You see, there are so many of them, one cannot possibly gather all. And to your superior Fouché, you will promise more courteous behavior to all ladies in your midst in future."

Vaillancourt bared his long teeth.

"News of your attack on the British second envoy and his wife, the niece of beloved Countess Nugent, will spread. Of course, the story includes your failure, and our defeat and capture of your men."

"I will retaliate."

"You can try, *monsieur. La France* will not approve." The use of the affectionate term for the old Bourbon kings spiked Vaillancourt's spine. Bonaparte had not yet used the phrase for himself, but Parisians began to credit him with it. The move to greatness by him and the public's need for a leader whom they could venerate called forth the honored term to the lips of the citizens of France.

The doors swung open and Vaillancourt's butler, backed by one of Kane's watchdogs, appeared.

"How much will you pay them, *monsieur?*" Kane asked. "Do have your man fetch your strongbox."

Fifteen minutes later, Kane and Gus departed the townhouse. Four of Kane's men came with them. Four remained until the six they had subdued were rewarded for their service and sent, minus ties and gags, to the street.

OUTSIDE VAILLANCOURT'S HOUSE, Gus accepted Kane's hand up into their rented carriage. She watched as he conferred in low tones with one of his men, then climbed in to sit beside her.

In the confines, she sank into his embrace. "I will sleep for a year. You should come with me."

"After we arrive home, I have a few things to do, and then I will follow you."

"First thing, though, we must find our coachman."

Kane's coach, in hideous condition, had been dragged away to a stable by a team of horses one of Kane's men had hired after the incident. Another guard of Kane's had found an open cart near the Louvre and appropriated it to take the six attackers to Vaillancourt's house. Kane had given one of his men orders to return the cart and old nag to the street and wait until the owner appeared. He was to pay him an old gold louis for his kind service to a lord in need.

Kane told her not to worry about their man. "One of our guards tells me he is well. Saved. They saw him being attacked as he climbed onto the box in the street. They witnessed that our groom was badgered, too. All waited until they could capture all the culprits. Our coachman was drugged. He awaits us at home, as does our groom. Both are shaken, of course. But they are well."

"Good to hear. Now tell me about this other business. I had no idea you have pamphleteers in your pay." She arched both brows at him.

"Why, *Madame la Comtesse*, I will have you know that I am the second British envoy, and I am charged with increasing commerce between our countries."

She laughed. "And increasing the numbers of prosperous printers and street *chanteuses* in Paris."

He laughed, not quite humble. "So many need employment."

She chuckled. "I guess you began your patronization long before the contretemps at Castleton's last night."

"You'd be correct."

She exhaled and settled nearer to her husband. "I was afraid last night when they attacked us. I cannot lose you, Kane. You are my everything, and I have not told you so. But now, I will. I must."

He fisted his hand in her hair. "Look at me."

She smiled into his mellow eyes. When he looked at her like that, she was not unto herself, alone. She was loved and belonged to him as much as to herself.

"I love you, Augustine. You are my wife, my treasure, my beginning of a new life, and you will be here at the ending of it. I will not lose you. We have decades more to live in happiness and peace. I lost half my sense in Varennes when that man attacked you. Tonight I nearly lost the other half." Tears dotted his lashes. "I love you, and I will never allow any man to take you from me."

"Only God," she murmured, nigh unto overwhelmed with her husband's admission. "Only God, who gave me you, can ever take you from me."

Their coach came to a stop in front of their house.

He took her lips in a swift declaration. "Come inside. Let me prove how I adore you."

Corsini had the door open wide for them, his face white with concern.

Gus took one look at him and grabbed him into her embrace. "Thank you, sir. You are unique, and we are so privileged to name you ours."

The Italian foundered. *"Grazie, grazie,"* was all he could manage as she kissed both Kane's cheeks.

Kane beamed at him. "I will take my wife up, but I want coffee in my study when I come down." Then he took Gus's hand.

The two of them scampered like children to their suite.

# Chapter Twenty-Six

KANE DID NOT appear in his study until after nine. He had bathed with his wife and taken her to bed. The two of them were exhausted from the night's events, but not quite tired enough to postpone the intimate joining that celebrated their relief at their escape.

Corsini appeared like a genie from a bottle at Kane's study door.

The man's frown alarmed Kane. But he had no time to ask the reason when from behind him a vibrant, red-haired siren rushed toward him. Kane recognized her at first sight. The lady from the road to Malmaison. The lady whom Scarlett had sent him to find. The one in the sketch that Gus had drawn. Amber St. Antoine.

And on her heels strode an anguished Ramsey.

"Good morning, Lord Ashley." Amber stood ramrod straight, her hands folded before her, her heart-shaped face placid. "Forgive the intrusion, but I know you will receive me."

Kane circled his desk to approach her and shake her hand. "I am pleased to meet you, although, I do believe, not in these circumstances."

"You have that right, Whit." Ram bit off his words, not so much dismayed now as downright angry. "I have fought this, but she will not listen to me. I hope you can persuade her otherwise."

Mystified, Kane nodded. "Please sit down, Madame St. Antoine. Ram. Corsini, please ask my wife to join us."

"Yes," said Amber as she took a chair near the fireplace. "Do summon Gus. I wish to see her, congratulate her on her marriage. I do hope, sir, this is a love match."

Because the last was more a question than a statement, Kane was happy to affirm it. "None other than that, *madame*."

She flicked a hand. "Let us dispense with formalities. We are too much in each other's pockets to be otherwise. I am Amber. You are Kane. Save for Godfrey here, who remains Ram." She gave the man a small, intimate smile that told Kane she had more affection for him than her words denoted. "Let me begin by telling you that we've seen the scandal sheets. Our servants collect them each morning. It is how Ram and I have avoided the *gendarmes* of Vaillancourt. A very thorough job done on that man in those broadsheets today. I assume the work is yours."

Kane would never admit to such a thing. What little others knew protected them as well as him and his wife. Besides, he did not yet know Amber as well as his wife, or even as well as Ram. He had no reason to trust her until he gauged her dedication to her former role. Even Ram might now know more than Kane on that subject. Kane would not learn it by intuition. Not in a few minutes.

"What you read in those sheets is rumor," he said as he braced his hip on his desk. "Not all is to be trusted."

"Very well," she said, brushing aside his failure to admit guilt. "Define it as you will. I am not here to argue with you about your work."

"My work is to negotiate commercial contracts for British citizens and, when I can, to buy agricultural products for them."

"Of course it is," she said with a smile.

"Amber!" Gus flew into the room, her morning gown of white muslin aflutter beneath her banyan as she ran to her friend, arms out.

GUS COULD NOT believe Amber was real. She gazed at her, her hands to her cheeks. "Oh, you look wonderful. Healthy. I was so worried about you."

Tears clouded her vision of her friend. But Gus could see the shine of her bright red hair, the clarity of her dark brown eyes, the perfection of her pale complexion, and the smattering of freckles on her nose. She hugged her...and felt the resistance in her body.

Whatever Amber's reason to appear here today, she expected an argument about it. She would fight for herself—and do it fiercely.

Gus stepped backward.

Kane put his arm around her waist. "Join us."

She nodded, agreeing as she saw Amber resume her chair. She welcomed Ramsey and took a seat across from Amber. "You come unannounced," she said to her, and a quick look at Ramsey told her he was not pleased to be here.

Amber pressed her lips together and glanced down a moment to trace the folds of her pale yellow cotton gown. She wore a pelisse of forest green, which meant she had not stopped at the front door to allow Corsini to take her wrap. Ramsey, too, looked like he had just flown from hell to keep up with Amber. His dark brown hair fell over his brow and his gaze was clouded with some torture.

This next, whatever it was, would not be pleasant. Gus wanted this over and done. "Tell us quickly why you are here, Amber."

"I know what happened to you last night."

Gus inhaled. "News sheets on the street, I suppose?"

"A new song by the rabble, too, tells the tale of the Englishman who married Nugent's niece, both of whom were attacked by peasants hired by Vaillancourt."

Gus added nothing.

Neither did her husband. Kane sat beside her in his own chair, his gaze never wavering from the woman whom he and she had sought for so many months.

"This," added Amber, "comes on top of the reports that you Augustine did away with a fellow in Varennes. He, sad to say, died of a severe cut to his groin. He bled to death."

Gus held her tongue.

"I see neither one of you will admit to these acts."

"Why should we?" Gus asked. "You seem to have the answers you want." *Or not.*

Amber's dark gaze slid from Gus to Kane. "I have a plan."

No one urged her on.

"I will return to Society. Open up my house again. Announce I am ready to receive once more. Then I will send out my invitations to dinner parties and balls."

Gus said, "No."

"You have no say in the matter, Augustine."

"The same way I had no say in your departure from Paris? Your extended absence? Your failure to perform your duties?"

"My duties," Amber blurted, "did not suffer."

Gus scoffed. "I beg to differ."

"No catastrophe has befallen anyone in my group in the time I have been gone. While I take no credit for it, I take no offense either. Neither should you."

"Oh, yes," Gus offered with sarcasm. "The only catastrophe is that the man in Varennes is dead...after he tried to kill Kane and me."

"Exactly," Amber said with vehemence. "And now nothing like that will happen again."

"You will stop such things from occurring?" Gus taunted her.

Amber gave them a secretive smile. "I will."

Gus fumed. "Even you cannot have the audacity to expect a dinner party and a ball will set any of us free from Vaillancourt's determination to have you as his own."

At that, Ramsey, who had sat throughout this spat like a

marble statue, closed his eyes.

"No. It is the beginning."

Gus feared the next. "Of what?"

Amber had always had a clear understanding of her own nature. More than Gus ever had, and at an early age, too. Gus had seen it, emulated her dear friend's courage, and followed Amber's unerring ability to make decisions based more on fact than on any other element, except emotion. Even Amber's decision to marry Maurice St. Antoine had been a quick study for Amber. Her logic was sound: she loved the man. What was age but a number? She could as easily die before Maurice as he before her. She would have him, enjoy him and their love for the moment, in the ripeness of lust and love.

Amber got to her feet.

Gus noted the move was not smooth. Amber had a hitch in her knees.

Ramsey grunted at her movements.

So what Amber did caused her pain.

"I will open up my house. Receive guests. Return to the work only I can do. Examine what is left, what needs repair, what needs addition. I will invite Society to my door."

She blanched all of a sudden, as if she were drained of any valor.

Ramsey cursed, then shot to his feet and took her arm. "Tell them. Do it quickly and we will leave."

Disaster lay before Gus at whatever Amber would say next.

"I will become Vaillancourt's mistress."

Gus was out of her chair. "No."

Kane was beside her. "Why that, of all things?"

"Because it is the only way the man leaves everyone alone. Because it is what he has wanted for years, even before Maurice and I met. I have refused Vaillancourt time and time again. He grows more ruthless as he grows more powerful. He will not be denied."

"Amber," Gus pleaded, "do not do this!"

Kane looked at Ramsey. "What say you to this?"

"Whit, whatever can be said, I have argued. To no avail. Amber refuses. In this matter, I am without power. Though I wish to God I had it all."

Amber looked each one of them in the eye, then turned and walked away.

Her footsteps resounded down the hall toward the staircase and the foyer.

Gus broke into a run.

On the landing, she caught Amber's arm and spun her around. "Don't do this. Do not throw your life away. You are young. Vaillancourt will hurt you. Defile you. Destroy all you have built. Do not reappear. Someone will rebuild the network that you and I can no longer serve. Trust in that. Live your life. I detect Lord Ramsey wants you to live it with him."

Amber stood, facing her, tears silently streaming down her cheeks. "I would do it, too. Accept Ram's offer of...life and love. Especially love. But I know of what Vaillancourt is capable. You only know a small bit. I will not have you hurt." She would have turned, but Gus tugged at her.

"He cannot hurt me now. Kane will not permit it."

Amber rounded on her. "Do not believe it. Where evil lives, it is capable of destroying the finest, the fairest, the worthiest of any of us. Each of us fights with the weapons we have. You have your own skills, your knowledge of what you and I and our network has done. You have Kane, who has another entire cadre to support him. Use it. Employ it. Never abandon it. As I do not abandon what I know, what I have, what I must do to strengthen the work I have done and what I will leave behind. I must fight as I can. For the love of a freedom I can only imagine. For you to live in the love that can bring you peace and joy."

"Amber, you told me once never to fail to take love where you find it."

She ran her fingertips through Gus's hair. "I did."

"You can again."

"Could? Might. Should not. Cannot." She got a dreamy look in her vibrant eyes and gazed back in the direction of the study and Ramsey. "Perhaps one day I might take the love I'm offered and live in peace. But that day is not this one." She took the stairs down.

Gus could not move.

At the last step, Amber stopped and lifted her head to regard Gus with a smile. "I love you, sweet Augustine. You have been my dearest friend, my colleague, my collaborator, and my darling sister. Go seize your love and live in peace. You deserve Kane and all the happiness you both will find together."

Then she picked up her skirts and fled.

RAMSEY STARED AT Kane. But saw nothing. "She does not listen to reason."

Kane had never seen him so depleted. So undone.

"I have tried everything."

Kane put a hand to his friend's shoulder. "Find yourself."

Ramsey blinked. "What?"

"Find yourself, and then you will find a way to help her."

"I doubt that."

"*Don't,*" Kane said with the perception of one who had known another through many trials and tribulations. "You will find a way."

A spark of vigor lit Ramsey's blue eyes. "Never easy, is it, loving another?"

"Never. But then the rewards are more than you imagined."

Ramsey embraced him once, then turned on his heel to follow the woman he loved.

A MINUTE LATER, Gus flew into the study and halted before Kane. "She has lost herself."

"But she is strong," he assured her.

She glanced toward the door. "He loves her."

Kane nodded.

Gus swallowed her tears. "And still she will do this."

"She has the means to keep those she loves from harm."

Gus shook her head. "She will save many, but not Ramsey."

"Not now. Not today," Kane said. She went into her husband's arms. "To those we love, we never stop trying to save them, help them help themselves." He kissed her lips.

"And we go on."

"We do. We walk on through storms we did not create, through winds of fate we cannot avoid, and we stand by those we can, most especially those we love."

She cupped her husband's cheek. "And if we cannot convince them that we need them beside us through those storms, we wait and pray and love them all the more. We go on."

## Chapter Twenty-Seven

G US PUT ASIDE her inability to dissuade Amber from her course, and threw herself into those things she could change. She devoted herself to planning grand dinners and balls. All of Paris came, and her husband benefited by making new friends and associates.

She tried to repair the damage done to her chain of information, but Luc Bechard continued to fail to appear on the twenty-fifth of each month in the bathhouse near the basilica of St. Denis. She busied herself with aiding her husband to buy porcelain and stoneware, rugs and porcelains, and the occasional load of corn or barley or wheat. She introduced him to a friend of hers and Amber's who ran a fleet of barges up the Loire from Blois to St. Nazaire. She knew a clerk in the port of Rouen whose mother had been British. That lady sent letters written in code to Gus. They described troops who marched past her home up to the Citadel of Lille.

Kane welcomed all the recruits and knowledge he could get. But he knew his time—and that of all British in France—grew short.

By Christmas, the city of Paris bulged with the high and mighty of London. Charles Fox, a politician, had come to town with his entourage and had dined with Bonaparte in the Tuileries.

The notorious Earl of Egremont had come, too, trailing three of his lovers. The Earl and Countess of Cholmondely spent the entire winter in Paris. The Earl of Elgin stayed long past his original plan. His wife, too, remained. But then, of course, she maintained a separate household. After all, she was pregnant by her lover and not welcomed in her husband's home.

The night before Christmas, another attempt was made on the life of Bonaparte. Kane had nothing to do with this one. Bonaparte acted quickly to punish those who attempted to destroy him.

Kane and Gus attended many court functions during the colder months. But Gus's condition, delicate as it was with the impending birth of their first child, meant she chose more and more carefully those events requiring their presence.

Aunt Cecily kept Gus up on the news. Bonaparte recently cut his hair, a more attractive mode for him. He had his tailor improve the style and fit of new coats. One was a fine red, which he favored. He then had a few duplicates made. Another coat, a purple satin velvet, was one Gus and Kane saw him wear one evening. Gus told her husband she found that more suited to Bonaparte's complexion.

"It is true," Gus's Aunt Cecily told Kane and Gus as they took her home in their coach one evening, "the first consul presents much better now that he is close-shaven. When he smiles, his lips are drawn back at the corners of his mouth and his teeth show. They are large and straight, but he must be careful, as they are not very white. I declare that his chin projects a bit too much to make him handsome. But he is courteous and inquisitive of his guests."

"I guess that makes up for his teeth," Gus remarked to the laughter of her husband.

Bonaparte took other airs unto himself. Kane returned home one night from a dinner party with British colleagues and reported to Gus that Bonaparte had ordered attire at Tuileries be that of a formal court. "Starch is the new order of the day. He wears white silk stockings and hangs a little sword from his belt even at dinner parties."

The first consul was becoming enamored of prestige, place—and his own power.

By February, Kane told Gus that relations between the first consul and the newly arrived British ambassador Whitworth were testy. Bonaparte had asked for troops from German princes, one of whom was the former Margrave of Baden, now a newly minted duke. Dirk Fournier, who was still in his grandmother's home, wrote often to Kane in code. His letters were filled with the promises the first consul made to the land-hungry German. An agent of Kane's in Amboise wrote of Bonaparte's movements of troops to the Atlantic Coast.

"The first consul has ambitions," said Kane to his wife one night in March, "that we will never accept."

Gus had ordered Corsini to begin to pack their belongings. Kane had begun to arrange with Corsini for the household staff to have pensions and a plan, should he and Gus have to leave Paris in haste.

Then, one night in mid-March at the Tuileries, Bonaparte and Whitworth openly argued.

The next few days, the air grew raw with speculations that the Treaty of Amiens drew to a close.

Kane ordered Corsini to ready them all to close the house and depart at his order. "I will want everyone prepared well. Traveling reticules packed. Money at the ready. Destinations they have decided upon. And no traces left in the house of where anyone has gone. The gendarmes will come for me and my wife to see if we are in violation of any passports. They will also come for any employees here, Corsini. I want all of you safe and compensated."

Indeed, Kane had used Scarlett's money well. He depleted the entire amount she had given him, again as much as her original this year as last. With it, he gave each member of his household enough funds to live on for two years.

"I fear it will not be enough," he whispered to Gus one night as he held her close in their bed. "This war to come will not last one year or two, but much longer. Bonaparte wants the world, and we British will not share it."

"The staff will remember with gratitude and respect what you did give them, Kane. Perhaps, over time, we can find a way to give them more. Besides, you have built a good network."

"With your help."

Gus grinned. "If it can pass secrets, it can certainly pass coin."

"I do like the way you think, my darling."

THOUGH THEIR WORK in Paris drew to a close, their relationship with Ramsey continued. He came to dinner, he came to visit with Kane, and he performed his assigned work for him. Ram had moved back into his own house not far from them. Kane and she did not ask why. They considered the move illustrative enough of his and Amber's relationship. Ram spoke rarely of Amber, but Kane and Gus understood that he followed her actions.

Kane feared it was the end of all their time in Paris.

*May 2, 1803*
*Paris*

ONE AFTERNOON WHEN Kane returned home from a meeting, he barged into their sitting room and announced that they were leaving for Dover in two days' time. "The British ambassador and Napoleon are at odds again, We must leave Paris, darling. I trust nothing about what may happen here."

She sat quietly for a minute and then said, "Have Corsini bring round the carriage. I will see Amber."

"Gus," Kane said, "you cannot go in your condition."

She was near term and very big with child. "I will go. If I can leave Paris in a coach, I can travel in one to say goodbye to my dearest friend."

Kane sighed but had the butler summon the coach.

An hour later, Gus marched past Amber's *majordom*. "Do not tell me no, sir. Show me to your lady."

The man took her to Amber's small sitting room.

"What in hell are you doing here?" Amber shot to her feet. "And in your condition?"

Gus blew out a breath. "Allow me your chaise longue, will you, and do be quiet." She lumbered over to the large pink couch and sat heavily down.

"Water? Tea?"

"Nothing, Amber. I come to tell you we are leaving Paris."

Amber slowly smiled. "I am thrilled. Good for you."

"Come away with us."

Amber's good humor fell away. "You are heavy with child, and I see the stress has affected your mind too."

"Don't be flippant with me, my friend! To the matter. Come away."

"You know my answer."

"Why?" Gus set her teeth. "What can you do now?"

"Continue."

"You will be arrested. Vaillancourt will not allow an operation to continue if France and Britain are at war. Be sensible."

"He does not know."

Gus scoffed. "Are you blind? Deaf? What is *wrong* with you? Come away."

"Aunt Cecily does not go."

"Aunt Cecily *never* goes!" Gus spat. "Not under *any* threat. Why will *you* not go?"

"I do better work here."

"Unto your death."

Amber nodded. "So be it."

They stared at each other.

Gus struggled to her feet.

Amber looked pained but did not rush to help her.

Gus took one last look at her friend. "You have a chance of love and laughter. A long and happy life."

Amber got a wistful look in her eyes. Then suddenly there were tears there, too. "I do."

"You will not take it?"

"No."

"Oh, Amber. You did once. You loved Maurice and valued every day with him. Ramsey loves you, and I know you love him."

"I must do this alone, Gus. I must."

"You think you are invincible," Gus accused her.

"Like you?" Amber taunted her. "Did you not once tell me that? You were an island. A creature alone. No, Gus, I am not a creature alone. But I do what I can. Go. Leave me in peace."

How she left Amber with the tears streaming from her eyes, Gus did not know. Yet she left.

But by the time she arrived home, she knew with crystal clarity one true thing.

At the door, seeing Corsini, she asked for her husband.

"The library, *signora*."

Off she waddled up the stairs, down the hall, into the large, lovely library where her handsome, dashing husband worked.

At the sight of her on the threshold, he shot to his feet. "Are you well?" He rushed forward. "You look terrible. I should have gone with you and—"

She put two fingers to his lips. "No. No. You should not."

"Tell me what happened," he said as he helped her to the settee and sat down beside her.

"She will not come with us. She is so stubborn devoting herself to her work. She is noble, foolhardy, and sad."

Kane lifted her chin. "She does what she must. For many reasons, I daresay, that we know not. Now we must leave her to

God."

"Yes, yes. You are right. But there is something I learned from her. Something I must tell you. And you must listen. You must." She traced the arc of his cheekbone, the contour of his jaw. "I have not said this, and I must. It is a truth I have come to know in my heart and you must hear it. I must say it."

Dark fear laced his ice-gray eyes and his hands gripped her. "No. You will not stay in Paris. You will not listen to her."

"No, no." She shook her head. "I have shocked you. I don't mean to. I am not leaving you. Not staying here. I go with you away to wherever you are, wherever you go. And I want to tell you, share with you what I am. But I want to tell you. For all my life, I thought I was a creature alone. An illegitimate child no one wanted. Oh, perhaps I am the Boltons' child, as it says in the records. But I always doubted it. Still, the idea affected me. I saw, I *perceived* that I belonged to no one but myself. That I belonged wherever I was. A creature of every place and no place. Everyone's and no one's. But I have learned, these past joyful months, that I belong with you. You are my completion. You embody my aspiration and my hope. You are my one and only love, Kane Whittington. I love you, my darling, and I am so happy I have you and you have me."

He wrapped her close, his words muffled as he buried his lips in her long black hair and said, "At last. You love me at last."

She pulled back and smiled at him through her tears. "I do. I will. Forevermore."

# Chapter Twenty-Eight

THE NEXT MORNING, Corsini came to Kane in the breakfast room with a plain linen bag in his hands. *"Conte,* this bag we found in the back of your wardrobe."

"What do you mean?" Kane had seen no such bag there. Ever.

"When we began the packing for you yesterday, the old wardrobe was jostled in the doing. One of the rungs fell to the bottom. I worked with Clement to repair it, but behind it, we found this!"

Kane took it from his man. Heavy. Malleable. With tiny items of varying sizes inside, all of them rustled. "Have you looked at the contents?"

*"Si, conte,* one is more curious in such cases than prudence allows." He grinned like a village thief.

Kane placed the bag on the dresser, then drew the strings. Inside, what glittered was every color of the rainbow.

He dumped the contents to the top. With a finger across his lips, he smiled. "The Rohan jewels."

"My conclusion as well, *conte."*

"Thank you, Corsini." Kane strode away but turned back. "One question."

*"Si?"*

"Have you been able to repair the wardrobe?"

"*Si, conte.*"

"As I thought. Put these back where you found them. We leave, but one day a remaining member of the Rohan will come and need money to live."

"Ah, but, *conte,* do they deserve such fortune?"

"Do any children deserve to pay for the sins of their fathers?"

Corsini nodded. "No, *conte.* Never."

⪼⪻

KANE HAD FINISHED his instructions to Corsini and took the stairs two at a time. He flung open the door to his and Gus's master suite, passed their sitting room, and headed for the bedroom.

She sat in her favorite wing chair, drinking her morning cup of chocolate and picking at an apple crumble.

"Good morning, sweetheart." He beamed at her and went to kiss her cheek. "How are you?"

She regarded him with wry humor. "Big. This baby is sitting on my bladder. And he does not like bacon!"

"Picky little bugger." Kane took the chair opposite and gathered her hands in his.

She traced his features with her beautiful green eyes. "What has happened?"

"Bonaparte and our ambassador have had another falling-out."

"When? Where?"

"Last night. The Tuileries." He stroked his fingertips over her knuckles. "Listen to me. I—"

"You hate to say this, but you want to leave."

"I do. We must."

An urgent knocking came to their bedroom door. "*Scuzzi, conte?*"

Gus pulled her woolen robe around her more securely. "Corsini. Let him in, darling."

Kane went to the door and opened it. "What is it?"

Countess Nugent met him with wide, worried eyes, but swept past his *majordom* and around him. "I've come from the Tuileries, Ashley. Good morning, sweet girl! How are you today, hmm?"

"Well, Aunt," Gus said with a resigned laugh. "Very well. And you? Do sit, Aunt. Kane, tell Corsini to send us another pot of chocolate for Aunt Cecily."

"Ashley, do not bother. I am here only for a minute." Cecily marched over to sit in the wing chair near Gus and, much as he had moments ago, took Gus's hands in hers.

Gus smiled, and within it was consolation and much sadness. "We know what's happened. Kane told me the ambassador and Bonaparte had words."

"More than words, dearest. I hate to say it, but—"

"We are leaving, Aunt."

Cecily sat back in the chair, her resignation to circumstances evident in her collapse. "Thank heavens." Her gaze flew to Kane. "When and how will you go?"

He'd been at the preparations for days now. He'd not breathed a word to his wife because he would not burden her with the worry of it all. He'd found the planning as perilous as the journey would be for a woman who was nine months gone with child. A very big child.

"We will go up the Seine by barge."

"Barge? Are you mad? Augustine must have privacy, warmth, and comfort. What if she goes into labor as you travel? What of her nourishment? The baby's? No, no. You cannot, Ashley."

"Madam." Kane approached them both and leaned against the footboard of their bed. "I assure you I have taken care of all of that. Bed, chair, cradle, and food. If I could summon the god of wind and water, I would command the air to stillness, and the Seine and the Channel to serenity. But in the meantime, I have prepared so that my wife may board her vessel to England and not worry a moment for the hazards of the unknown." He smiled at his adoring wife and sent her a wink.

"There, you see?" Gus waved a hand. "I am in the best of hands. Fret not at all. But I worry for you. Tell me, my dear aunt, what of you? What will you do?"

"I am in no peril."

"Madam, you are English," declared Gus with stern trepidation. "Your special friend loses her influence daily beneath the self-importance of her husband." Kane crossed his arms and stared at his wife's dear aunt. "Gus is right, madam. Come with us. Home to England. There you will be safe. Live with us. You can be our witness to our wedding."

"Another one?" Cecily trilled a laugh, and for a moment the air was bright with comic relief.

"Yes," he said, "Gus and I will marry again."

Gus joined in. "I wanted to marry him—little did I know it would take so many tries!"

Cecily chuckled. "For such a sight, I might even be tempted to join you. But no. I remain."

"Oh, Aunt! What is there here for you? Your influence is only as strong as those who are your friends. And in this atmosphere, friends who have sway today can be dead and gone tomorrow."

"A man as self-important as Bonaparte will do whatever he wishes, when he wishes," added Kane. "Make no mistake, madam. Stay at your risk. A very large risk. Sail for England with us. Our countries are on the march to war, and you know it. Once this treaty is declared null and void, you will be the enemy. Come away."

Cecily set her teeth. Her green eyes, so like Gus's, grew harsh and sad. "I cannot."

"Friendship is one thing, Aunt."

Cecily arched both black brows and, with a stance as staunch as a cannon's, stared hard at her niece. "I do not stay for friendship, Augustine. I never did."

Kane felt the earth shift beneath his feet. The growing look of astonishment on his wife's face was one he sent to indelible memory. Gus did not gape. She did not gasp. But in a flash, she wore her heart on her face as she stood and reached to take her aunt in her embrace.

They held each other as if statues molded from the marble of the earth. Time stood still. Then, as tears wended down his wife's cheeks and her aunt's, they drew away from each other, neither looking in the other's eyes—for fear, Kane surmised, that each would see too much truth there.

"I must return," Cecily said, sniffing back her sorrow as she dug a handkerchief from her dress pocket. She gave Gus a thorough once-over and grinned at her. "My beautiful girl with the heart of and courage of a lioness. I am so proud of all that you are. Go and be happy, my dear. Have many perceptive, stalwart children and tell them who you are, all that you are."

She looked at Kane with more adoration and benevolence than he had ever seen her reveal to any man. "I love you, Kane. You are more than I expected. Far finer than I predicted. I know you will take care of my girl and your children. Continue to secure all our futures, please. I depend upon you, sir, to save what I treasure most in this world and the next."

Then she glided from the room.

Kane and Gus were left to regard the empty space she had vacated, but filled with all the tiny revelations that would leave them both questioning all they had known and all they would never know about the English Countess Nugent.

THEIR SAIL UP the Seine was the calmest Kane had ever taken.

The merchant barge on which Kane had bought passage for them was a newly registered one docked below Mount Valerian to the west of the Periphique of Paris. Yves Pelletier, whom Scarlett Hawthorne had put to work the same day as Kane over a year ago, aided in obtaining the barge. Pelletier sailed with Kane and his wife to Rouen because the old port master whom Yves knew had recently died. If the new port master at Rouen docks found the crumpled license watermarked and stained and the handwriting difficult to read, well, then, the barge's owner, a British fellow with a good Norman accent, shrugged. *"C'est la vie. What can one do, eh?"*

They docked in Rouen only for a few hours, as the captain loaded provisions and let go of the ropes again before the sun rose the next morning.

A certain Monsieur Bonfleur and his wife, who was heavily with child, left the barge at Le Havre and transferred to an old refitted schooner whose papers said it hailed from Bordeaux. This, the harbor master at Dieppe debated. But filled as his harbor was with craft of all sizes and nationalities, his confusion led him to allow the sleek ship to sail without much ado. After all, his wife could be a woman of great consequence if he was late to home and her stew had gone cold.

The Channel crossing for the married couple Bonfleur was secured by a man whose reputation was that of smuggler. His looks, that of a handsome rogue with only one eye and the swagger of a bounty pirate, disturbed the husband. But the fellow, by name of Jacques Durand, promised to land the couple quickly in Dover. Amazingly, Madame Bonfleur took to the storm more easily than her husband. He was very ill over the rear deck in the ten-hour sail that blew them north, then south into Dover.

After hiring the best carriage available in the crowded port, the Earl of Ashley sat in the well-padded coach for the drive to Grosvenor Square, number 20, praying for speed and no breakdowns. His wife was suddenly in labor.

Hours later, immediately upon entry to his townhouse, the earl sent his faithful old butler, Friendly, and a young footman, whose name the earl did not yet know, to Doctors' Commons for a special license. Friendly's orders were that the footman speed home as soon as word came that the earl could have an audience with the archbishop. The earl needed this license to marry, as his wife, whose own birth was recorded in St. George's registry, was about to deliver their first child.

Yes, he gave his butler the papers to show that he and his wife, for he did name her that already, had been married by the British envoy, Anthony Merry, in Paris last July. However, they wished to have the blessing of the Church of England. Ashley's marriage was of such importance to him, said the letter Friendly presented to the archbishop, that he would marry this woman every day of his life if that was what it took to make her truly his wife by the law of England.

By the law of man and of God, she was his beloved, and he needed their marriage legitimate as the air and sky and grass, so help him God.

The archbishop sent not only his writ to number 20, Grosvenor Square, but also one of his younger clergymen. The marriage, the second for the Ashleys, was declared three major pushes before the earl and his wife were delivered of a squalling baby boy. They named him Piers Alfred William Whittington. He slept in the Ashley family rocking cradle, his mother's curiously crafted purple knitted blanket across his chubby little body.

At labor's end, the earl—not in top health from the worry, the rocky Channel sailing, and the fear for his beloved wife—kissed the woman he adored and buried his lips in her long black hair. There for a scant minute—because a man did not wish to appear daunted by the vicissitudes of life—he shed happy tears.

And when he raised his face, his beloved, *legal* wife, twice over, brushed his tears from his cheeks. "My darling husband, you are my fondest treasure, my dearest hope, and my most surprising mate. I love you now and will every day of life. Beyond, as well. Now go leave me and organize us all so that we all may live in freedom and in love from this day forward."

Minutes later, the clergyman gone, the baby sleeping, the countess napping, the earl jogged down the circular main stairs to the kitchens. There he poured everyone in the servants' hall a hefty three fingers of the scotch whisky Friendly had dutifully kept in the wine cellar for such an occasion as the master's return.

"To us all." Kane raised a toast to the four assembled before him. "May we have courage and strength, valor and might to fight for the success of our country, and the health and happiness of us all forevermore."

## THE END OF THE BEGINNING

# Travels with Cerise~
## Spicy Romance and Vivid History
## in *Scarlett Affairs*

We read romance for the joy of falling in love. But we read historical romance for the drama of living in different eras.

In my new series, SCARLETT AFFAIRS, I give you sixteen spicy historical romances. Each one will come with a kick of loads of accurate historical detail. The agents of merchant Scarlett Hawthorne will not only fall in love amid actual events, but some will participate and solve mysteries many experts ponder even today.

Sweeping you from London to Paris during the years Bonaparte ruled, I am tickled to open the series with a trip down the road to Malmaison and show you the problems of navigating Josephine and Bonaparte's court. The intrigues of spies, ambassadors, merchants, military men, and the women who loved and aided them create a canvas of actual events that shaped the fate of millions.

Over the years of Bonaparte's rise and reign, espionage agents of all nationalities tried to stop him. Many failed. Like the attempt in LORD ASHLEY'S BEAUTIFUL ABLIBI to abduct Bonaparte in June 1800. A few succeeded, like the attempt of the British government to plant agents throughout the Continent during the peace of the Treaty of Amiens.

Some of these events were documented, like the abduction of the duc d'Enghien. Others still remain mysteries, such as the identity of the mysterious Englishwoman who for decades sent thousands of coded secrets home to London. And the lady who stole documents from Talleyrand in Vienna during the Congress of 1814.

In SCARLETT AFFAIRS, I take you to those cities that live in our history books—and palaces, churches, and streets I have walked. They are places that exude their own charm—and hold for the people of that time secrets and challenges for agents of all countries.

You will go to the tunnels beneath Compiègne and to the palace where Napoleon met his second wife and within minutes escorted her to their bedroom. You will go to Reims, where kings were crowned, and enter the caverns of St. Denis in Paris where they were buried. You will go to the church in Varennes where *gendarmes* captured Louis XVI and Marie Antoinette and sent them to Paris to die. You will go to Baden, where a greedy German margrave sold out his subjects to Bonaparte for land and money. You will track Bonaparte and his aide Caulaincourt as they race away from Moscow and are tracked by agents all the way to Paris.

I will also take you to other seemingly insignificant places that really existed. A public bathhouse, the smelly abattoir of Montmartre, then south to the huge fortress of Amboise and the vineyards of the Loire. To Verdun, where the citadel becomes the prison for hundreds of British trapped inside France by the wily new emperor.

A panoply of stories, the series will be a rich discovery of the challenges of fighting an enemy while falling in love with one irresistible person. I hope you enjoy them all, from this first search for a missing friend, to the action-adventure of saving an entire family from death, to the rewards of stealing Bonaparte's gold and more. Through each story, one man and woman will try to save the world from a despot—and save each other and the love they treasure above all else.

I hope you have enjoyed your tour of Paris and Northern France in this first novel of the series. Come with me as I take you to those times and places where kings walked, Bonaparte reigned, and where espionage agents of my fictitious merchant Scarlett Hawthorne will attempt to topple the Little Corporal while they fall delightfully in love.

*Happy Reading,*
*Cerise*

# About the Author

Cerise DeLand loves to write about dashing heroes and the sassy women they adore. Whether she's penning historical romances or contemporaries, she has received praise for her poetic elegance and accuracy of detail.

An award-winning author of more than 50 novels, she's been published since 1991 by Pocket Books, St. Martin's Press, Kensington and independent presses. Her books have been monthly selections of the Doubleday Book Club and the Mystery Guild. Plus she's won nominations and awards for Best Historical of the Year, Best Regency and scores of rave reviews from *Romantic Times, Affair de Coeur, Publisher's Weekly* and more.

To research, she's dived into the oldest texts and dustiest library shelves. She's also traveled abroad, trusty notebook and pen in hand, to visit the chateaux and country homes she loves to people with her own imaginary characters.

And at home every day? She loves to cook, hates to dust, goes swimming at least once a week and tries (desperately) to grow vegetables in her arid backyard in south Texas!